CW01369800

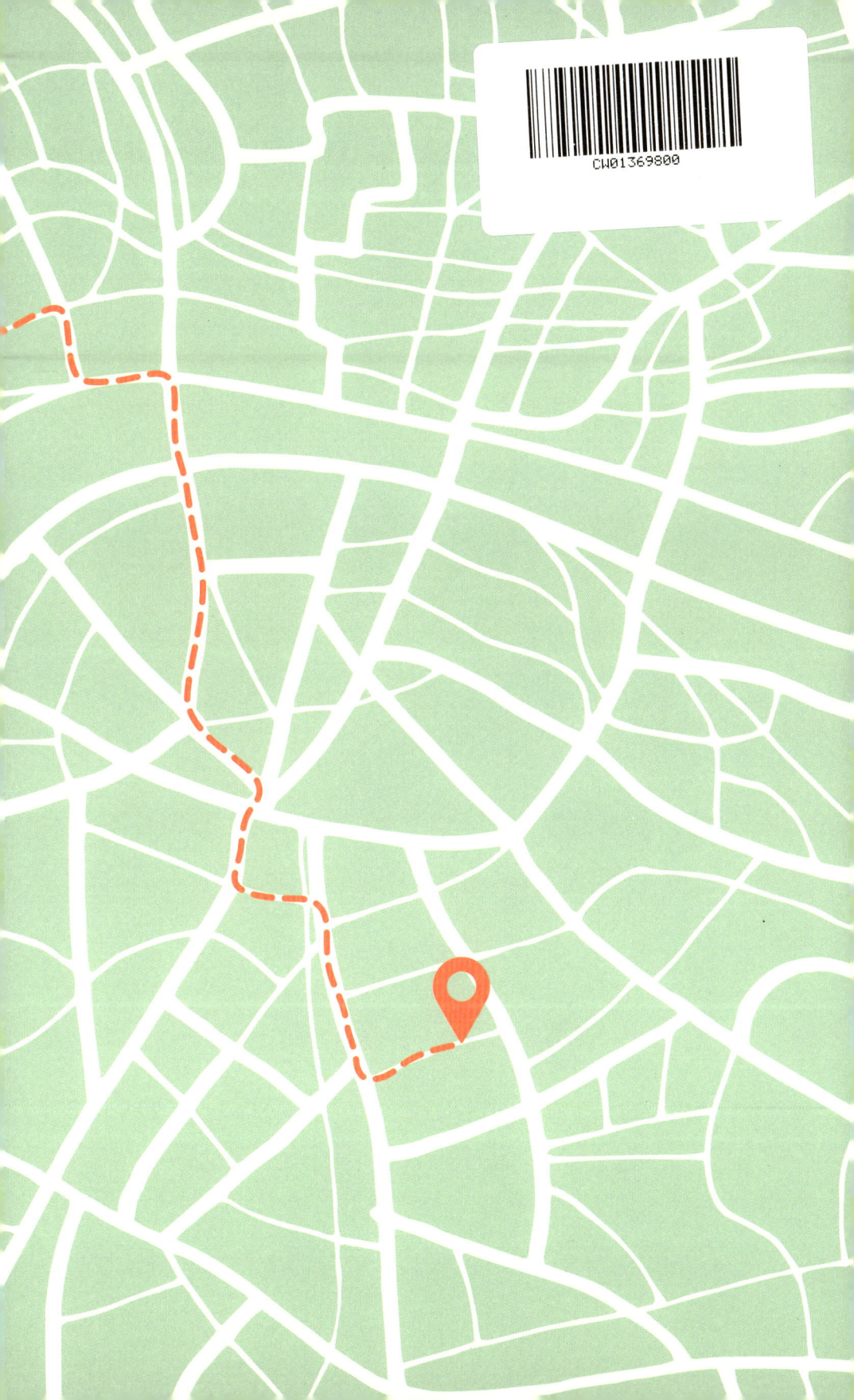

One Minute Away

MARK WATSON is the acclaimed author of nine novels, which have been published in twelve languages. He's also a stand-up comedian who has won numerous awards in Britain and Australia, and performed at every major comedy festival in the world. He was a celebrated contestant on *Taskmaster*, is one-third of the YouTube phenomenon *No More Jockeys*, has had multiple Radio 4 series, and has been one of the biggest-selling acts at the Edinburgh Fringe for twenty years. He lives in East London.

@watsoncomedian
@watsoncomedian
@watsoncomedian.bsky.social
@markwatsonthecomedian
markwatsonthecomedian.com

Also by Mark Watson

A Light-Hearted Look at Murder
Bullet Points
Eleven
The Knot
Hotel Alpha
Dan and Sam: A Graphic Novel
The Place that Doesn't Exist
Contacts

ONE MINUTE AWAY

MARK WATSON

HarperCollins*Publishers*

HarperCollins*Publishers* Ltd
1 London Bridge Street,
London SE1 9GF

www.harpercollins.co.uk

HarperCollins*Publishers*
Macken House,
39/40 Mayor Street Upper,
Dublin 1
D01 C9W8
Ireland

First published by HarperCollins*Publishers* Ltd 2025

1

Copyright © Mark Watson 2025

Mark Watson asserts the moral right to
be identified as the author of this work.

A catalogue record for this book is available from the British Library.

ISBN: 978-0-00-834700-0 (HB)
ISBN: 978-0-00-834701-7 (TPB)

This novel is entirely a work of fiction.
The names, characters and incidents portrayed in it are
the work of the author's imagination. Any resemblance to
actual persons, living or dead, events or localities is
entirely coincidental.

Set in Dante MT Std by Palimpsest Book Production Limited, Falkirk, Stirlingshire

Printed and bound in the UK using 100% Renewable Electricity by CPI Group (UK) Ltd

All rights reserved. No part of this publication may be
reproduced, stored in a retrieval system, or transmitted,
in any form or by any means, electronic, mechanical,
photocopying, recording or otherwise, without the prior
written permission of the publishers.

Without limiting the exclusive rights of any author, contributor or the publisher of
this publication, any unauthorised use of this publication to train generative artificial
intelligence (AI) technologies is expressly prohibited. HarperCollins also exercise their
rights under Article 4(3) of the Digital Single Market Directive 2019/790 and expressly
reserve this publication from the text and data mining exception.

MIX
Paper | Supporting
responsible forestry
FSC
www.fsc.org
FSC™ C007454

This book contains FSC™ certified paper and other controlled sources
to ensure responsible forest management.

For more information visit: www.harpercollins.co.uk/green

For Delyth

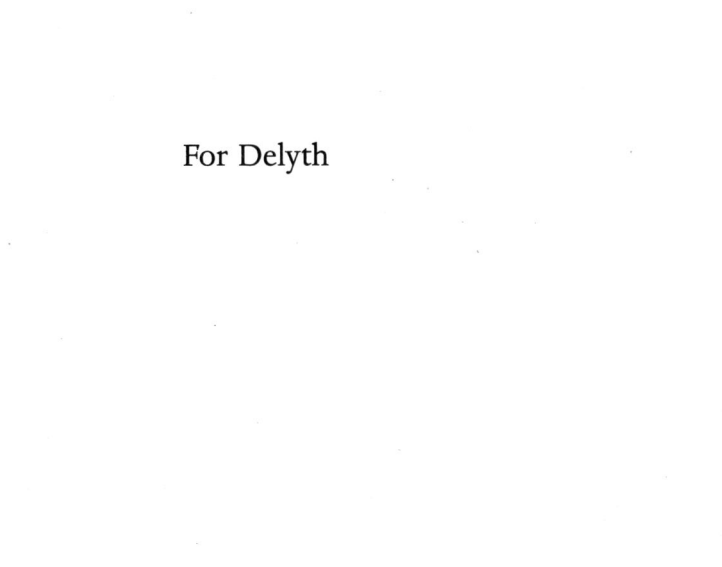

PROLOGUE

From the bar at the top of London's tallest tower, where I have been only once, you can see the whole city like a model village. Train tracks stretching out towards the suburbs. Streets that do not form a nice grid, as I imagine New York or Tokyo do from above, but wind around, run into buildings, seem to disappear into the river. Confusing if you are on the ground. A ball-ache if you are riding around trying to find addresses, every minute worth money, every wrong turning costing you. But from high up, things make more sense. You can see how the city works, how it breathes.

If you are gazing down from that tower, you might think things are pretty much the same in London as they were fifty years ago. The cars are better and the lines of traffic are thicker, and there are steel and chrome buildings where there probably used to be low-rise concrete blocks, and everyone is carrying a phone, but people are doing what they always did: getting themselves to work, earning money, going back home from work. Under the ground where you cannot see them, even more people are doing the same thing. In the sky above the tower, some of the luckier or richer ones are escaping the whole game for a little while, going somewhere else. So far, so familiar.

But on the roads themselves, things are not the same as they have always been – not even the same as they were ten years ago. There is one massive change, which would be obvious straight away to someone who had time-travelled from 2010 and been brought back. It is that one in four people on the roads now is a cyclist, or a motorcyclist with a backpack, and another one in four is a private taxi driver. And these people are not just working for a boss in an office; they are working for you. You click a button if you want a book, or a vintage dress, or a microwave, or more or less anything else. You get them to pick you up if you are out drinking and it is too much effort to catch a bus home. You select a restaurant, and one of these guys goes there for you and brings you dinner in a bag.

The system is a fair one –you have earned your money; you pay another guy to ride to your house with a pizza. But it is even better than most transactions of the same kind because you hardly have to see the person doing the work. You just get a notification on your phone that says, 'Your order is being collected by Damir.' Who Damir Kovačevíc is, why he needs the money, what he is thinking: none of this has anything to do with you. In fact, at the time this story begins in 2021, you can select 'contactless delivery' and you might not see Damir at all. Whoever he is, he will leave the bag on your doorstep and ride away on his silver bike. Even if you do not select this option, he will hand the bag over as fast as possible and say thank you before turning away and disappearing.

This is not just how London works now, it is how everywhere works. And do not think I am criticizing you for taking part in it, for calling me over to your house. It is nothing personal, this system. That is why people love it.

But we have to talk about what happened when it did get very personal. When it was not just about your food coming quickly. When the guy on the bike became a real human, for that one summer at least.

PART ONE:

OUTSIDE

1

Quack! Quack! Quack! Quack! Quack!

It is the most irritating alarm on the iPhone, which is why Goran and I both use it; you cannot ignore it, have to turn it off straight away. And that means getting out of bed, because the phone needs to be charging overnight. Without phone charge we cannot work, and the only socket is on the other side of the room. If the landlady Caroline had her dream, there would probably be none at all; we would be communicating by writing letters and using a generator to watch TV.

I slide off my mattress, which is on the floor, and walk over to turn off the ducks. Eight a.m. exactly, but part of me has been half-awake for a couple of hours, the way it always happens when the body is expecting an alarm. Light has been coming through the cheap blackout blind for some time, falling on my guitar in the corner, my clothes folded neatly by the mattress. Lorries have been rattling past for a while, too, making the windows shake; although ours is only a side street, in the mornings you would think it was the busiest road in London. None of this is a problem; it is good to be awake, good to be ready, when you do what we do.

Across the hall, in his bedroom, I can hear Goran doing exactly the same – except he catches his toe on something, one of the multiple items littering his floor at all times, and swears in the language of Dalmatia, where we come from, using a word so strong you would be surprised to hear it in prison. We are out in the hall to say hi at exactly the same moment, like synchronized dancers.

'*Di si.*'

'*Di si.*'

The bathroom is next to my room, the kitchen next to his. That is it: you have had the tour. My bike, the Silver Fox, stands in the kitchen, waiting for action. There is only one chair. But it is not as if we sit down for breakfast. We do not spend much time in the kitchen at all, in fact. For a start, there is a part of the floor where if you tread too hard it feels like you will go straight through like Alice in Wonderland, except without such fun consequences. That is not the main reason, though. The main reason is time. Time is what we sell.

Every second counts. That is a phrase I have in a note on my iPhone. Only a couple of months after I arrived from Split, I went into an Indian restaurant for a pickup and a man was saying it, laughing: 'Every second counts, mate!' I did not know what he was referring to, but I liked the sound of it, and noted it down. Ever since then I have been adding to the list of English phrases, things you hear outside a pub or in a crowded pizza place waiting for your order number to be called. The expressions you do not learn at school. *Ball-ache. Fuck this for a game of soldiers* (I heard a customer say this when he was turned away from a restaurant). *It's gone down the absolute shitter* (a man in the pub referred this way to county cricket, although even now I do not fully know what that is). But 'every second counts' is my favourite. It is perfect. If you are one second too slow in pressing the screen to accept a job, someone else will take it. Sometimes it feels like you only have to be one second late knocking on a customer's door with food before they start to complain, your rating goes down, the algorithm selects other riders over you, and soon there is less food on *your* table.

Often Goran burns the toast and the smoke alarm screams. The alarm is one of the only things in the flat that works; in fact it works too well, it is terrified if you cook anything at all. Goran is one metre ninety, so although he is always the one to disturb the alarm, he is also able to shut it up with a punch. This morning, though, the alarm is quiet. I eat an energy bar. We get these in a box of twenty for £1.49 and you sometimes do not need to eat lunch after them. The coffee is also £1.49, for a jar the size of a barrel. It is a brand from a country we cannot be sure of, and it does not exactly taste like coffee, just like the beers in our fridge are not quite what you think of when you think of the taste of beer.

Into the bathroom. Again, not much time for a beauty regime, we are not the Kardashians. A Kardashian, for example, would probably have a toilet seat which stayed in one place, and a shower which did not give them an electric shock, but that is not how things go around here. This morning I am lucky with the shower; no shock, and a steady flow of water, which means the couple downstairs are not using *their* shower. If both are running at the same time, it is a tug of war to see who actually gets wet. But Goran slides several centimetres to the left as he sits on the seat, even though he only fixed it the other week. 'Jesus and Mary Christ,' he mutters; this is his normal sort of curse, even though I do not think this was her surname because of the unusual family situation. 'The rodeo, again.'

'We'll have to ask Caroline to sort it,' I say, and we laugh: it is a running joke. We both know if we want the toilet or shower or kitchen floor fixed, we would be better off rubbing a lamp for a genie than calling Caroline, whom we have never met. Goran is in the shower next and I get my jacket on, my backpack ready. The uniform is important, like every detail. Goran and I are elites, which means the algorithm sends us more jobs, and better-paid ones; especially Goran, because of his motorbike. He picks up his biking trousers and socks and boots from the floor of his bedroom where, as usual, they are lying in a heap like a dead man's clothes found by a river.

Phones charged to 100 per cent. As soon as we select 'Begin Shift', they will start to chat at us about where the hubs are, what is the volume of drops so far today. I clatter my bike down the stairs, where there is always a pile of leaflets for

ONE MINUTE AWAY

food places. SPECIAL NEW DEALS AT ORCHID. Every week for two years, even in lockdown, they have put this leaflet through our door. The special new deal is always the same: free Coke or Fanta when you order two mains. There is a good chance that Goran or I, or both of us, will visit Orchid at some point today, but not as customers.

In the narrow stairwell we can hear activity from the flat beneath ours, a similar set of rituals going on. The occupants of this flat are a British Asian couple; now and again we see each other at one end of the day or the other. Goran once got into a conversation with them and found out that the guy drives for Uber, as well as the woman's occupation, and both their names. But that same night we went out drinking and he lost all the information except the Uber part. With every day that passes, it feels less likely we will get a chance to start that conversation again.

Out of the door, next to the sign: CECIL COURT. There is a much more famous Cecil Court you can find on Google, near Leicester Square, with fancy bookshops and cafés, and I think my father believes that is the one we live in. I walk Goran to the lockup where he keeps his beloved motorbike, the Empress. There is just about room in this shed for three bikes. One day, when I have saved enough, we will need a place with room for four. I am not too far away from getting the money. Not for the first time, the place has not been shut up properly; the door opens without Goran having to work the padlock. 'It takes *thirty seconds*,' he mutters, 'fuck my life, what is wrong with them?'

By 'them' he means Mario and Bartosz, our two friends who share the lockup. These two guys are such opposites physically that they could be out of some folk tale where there is a moral about not judging by appearances. Bartosz is from Poland, so thin he could be made from coat-hangers, and he has rosacea on his face so always looks a little hot or embarrassed. He and another rider used to keep their e-bikes in the hallway outside their rented flat; they were not in the way, and the landlord had agreed on this when he showed them round. But then the guy read on Twitter that e-bikes can be dangerous if they overheat, and said they had to find somewhere else for them. They politely complained about this and he threw them out the next day with no notice.

Mario found space for Bartosz at his own flat: in some ways he is the team captain. Mario is a powerful man with no hair and has the kind of playful aggression where his idea of fun is to punch you a little too hard on the arm, or make you drink four shots even though you were hoping to go home. He is from Split, like us, and he was the first person we heard of who came here to London. Goran was next, in 2016. A couple of years after that, it was my turn, because I go where Goran goes. He says, 'I have a plan,' and I listen.

'Good luck, bro,' Goran says now. We are not brothers by blood, but with every day we spend here, it feels more like we are. We high-five, as every morning, and Goran straddles the red-green motorbike – a pat on its side, like it is a favourite horse – and roars around the corner.

Maybe our paths will cross. There are hubs – the burger

place, Superior Pizzas, Orchid Chinese – which come up many times. Or it could be the kind of day where we just stay in touch by texting, between drops: *quiet one today. Speak for yourself, I am doing great. Fuck you, bro.*

As long as one of us is having a profitable day, both of us are.

In the evening, perhaps we will hang out with the others. Since we have been here – except for the part last year when it was illegal – Mario has always sent out regular drinking invitations on the riders' WhatsApp group. You bring your own beer, bitch about the day you had, maybe celebrate something with a toast. Mario has always got some reason to celebrate. A cousin is here. A cousin has graduated, back home. Someone we don't even know has graduated. Someone *Mario* does not even know. The way he phrases social invitations is like the way he grabs you and offers you the shots in a pub: it is kind, but also, you do not have a choice. Sometimes there are riders from four or five countries, and we joke and laugh in English although none of us is thinking in it. It can be midnight, even one in the morning when we head for home. There is no boss to worry about; you are the boss. Anyway, we know we will be up when the alarms go off. We are a team.

More likely, tonight it will just be me and Goran, back where we started the day, sitting on one of our mattresses with the budget beers. Even if there is an invitation to the group, it will only come at the last minute, because none of us can really know how long the work day will be. We will go where the algorithm tells us, and only stop when it has nothing more for us.

I select 'Begin Shift' and my feet are on the pedals, waiting for orders which might come from anywhere, from any of those people seen from the top of the tower.

Every second counts. The race is on. And we love the race. We love the fun parts of the lifestyle here, sure: getting a little drunk at Mario's place, sending messages back and forth, having bike races, planning future holidays, future adventures of all kinds when we have a little more money saved. But whether we admit it or not – whether we even really know it – we love the race itself.

2

The familiar vibrations of the phone and the little noises. *Bloop-bloop-BLOOP*, a three-parter, means a job is available. And then a sort of 'ting' when the app confirms you have got it, and gives you the pickup address. Sometimes the *bloop-bloop-BLOOP* is the only thing I can hear in my head, when I shut my eyes at night. It feels like a musical phrase, like an electronic fragment in a pop song. I build tunes around it in my brain, imagine words going along with the rhythm of it. *I-want-YOU*. Or *Here-we-GO*. When I am composing lyrics, my brain goes automatically into English, because that is the language of pop music. The dream is not to be a folk singer in some shitty basement in Zagreb, playing to twenty men with beards who nod solemnly at the technique, go home and write a blog nobody reads. I want to be big. In London everything is big. That is the point of London. That is what we came here for.

There are riders out everywhere already, even on a Sunday. At the start of every morning I see other people like me, pulling the invisible levers that make the city go round. The guys collecting the bins, leaping down for them, emptying them, never meeting whoever made all that rubbish; the Uber drivers whose names you are unlikely to read, certainly not to remember. It feels good to get my first couple of orders in the bank: a couple of pounds for this one, a couple of pounds for that – although we never quite know how much we have earned until later, because there is no time to stop and do math. On this Sunday, like most Sundays, there are an hour or so of breakfast orders: coffees, bacon rolls. When I first came here, it surprised me that people would pay for the delivery of two coffees in a tray instead of walking a couple of blocks, but the surprise has long gone. And the lockdowns have made everyone used to staying indoors, summoning us.

Coffee orders are annoying because they have to be zipped into the compartment of my backpack to stay upright, and even then they can spill if they have not been clingfilmed properly. Gradually, though, the drops get more interesting, more profitable. I pick up a whole roast lunch from a pub which has been doing deliveries since not long after the pandemic began. Lamb, potatoes, wilted greens; a bottle of white wine. 'Keep it as level as you can,' says the publican, who has a small, neat moustache. We have had versions of this conversation before; he talks about his roasts like I am delivering antique furniture. 'And be as quick as you can, this stuff needs to arrive hot.'

This, of course, is a needless thing to say to a delivery

rider, to someone for whom time and money are the same thing. Does he think I am going to take a detour to the park and wander around the flowerbeds for a little bit before dropping off the food? Nobody wants this job done quicker than Damir Kovačević. Less than ten minutes after leaving the Old Oak, I am leaving the bag on a doorstep just off Roundwood Street. I have been to this house before, two or three times. A dog is barking in the next house every time. The doorbell rings in a three-part phrase which reminds me of a couple of different pop songs. You could almost say I am a regular visitor here, but not a visitor who would be recognized.

Mask on; contactless delivery. As a customer, there is a box you can tick to request this. Fewer people are doing it now, compared even with a few months ago, but the app is still very keen to remind you. Your safety is paramount to us. (This is where I learned the word 'paramount'; before that it was just a film studio.) I see movement through a window; they will come and grab the food when I am on my way. No interaction. No problems. Almost certainly no tip, either. The app gives an option to tip me, but why would they do that if we have not even spoken? Why would they do it at all, is probably the real question. They paid for the meal. They are paying for it to be delivered. I am not serving them in a restaurant; that is the whole point. I am removing the need for them to go to a restaurant.

By late afternoon it has got warmer but also started to rain, a trick which London does all the time in summer and an uncomfortable combination for someone trying to cover the city as fast as possible. My jacket is the lightweight version – there is another one for winter. There has not been a day since 2017 I did not wear one of these two jackets, including Christmas Day. You might be surprised how many people order on Christmas Day. London is never all on holiday at the same time.

I have removed the jacket and am leaning against a wall, sipping from my water bottle – which I refill from time to time in restaurant bathrooms – texting Goran, and Petra, my sister back home. We confirm our weekly Zoom call for late that night. I have not been back to Croatia since I arrived here, and I miss sitting in the kitchen with her at one a.m., hearing about her shifts at the pizza place, Petra normally (to dip into my iPhone note) *off her tits* after a couple of joints. If she could get her shit together, maybe she could be working over here, too. But if anyone in my family had their shit together, which has not been the case since Mum died, maybe we would not have come here in the first place.

Bloop-bloop-BLOOP. Come-to-ME. A Japanese restaurant, a fifteen-minute ride; a little out of the way, not a place I have been many times. 'Accept Job.' The 'ting': I have got in before anyone else. The place is called Tokyo Kyoto. Because of what happens next, those are words which will live in my head for ever.

Even before I reach the address, the company's app has already sent the customer a note saying, in a tone like they are friends: congratulations, your food is on its way! This, in turn, is because the restaurant has told the app that the order is all done, whether it is or not. Everyone in the chain is doing this; everyone is lying slightly. If the customer gets angry because something goes wrong, nobody will blame the restaurant or the app. They will blame the guy who shows up at the door.

Rain in my bike lights as I pedal; sweat down my back. As soon as I walk in: problems. The bag is not on the counter. I call out. A man comes out who looks so hot he might have been in the oven an hour himself. He says sure, OK, give me a minute, we are up against it here. I am standing helplessly by the counter, smelling food. My stomach gets the wrong idea and starts to say: good man Damir, I assume we are about to eat. I have tried to train my body not to anticipate a meal like this every time I smell food, but sometimes it cannot be avoided. Since the energy bars, I have had nothing; I approached a Subway at one point, but a notification came.

The sweating man comes out of the kitchen with a large package. I thank him, like I always do, even when I have been screwed as hard as this. Look at the app for the destination, which pops up when I input the code on the delivery bag. Backpack on and I am pedalling like the Slovenian cycling prodigy Tadej Pogačar, whom Goran and I like to watch in the Tour de France. *I could do that*, says Goran as he watches Pogačar slamming through the gears and rocketing up the mountain. He is only half-joking. I was never as fast as Goran, never had piston legs like him, but I can move pretty fast when I have to – which is always. The trouble is that, especially in rain, you also have to be a little bit careful.

Water is streaming out of my hair, which is long at the moment; there is never time to see a barber, and anyway, that costs money. I have to keep reaching to wipe the streams out of my eyes, because my eyes are pretty important if I want to stay alive. Everybody on a road makes little mistakes, but cyclists are at the bottom of the chain, like the little fish that get swallowed up by the whales. My mistakes will not kill anyone else, but theirs could kill me. An Uber in front of me slows without warning – taking people to food while I am taking food to people. Someone wanders across the street where they should not, or a lorry rumbles behind me: I perceive these things so quickly that sometimes I feel I almost looked into the future; I reacted to them before they even happened. On a motorbike, Goran says, this feeling of being wired to the streets is the same, but faster. One day I will know. I have ridden on the Empress, of course, clinging to Goran's back, screaming as he wove between a bus and a van, but to be in charge of the machine is what I want. To *be* a machine, a money-earning machine, with the wheels underneath me.

40 Laurel Gardens is in a smart part of the neighbourhood, very much smarter than where we live. The houses are more widely spaced. Trees are planted all along the pavement. This is very nice for the homeowners, and a source of oxygen as we learn at school, but what they did not teach you at

school was that trees are a pain in the ass for delivery riders because they make it difficult to see house numbers. To make it worse, Laurel Gardens' numbers do not seem to be laid out in a normal way: a psychopath has arranged it so that they go up one side, but down the other, and many doors do not have a number at all. The app's GPS has got me this far, but now the little dot is flicking around the screen and the phone is shrugging its shoulders and saying, good luck, Kovačević, my friend. Every second counts. Sweat is starting to run into my eyes along with the rainwater.

Big dark blue door. The number '40' in brass. This cannot be a contactless delivery, because I need to explain the lateness, explain it was not my fault. I knock and, almost at once, the door swings open. It is like someone has been crouched there waiting to kick it open, as in the war that was happening when Goran and I were born. A man is standing there. He is about forty-five years old. His hair is dark and turning a little grey at the front; he has keen blue eyes, a handsome face. He is wearing a white T-shirt which shows off significant pecs, three-workouts-a-week muscles.

'Sorry for the delay . . .' I begin.

'What a joke.'

'Sorry,' I try again, 'but unfortunately the restaurant was not ready, so . . .'

'I mean, it would have been quicker to go to fucking Japan and pick it up from there.'

'The order was not ready when I arrived,' I persist, 'so again I apologize if . . .'

'Sure, sure.' He is nodding sarcastically, like my story is the maddest excuse he has ever heard. 'Well – good luck with your review.'

He turns to go back into his big house, shuts the heavy blue door. I almost stumble physically at what he has said. Whether he knows it or not, he has struck at the most vulnerable point of a rider's brain. My rating is all the power I really have. If it stays high, the algorithm keeps pushing jobs to me, because I make the company look good. If I remain in the 'elite' bracket – over 4.5 average – my pay rate is slightly higher and there are little bonuses. Already, the way we live is tight; if I lost these bonuses, it would be almost impossible.

On top of this, even if it seems stupid to say, there is my pride. Sure, maybe what I do is not full of glory. I am not walking down the red carpet with paparazzi yelling *over here Damir, great burger you dropped the other night!* But I do my work well; I make sure people are satisfied. My rating is a badge that shows I work hard and care about my tasks. And now a man is threatening in a casual way to stick a knife into that reputation, which I have built up over hundreds of deliveries in rain and snow, through rude customers and shitty incompetent restaurants, through being ill or injured or just tired as a dog. And all for something which, really, I have no more control over than I have control over the winner of the dancing show on TV, which I see through windows on Saturday nights.

I need to confirm with the app that the drop is done:

it will be logged in My Jobs and a small amount of money will appear there, with a green tick. My finger slides around uselessly on the screen, though, because of the rain; I cannot make contact with the button. It is a restless feeling; no more jobs will be offered until this one is officially completed. All these minutes add up. Plus, because I am still across the road from number 40, from the angry man, I feel like I can still see him, his contemptuous face. Ten seconds later, like this is an anxiety dream, I *can* see him. The front door has opened again.

'Hey! Hey!'

My customer is holding out the package like a bag of dog shit. 'This is the wrong order, mate! Does this look like three people's food to you?'

Ajme! I say in my head, an exclamation that can mean almost anything you want it to. What it means right now is that I am starting to wonder if the man has psychological difficulties. How am I meant to know that there are three people in his house waiting to be fed? Does he think that when he places his order, an assistant comes out of my phone and says, 'This is for Mr Smith, who has a wife and child'? Does he imagine I sit, when I have collected each order, and count exactly how many grains of rice are included?

'I don't know.'

'You don't know.' He is opening the bag now, taking items out, shaking his head. He opens one of the little containers and holds it out to me. 'I mean what are *these*?'

'They are edamame beans,' I say, my stomach sighing at the thought of what they would taste like in my mouth.

'I can see that they're fucking edamame beans!' he snorts. The words sound crazy together; who in history has been this angry over edamame? 'My point is, this is *not the order!*'

And here a thing happens which is over very quickly, and yet feels to me like a moment of real brutality. He clatters open the black bin, partly hidden by a big bush; he throws the entire box in, and slams down the lid. I lose my breath for a second.

'Would you like me to – should I go back and . . .'

But the guy is waving his hand in the air to dismiss it, to dismiss me; he is moving away. 'Forget it. Absolute clown car.'

As the blue door slams for the second time, I try to make my brain understand everything that I have seen. That the guy either holds me responsible or is too angry to care; that he is prepared to throw away good food in front of me. And that he can afford to waste it like that, probably not even get a refund; simply order a second dinner.

I find my hands are shaking a little on the handlebars and the wet uniform T-shirt feels like it is stuck to me, like – although this is stupid – it will be impossible to take off even when I get home. I wheel the bike into where there is a sort of gap between some houses and the others, which turns out to be a tiny street of its own. VINTNER MEWS. I shake rainwater out of my hair, again. I want to text Goran but I do not even quite know what I am thinking.

★

I go to the riders' drinks, but it must be pretty obvious that I am not in the mood. Mario puts a massive arm around me. 'You're quiet, man.'

'Yeah, just had a shitty customer. Blamed me for the wait, when . . . you know.'

'Some of the people here,' says Bartosz, rubbing his red cheeks, shaking his head.

We do this every drinking session, but usually complaining about Londoners is a kind of sport, the way old ladies complain about buses, or Goran about the lockup and our bathroom conditions. We enjoy it, the same way people in every profession probably enjoy it; it is almost disappointing if someone has *not* had a nightmare customer, a psychotic taxi driver, an idiot restaurant, to deal with. Tonight I cannot feel the fun of it, somehow; do not want to dramatize the story for my friends to laugh, or shout and swear. I tell Goran I will be going home early.

'Are you OK?' When he asks, it is in a different tone from the others; it is like the answer really matters.

'Yeah. Got to do a Zoom with Dad, that's all.'

'I'll see you back there, man.'

My pace, as I unlock the Silver Fox from the bike stand and get back in the saddle, is nowhere near the great cyclist Pogačar anymore; more like Pogačar's elderly aunt going for the newspaper.

Plenty of people have been rude to me, these three years. If the toppings have bled from the pizza because it went on its side, the customer will not be toasting you with a gin and tonic when you arrive. It does not matter that you are probably blameless. You accept the criticism; it is the job. But what has happened this evening feels different from most of what I have encountered in London so far.

I feel I have learned something about how some people see us here, something that has not presented itself so strongly before. And that it is something I did not want to know.

*

As usual for a Zoom call, Dad is sitting in the study, near Mum's electric piano, which we could not bring ourselves to sell after she died. I check that his back is feeling OK, that he is doing his physio exercises. He lies and says that he is; Petra makes a face at me behind his back. We talk about the Euro football: England will be playing Croatia soon. Dad is confident. 'It's the thirteenth, the suckers.' He has always claimed the number thirteen is lucky, not the opposite. It is something to do with Jesus and his twelve apostles although, as Mum once said, Jesus himself would have been a lot luckier if he had one fewer of them.

A couple of times a month I send cash at the MoneyGram place in the Post Office. Partly so they can buy useful things, a new orthopaedic cushion for him, a servicing of Petra's car so she does not kill herself driving to the pizza place. And partly so that Dad is reassured that things are good here. That the plan is working. I am sending money so that they see I can send money. To back this up, I always make sure I am very upbeat when the conversation goes on to work. *Yes, a really busy week!* Normally this is true, but it takes energy to hit that upbeat tone, and tonight my heart is not quite willing to do it. To make things worse, the call keeps glitching. They need a faster connection, one of those boosters, but I cannot do everything.

'. . . sorry, Dad, I lost you for a second there.'

'I just said, anyone I should know about, anything happening like that?'

Petra makes a stupid teasing noise, kissing the back of her hand, and my thighs feel sore from the bike, and I snap a little. 'No, Papa, there is not "anyone" to tell you about because I have been on the fucking bike twelve hours a day as usual.'

There is a little pause and I immediately want to stick a fork in my eye. He clears his throat. 'Well, I'm sorry, Dam, I just like hearing about what's going on.'

Even though of course we make friends again, the conversation keeps coming back to haunt me as I lie on the mattress, having eaten a bowl of reheated pasta and said goodnight to Goran. Across the hall come the sounds of his favourite YouTube channel, wrestling commentators going wild over something I cannot see. Soon, his animal snoring, which I do not mind: the sound is kind of comforting, like rain on the windows. I think of Dad lying in the half-empty bed, wondering when he will next get to chat to me.

When I close my eyes I see the guy dropping the edamame

beans into the black bin, can hear again and again the sound of them hitting the bottom of the bin. And this is not a sound I can make into a song. It is more like an itch on the skin, something I can feel even through sleep.

3

I have various tactics to trick the brain out of focusing on being hungry, or too hot: biting my lip till it hurts a little, thinking of cycling races, remembering one day the planet will die, et cetera. The best one is something Mum taught me. Spot an ant, in a pool of partly dried Coke on the floor, in a crack between paving slabs – wherever. By concentrating hard, focusing intently on that one ant, I notice a dozen others in my peripheral vision, and my mind settles for a few seconds on their little lives instead of being trapped in mine.

I am doing this, staring at a busy colony outside the burger place, Bartosz next to me, drinking from my water bottle. I shared it with him because it is a hot day, and his face is even redder than usual; he looks a couple of degrees away from actually setting on fire. There are two thoughts to hold off, at least for a few minutes. The smell of frying food is making my stomach beg for things it cannot have, and – having hydrated myself very well – I feel like I need to piss for ten minutes straight. It was a long wait to get an order, because several riders converged on the burger place at the same time, and the queue has been long, too. We are not allowed inside until they call the order number. We stand in our helmets, with our backpacks, in our sweat, while real customers walk past us without looking. A crazy drunk guy in the square is playing Bob Marley from an old-fashioned stereo, dancing in a jerky, unhinged way. I feel my feet going with it. I want to be singing; I want my guitar in my hands, not the greasy white bag I am waiting to receive.

'Forty-four!' yells the man behind the grill. 'Two patties, no cheese; American extra!' Bartosz nudges me. This is his, the next will be mine. I go towards the bathroom; I am not going to be one of these riders who do it in an alleyway and are criticized on radio phone-ins (the riders' WhatsApp group discusses this sometimes). But the door will not give when I push it: there is a code. I look for help at the man behind the counter: tall Black guy, mask, sweating, steam in his face.

'Toilet's customer-only,' he says, not looking up.

'We are customers, man.' Bartosz is standing up for me. For a skinny guy he has a lot of physical courage; he once deliberately rode his bike right into someone who had just stolen a woman's bag. She took his number and said there would be a reward, but he never heard anything. 'Pickup is still customers.'

'You got to be dining to use them.'

'Piece of crap,' mutters Bartosz, shaking his head. The guy is not even listening; he continues shouting out the orders to be collected. 'I guess we just go through the possible combinations?' Bartosz wants to take a degree in advanced math back at home one day; that is what he is working for. He specializes in doing the sums on what are the best times of day to work; when you are making the most. 'Four digits means there's ten thousand options, so I hope you are not too desperate.'

I laugh, gratefully; any time he spends backing me up is time wasted for him as well as me. 'I'll be OK, man. Get out there, see you soon.'

Bloop-bloop-BLOOP. What-is-THIS? I glance down at the phone: another order has come in for this place. I am quick as a snake; I take it, and will now leave here with two lots of food and get paid twice for a single pickup. These are the moments you hope for. I can wait to piss. A bad moment has become a good one.

Backpack on, the bags neatly side by side. I get the first order dropped off – nice guy, answers door with a beer in hand, a possible tip – and I mount my bike again. I look at the postcode for drop two. I blink and read it again: 40 Laurel Gardens.

It is the angry man's house again. Jesus, Mary and Joseph Christ, as Goran would say.

What is there to be done? I take a breath and wipe my forehead, and even though I want to see the guy's face again like I want a second hole in the backside, I am pedalling towards his place. Of course, no trouble this time finding it. At the sight of the blue door and gate, the brass number 40, I briefly feel myself tense. But a part of me is saying, come on, Damir: we are on the side of right. I will not shuffle about like some rat. I am providing a service.

The bag in my left hand, I knock three times. The noise sounds loud on purpose, like I am a drummer. I shift around on the doorstep, conscious of my heavy bladder. Come on, for God's sake. You are the one who ordered the food. I have not invited myself here for cocktails, man. Again, I could just leave the bag but, after what happened here before, I need to know they have collected it.

A voice. But not the man; a younger person, a girl. 'The bike's here.' That is what the newcomer at the door is, to a customer: a bike with their food, which just happens to be piloted by a man. Someone else speaks: a woman. 'Do I have to do literally *everything* around here?' Humour, not anger, in her voice. I feel myself exhale as the door opens. I put the bag into the woman's hands. She has a large amount of wavy black hair which hangs loose over her shoulders; she is wearing a black jumper with a coloured image.

'Thank you!' she says. 'Have a nice night!'

A tiny moment, but very different from what happened here before. To her, I was not just a bike after all: I was a human, even if I would never feature in her life again. My body registers this in a way, low down, that I cannot quite identify, but it leads to a feeling of relaxation. And *because* I am a human, what I need to do cannot be put off any longer.

I glance to the side of the house, sneak into VINTNER MEWS. Down on the floor goes my backpack. Sixty seconds, I say to myself, come on, get it done and we roll. I stand hunched, facing the fence, aiming for shrubbery. It is hosing out of me, a tremendous relief, and then from behind me: Thump! Thump!

I look over my shoulder and my stomach drops. There is a high part of the angry man's house I have not noticed: a loft conversion. There is a wide window and, from behind it, the teenage kid is hitting the glass to get my attention, laughing. It is not just embarrassing but dangerous to be caught like this, and as I strain to finish my task, my ears catch the sound of the dreaded blue door creaking open. My God. This house is cursed; my rating is dead. Maybe they will even make a formal complaint to the company. The Silver Fox might as well be at the bottom of the river.

'Hello?'

The woman's voice. A small consolation. At least it is not the sneer of edamame man.

'Hello,' I say, hauling myself back into my trousers so at least there will not be accusations of exposing myself. 'I need to apologize very much. This is not something I do; this was extreme. An emergency.'

'Are you all right?' she asks.

It is not what I expected, and in the moment of silence, of confusion, I am able to look at her properly for the first time. Her hair is, once more, the first thing that grabs the eye: thick, many curls. The image on her top is a rainbow. She is wearing flared blue jeans and she is almost the same height as me. Her eyes are dark brown.

'I am fine,' I say, 'but I have to ask, please do not complain, or . . . review me in a way which . . . I mean, if you do not mind.'

'Why didn't you ask to come in?'

Without meaning to, I laugh at this idea, and concern passes across her face. Her lips are big and full; she is a person of generous features.

'We cannot really do that, and I don't think your husband is so keen to see me again.'

The woman frowns; her face is like a cartoon of confusion. I watch as her eyes wrestle with the problem and she puts her hand to her mouth. Her fingernails are painted bright red, but on one finger the paint has chipped off.

'My God, that was you. He was *such* a dick to you.' She shakes her head and looks into the sky, like Mum used to when Goran did something stupid. 'I can't believe you came back again!'

'We don't get the address for the drop until we pick up the food.' It is a relief to bring the conversation onto something general, something that is not about me urinating opposite her house, which I had very much expected to be the main talking point.

'You don't get told where you're going?'

'No.' Because then, I want to explain, we might look at how far it is – or how near – and think, no thank you, fuck that for a game of soldiers. Take it back to the restaurant where it would go cold. In the early days of food delivery apps, when riders were paid an actual wage and the software was less advanced, riders sometimes did do this and get away with it.

ONE MINUTE AWAY

Mario had stories about guys not even working for the company who just got one of the jackets, went around restaurants, took the food and ate it. None of that anymore.

'So how do you know . . . how do you decide whether to take a . . . take a job or not?'

'My rule is: I just take it.'

This makes her laugh, her dark eyes lighting up, the eyebrows arching. The laugh is a surprise, just as it was a surprise to be asked a question about my work. The conversation has not gone the way I feared at all; my unwise act seems to have been forgotten. In fact, for a moment I feel I have forgotten all the context, the argument with the man who lives here, all the dread I felt half an hour ago. But then that awareness resettles and, as if looking at myself from across the street, I think: Damir, what are you doing, why are you giving a YouTube tutorial on delivery apps?

'I should really go and . . . go to the next one.'

'Yes, of course!' says the woman, slightly too loud and eager, like she is also feeling the weirdness. There is an awkward moment as we both start to say something else – I am trying to apologize again; she begins to thank me once more for the food – and our words trip over each other. She starts to walk back towards the house, number 40, and I am sort of following her for a moment. She turns back from her path.

'Well, have a good night.'

'You too,' I say.

The door shuts. I shake my head to clear it because

everything is odd and I am a little dazed, and the app is calling me again. Every second counts.

*

Nine days later: Croatia v. England in the football. As it gets closer to the start of the match, the app is vibrating like an insect is trapped inside it. People have lost their minds, ordering burgers and alcohol at eleven in the morning. It was raining overnight but is now stuffy and hot. For two hours before the game there is drop after drop after drop. I am hot in the saddle and the streets are crowded. Groups of men walk five abreast in football shirts, with serious expressions, as if they think they are going to play in the match themselves. There are songs I cannot decode. The atmosphere around town is fun and a little threatening at the same time.

As I am pedalling past the Cork pub, there is an enormous yell and cheer. My shoulders go down, this cannot be good news for Croatia, but all the same I hop off the bike and peep in through the window, wanting to be like everyone else for a minute, part of the game, part of the event. People are jumping around to celebrate. One man – who does not look a thug, more like a music teacher – is punching the wall, like he is so happy with England's goal it has somehow turned to rage. *Tits*, Goran has texted. On the WhatsApp group, Mario is raging, 'fucking onion', because he thinks the Croatian coach, Zlatko Dalić, has a head like an onion.

ONE MINUTE AWAY

Since the phone is in my hand, I glance at the app. On 'My Account' there is a little exclamation mark, which can mean a tip.

But something is not right. The balance is far too high. It is a mistake, I think. I refresh the app a couple of times. It is still there. The amount cannot be right. It is like I have been paid by accident several times over.

I go into 'My Jobs'. Down the list, through all the five-pound drops, until something sticks out so far you can see it from the Moon. It is the previous Friday night: 40 Laurel Gardens. COMPLETED.

Underneath it is the little green plus sign for a tip, and the figure of one thousand pounds.

I look away from the phone, then back; the unbelievable numbers are still there. There is another noise from the pub, but this time I only just hear it.

4

Keeping a secret from Goran is not something I have any practice in.

Our brains do not work exactly the same way. I am better at English, better with words and numbers in general; Goran types messages at about the speed a dog would. I am the one who makes budgets for food (it is quite easy; basically, try to buy as little food as possible). But emotionally, instinctively, it is as if we share one mental inbox. That is what happens when you see each other every day for twenty years.

There has only been one time we did not know each other's thoughts: it was the day that signalled the end of that twenty-year streak.

We had, as we did most weekends, raced our bikes to the top of Marjan, the hill that looks over Split. As usual, Goran got to the top first. Normally to mark his victories he would do a stupid dance, or a rude mime of some kind. That day, though, he was still and quiet. We stood together, looking out over everything we had spent our lives around: the hospital we were born at, the school where we met, the sea Goran encouraged me to swim in when we were little, the crematorium Mum was resting in now. That was when he came out with an odd phrase: *'Ko ovo može platit.'* This literally means, 'Who could pay for this?', but the sentiment is more like, 'You cannot put a price on this.' You might say it going out on a boat on a beautiful summer morning, or in the perfect moment of peace after an excellent sex session. It sounded strange coming out of his mouth, and I glanced across.

'Are you OK?'

'Yeah,' said Goran.

'Right, is something wrong with your neck then?'

'What?'

'Well, normally when you are OK, you look at my face like a normal human, but you are not.'

I could feel myself becoming nervous. Goran peeled off his sweaty shirt and cleared his throat.

'Would you . . . Dam, do you think you would be OK if I went away?'

'What?'

'To London.'

'What are you talking about?'

'Mario, you remember Mario? He's in London now. I was talking to him. He has a job delivering food for an app.'

'Like, pizza delivery?'

'*Everything* delivery.' He started to explain. At the time, things like Deliveroo and Uber Eats were quite new. 'You know. It can't always be this for me, cleaning toilets, chopping wood.' Goran's eyes were unusually soft and shiny. '*You* have your music, you have a dream. Me, I just want . . . I don't know – a family, kids maybe, a house. Something. A life. So at some point I have to do something better, right.' He pointed back to the bike. 'It sounds like if you can ride fast, you can make a ton of money. I'd like to be paid for something I'm actually good at, not be . . . you know, a human horse.'

I knew what he meant. Goran had not – to raid my iPhone list again – *set the world on fire* at school, although he did once set a science lab on fire. A lot of this was not his fault. His dad was killed in Dubrovnik, in the war, when we were only four. Goran has only one memory of his father, of him picking Goran up and swinging him around in the kitchen, and in dark moments he is not even sure whether it is a real memory or something he just wants to have happened. His mother was away a lot, trying to earn money to raise the kids, and he lived for long periods with his grandmother who had her own problems: she believed strongly in alien abductions and in old age this became her main topic of conversation. By the time we were sixteen, Goran more or less lived full-time at ours, sleeping on a couch in my room, and my parents became his parents. He paid a little rent by doing whatever jobs were out there; as he said himself, being a human horse. I had never really questioned whether he was satisfied like this; maybe I had not wanted to. We were twenty-four, messing around. Life was girlfriends, nights out. I worked in a music shop. But now this.

'Of course I'd be all right,' I said, 'don't be an idiot.' I called him an idiot again at the airport, a few weeks later, at the sign which said PASSENGERS ONLY BEYOND THIS POINT, and when he was safely in the air I locked myself in the men's room and cried for a few minutes.

We spoke every day, but time went pretty slowly without him. I had been seeing a girl called Téa, but she decided she was 'not ready for anything serious', and six months later got engaged to a tennis player with dreadlocks. Some days Goran would have no phone credit, or he would arrange to go to an internet café and chat to me, but then the deliveries would get too busy. I would sit staring at the computer screen like the *Guinness Book of Records* entry for Biggest Loser, thinking about the fun he would be having in London, which I pictured basically like a James Bond movie, Goran riding his bike across the top of red buses, leaping over Big Ben.

My boss at the music shop, Josip, was well known to be a bastard. He did not even seem to like music; it was more like a wizard had cursed him to run the place. He almost always played the same records, by an act called The Incredible String Band, whose stuff, in my opinion, was fine but not incredible. Part of my reason for working there was that it would inspire my own songwriting; I thought I would come home firing like Dolly Parton when she wrote 'Jolene' and 'I Will Always Love You' in one day. But it had been a couple of years, and it was fair to say I did not feel a lot like Dolly. My days were spent listening to this complicated British folk music, and watching old men come in, inspect the vinyl for hours at a time, then leave without buying a thing. Josip would roll his eyes if I was three minutes late, or even went for a shawarma at lunch, despite the fact the shop was so quiet he hardly even needed me: he could have put his Alsatian in charge and nothing would have gone wrong.

Mum had passed away a couple of years before. The atmosphere in the house was still strange, because without her we did not really know what to do with ourselves. And suddenly it no longer felt like I was in my mid-twenties, with all kinds of possibilities in front of me; it was as if life was getting away from me. Goran had zoomed off on his bike and I was stuck.

One day, not long after we had both got WhatsApp, there came a picture of a motorbike from Goran. Red and green paintwork.

What is this? I typed.

'This', I am calling the Empress.

What do you mean?

He was then typing for about a hundred years, of course.

I'm sorry, I did not realize your brain had been taken out and replaced with a passion fruit. What I MEAN is, I have bought this beautiful bike and now I can go everywhere as fast as shit. Isn't she amazing?

How the fuck did you afford a motorbike?

I told you, this job is like a video game. The better you get, the more money you get, you go up to the new level. So, I'm in a new level.

ONE MINUTE AWAY

Wow.

This could be you, Dam. Be your own boss. Work when you want, stop when you want. Earn money. London is amazing.

Don't be a dick. Where would I even live?

This time, the 'typing' interval was very brief, like he had been waiting for the question and had his answer all ready to go.

My flatmate is going to leave soon, going back to Poland. You could live with me, brother.

From then on, every time I complained about work, or said I was missing him, he would just send the same photo of the motorbike, the Empress. After a couple of weeks, he began sending it every morning, without even waiting for the conversation to start. I kept telling him to shut up, kept saying I could not leave Dad and Petra, had my music gigs here in Split, could not risk it all like he had. But he knew he was going to win. Like I said, he always knows. He has a plan.

*

But now, now there is a secret. The reason I cannot tell Goran about the money – or, of course, any other living soul – is that I must not raise his hopes yet. We can earn about four hundred pounds in a normal week. Three hundred if it is slow, maybe five when things are crazy: and then occasionally a few tips here and there. Half of this goes straight into the account of Caroline, the invisible lady who takes such good care of our place. I have a little fund I am slowly building for a motorbike, I send funds to Dad and Petra, Goran and I go to the Turkish superstore for our big bags of pasta. A thousand pounds out of nowhere would be like getting paid for two or three weeks or work that never existed. The trouble is, the money is just a number on my screen, not a bag of banknotes I can reach out and touch. At any moment it could vanish, like something from a fairy tale. Who gives a tip of a thousand pounds because their husband was a little rude? What if she pressed the wrong button, did it in error, will shit herself when the bank statement comes through?

If that does happen, though, she can contact the company, and I will be able to say: look, I have not touched a penny of it, have it back. That is what I tell myself for a couple of days. Goran and I swear at the shower, ride our bikes, text, hang out at Mario's place and laugh at his story about a customer who answered the door completely naked. Everything seems normal. And yet the money is still there. After a couple of days, it starts to seem stupid *not* to talk about it – especially because I am starting to be paranoid that Goran can sense I have a secret, and I am probably acting weirdly as a result.

I have to know whether this is real, and so I come up with an idea.

★

ONE MINUTE AWAY

In the café on our street, which normally we only visit on a special occasion, there is a rack of handmade cards by a local artist. Fuzzy images of birds in front of a sunset, footsteps on a beach. In my opinion they are slightly worse than normal greeting cards and cost slightly more. I choose one with a rainbow on the front because of her jumper on that night – perhaps rainbows appeal to her. £2.95. I borrow a pen from the woman from behind the counter.

Dear . . .

I do not know the name, of course. The name and phone number of customers are always encrypted, to make sure we cannot text 'fuck you, champ!' after deliveries like the edamame beans disaster. Dear 'customer'? It sounds about as friendly as the app's fake thank-you for your order. I might just as well write 'hey, asshole'. One word in and I am having a confidence crisis.

Dear generous person.

My name is Damir and I was your delivery rider two weeks ago (4 June). We had a conversation in the Vintner Mews and you were very compassionate.

(I look up several possible words for this, but it seems to be the right one, even though it feels like it takes half an hour to write.)

I then found you had paid me a huge tip. I do not know if it was a deliberate tip, so I am thanking you but also giving you the chance to take the money back! I have not spent any.

Anyway thank you again for the good conversation. My phone number is below.

MARK WATSON

Damir Kovačević

Even knowing what to write on the front of the card is a riddle. I do not want to leave it blank because it could be intercepted by a curious person in the family. I write 'CUSTOMER'. But of course, the angry man also has an account, is also a customer, and so I add 'FEMALE' above it. FEMALE CUSTOMER. What is that? I mutter to myself. The more I write, the more I hate it. Half of me wants to cycle straight to a bridge and drop my stupid note over the side.

I am now able to navigate to Laurel Gardens with minimum concentration. I pass a petrol station, and a playground, which is always quiet and a little spooky when I go past it. The roads becoming wider, darker, wealthier. The strange order of the numbers which I am now used to. I rest the Silver Fox against a fence some distance from the blue door, just in case I am seen coming. All this feels stupid, like I think I am a spy, rather than just a dweeb on an old bike. But perhaps I am enjoying it a little. A couple of bloop-bloops offering pickups; I do not really register them. For these five minutes, I am in my own life, not a small character in someone else's.

The gate creaks loudly as I open it, in a way I do not remember happening before. As usual there is nobody visible in the street at all, just the warm lights of other houses, the odd silhouette in a window; movements, conversations just beyond the edge of what I can know. I push the card through the letterbox. I am gone, silent, quick like any other delivery. I am 'the bike' again.

5

It is less than two hours later that something happens. A large Indian delivery is on my back, rain starting to fall in my face. The food smells unbelievable and I say to myself: maybe, when I have chosen 'End Shift', we could get a takeaway. If we only have starters, it is not too expensive. But I do not know whether I would be thinking like this if it were not for the phantom money in the app. Leaning against the wall after the drop, for a sip of water, I see a message from an unknown number.

FEMALE CUSTOMER here. Thank you for your gorgeous note. I'd love to discuss. Are you available to come back to number 40 yet again!? I will be up late, and no shouty husband to contend with (he's abroad). No pressure . . . and the money is definitely for you. Decca (it's a version of Jessica. I slightly hate it but it's a bit too late to change it now) xx

'The money is definitely for you.' My heart is out of its seat and running around the room for a second. I think of sending a big present to Dad and Petra in Split; of filling our place with a year's worth of food. But pretty soon these fantasies give way to questions, and to a vague unease in my stomach. What does she want to 'discuss'? And should I really be going back to the house?

I can quickly summarize the company's rules on personal relationships with customers: the rules are, do not have personal relationships with customers. Do not attempt to gain their phone number, do not converse with them away from the app, do not go into their house. But now there is a kind of tiny rebellion in my mind. I remember being in the record shop, a few days after Goran sent me the picture of the motorbike. The famous song by Tracy Chapman was playing and it seemed to talk to me. Either leave now, or die like this. Then I picture Decca standing at the end of the alley. Her rainbow sweater, her big thick bunch of hair. The big hands, painted fingernails. She seemed a good person then; she seems a good person in this message. I type a reply before I can talk myself out of it.

I can come in two hours? Thank you. Damir

Cycling to the address feels like a dream: the streets are familiar, yet I do not really understand what I am doing there. A large moon is rising, although the sky is still bright. A couple of foxes are lying together by a collection of bins; they glance up at me without much interest, more at home here than I am. When I arrive at number 40, I am unsure what to do with my own Fox. It feels a little strange to wheel it down Decca's path like I am proposing to stay for the weekend, go off into the countryside together. I try to turn off these thoughts and knock on the big blue door.

I hear her footsteps. The door swings open. She has on a big green turtleneck jumper, a strange thing for a summer night. And instead of the jeans, leggings, like somebody might wear on a bike. Her hair is all over her shoulders again. She smiles and clears her throat.

'Oh, hi, come in! You can bring the bike in, there's plenty of space for the bike.' She says all this very quickly, like it was a prepared speech and she was keen to get through it.

I am in a 'hall', but not a hall like our flat has, where the two of us can only just stand side by side. This is a wide space with fancy hooks to hang coats and hats and umbrellas. An enormous print, which is an old-fashioned map of London before they could spell words properly. 'This way,' she says. There is a giant sofa in mustard yellow, armchairs, a fireplace, a television as big as a train window, recessed Bose speakers, and a long low glass table with books about cities to visit before the end of your life. The place continues into a kitchen area with a green range cooker. Shiny white tiles, a large dining table. And even beyond this is a conservatory, which has more sofas and other furniture, and another TV which is walking distance, as they say here, from the original one.

I wheel my bike over the floorboards, which I am relieved are dark wood and so will not be stained by any filth I have collected on my treks around London. My hostess does a kind of embarrassed laugh.

'It's vulgar, I know.'

I do not recognize this word but also do not want to seem like an idiot, so I give a sort of careful laugh and look out of the glass doors towards the garden: a very large shed which I later learn contains a gym; a seat that swings back and forth.

'I've been – would you like a wine? My friend stood me up so I'm self-pity-drinking. Or a beer? Sit down, get comfortable. If you want.'

She still seems a little nervous, like she is trying too hard to be a good host. Almost as if she is wondering why she is hosting at all. And, for sure, most people *would* be nervous to have a guy in their house whom they do not really know from the drummer in the Muppets. For sure, this is an unusual situation: the first time, after hundreds and hundreds of drops, that I have properly been inside a customer's house. But, after all, she invited me here. I sit at the long, wooden table and glance down at the floor. Decca is barefoot, and her toenails are bright red, as if they have just been painted. For some reason this detail flicks a switch in my head. I have selected 'End Shift', I am not crazy. I have spent all day pushing the pedals, dodging the cars, earning my money. The company does not own me. I do not, as we know, even have a boss. Why should I not sit and have a drink with this new acquaintance, just like anyone else might do if they were asked? Well, there are probably ten or twelve answers to the question; Goran, I can imagine, would have a couple. But that switch will not go back. Something has shifted inside me.

ONE MINUTE AWAY

'If you are sure, I will take a beer. Thank you.'

Decca opens the fridge, takes out a bottle. She sits down at right-angles to me, her feet close to mine. She looks for a moment like she is trying to touch her glass against my beer bottle, as if for a toast, but then she seems to change her mind. Almost before I have taken a sip of my drink, she is checking on my satisfaction, like they do in movies when the lovers are at a fancy restaurant.

'Is that nice? We've got other beers; I'm not really a beer person, but . . .'

'Very nice.' It is true. The tang of a real-label beer is quite an experience for the tastebuds. In the moment's glimpse into the fridge, I saw bottles of wine packed in together, beers, shelves full of food. My stomach betrays me, making a grinding noise, and Decca turns her face to look right into mine.

'Are you hungry? Sorry if that's a bit forward. Just, I'm sure there'd be something . . .'

Of course, I *am* hungry: I have eaten nothing except a Tesco sandwich for ten hours. I would kill a man for a big plate of rice and meat. Even so, the alarm bells in my brain – which I managed to quieten down for the beer – are now rattling and shrieking. To sip a beer in this strange house: this is just about OK. To get my napkin on for fine dining: no, that is too far, too many steps down this unknown road.

'No, thank you, I am fine.' My voice comes out too formal. It echoes in this large room, this kitchen which takes up about the same space as our whole flat in Cecil Court. I feel a certain pressure to move the conversation on.

'What did you want to discuss?'

'Sorry?'

'You said you wanted to talk about the . . . about the money.' It is strange, embarrassing, to talk about it out loud. As I have said, the whole thing about the way the company works is that nobody needs to talk directly about what is being bought and sold; you do not hand over cash, you do not even bleep a card machine. It all happens by magic. Nothing personal. She has made it personal. Her tongue flicks out, plays with her front teeth. Her laugh is quite loud even when uncertain; it is loud in the same way her hair is big or her tallness is noticeable.

'I mean, I don't know that I had anything specific to say . . .' Decca says, sounding wary. 'I wanted to apologize, I guess.'

'It is not yours to apologize for,' I try to express. 'This stuff happens sometimes; people get angry.'

The beer is warming up every second; my hands feel sticky. For the first time I am conscious of her perfume, which is smoky like a bonfire. It is at the very edge of my senses, like when you can almost smell the coffee you know is being brewed in the next room.

'I just didn't want you to think we are *those guys*,' she says, 'even though we are.' Decca gives a short laugh. What exactly does she mean? There are so many unknowns, I think. Her life, their life, must be so different from mine.

'I don't think you are anything in particular.' Straight away this sounds like an insult. 'No, I mean . . .'

She laughs, this time full and bold. 'Seriously, these days I *feel* like nothing in particular.'

'I didn't mean . . .'

'I know, Damir – Damir, right?'

As I am confirming the name, her hand brushes against mine. Such a light touch that it could be seen as a mistake, but then, the thousand pounds have turned out not to be a mistake. The feeling changes my breathing a little. I swallow my beer in a couple of big gulps.

'Are you sure it is what you want?' I make myself ask. 'To give me this tip. There will be ways I can give it back.'

'No, no!' Decca sounds like she is almost panicking at this suggestion. I glance down again at her bare feet, which are moving up and down under the table like she is playing an invisible drum kit. 'No, look, my husband was so horrible to you. And I know it's hard on you guys. If it helps you, amazing.'

'Hard on us guys?'

'This whole thing of . . . you know. People working without contracts, without proper rights. Anyway, it's not my business, and I don't want to patronize you, either – God, I'm just talking nonsense.' She gets up to refill her wine-glass. 'Another beer?'

My brain is telling me I have to say no, this time. But not because I do not want to. On the contrary, it is a little alarming how much I do want to. How easily I can imagine, even though it is 100 per cent insane, staying here all evening, having more drinks, talking more about my life, finding out about hers.

'I really should go. It is very kind of you and it does not make sense, the tip, but it . . . thank you.'

I am not sure I can express to her in English the blessing of the money, or my incredulity that she can just give it away, or my confusion about whether it is really right to take it. In the end all these beginnings cancel themselves out into silence. Rising to my feet, I collect up the beer can – wanting to be polite – but am then left looking around the enormous kitchen with no clue where to put it. Decca laughs and reaches out for the can. 'Give it here, I'll . . . the bins are all hidden behind panels. *Opening up the space.*' She says this in a mocking way. 'At some point Niall talked himself into thinking he's an expert on designing houses, rather than just someone who buys them.'

'In our kitchen you would not really be able to hide the bin,' I say, 'unless you shoved it through the bit of the floor where there is a kind of hole.'

'You live with someone, with a partner?' Her back is turned as she asks. I watch her stoop to open a cupboard – the door glides at her touch, like it is automated – and I can make out some sort of tattoo on the back of her neck through the folds of her dark hair.

'Just with Goran. We work as a team.'

'Goran is your . . .?'

'Oh, just my friend. I do not have a partner.' Only in answering the question do I register that there might be something in it beyond mere curiosity and, to cover that thought, I babble some Goran trivia at her. 'We grew up together – his father . . . anyway, it was complicated, but he kind of lived with us, and it was his idea to come here to London and do this. The money is good. I mean, not always, but . . . better than we would probably do at home. And more fun.'

As I deliver this stream of words, my hands are on the Silver Fox, ready to wheel her back into the real world. Decca finally looks around at me, then down at her painted toes, and I cannot stop myself gazing the same way for a moment.

'So – I'm sorry if this is ridiculous, and I've got it wrong . . .'

She pauses, her eyes appealing for something, and I manage to say: 'I don't think you have got anything wrong.'

'I'll just be angry with myself if I don't ask: is there a way I could see you again?'

'You mean – like this, like a night?'

'Yeah. He's always away on Fridays, for example.'

'I could come another Friday, like next Friday.'

'Or – I mean, there are other times, too,' she adds, quickly.

They are strange, these negotiations. She has a husband and a teenager, and a job; she will have social commitments and places to go which I cannot easily imagine. Me: aside from the rider drinks, which we make up as we go along, every day is really the same. But I surely have to play *hard to get* – a phrase in my phone note, from a Netflix show we streamed illegally – at least a little.

'No, I think next Friday works. I will have to check.' I

almost laugh at myself: check what? I am pretty sure Goran and I are not booked for the opera. Still, her dark eyes sparkle at me and I feel like we have handled this well between us, somehow.

'Amazing. Well, I'll . . . see you then.'

As quickly as that, whatever relationship we had when I arrived – a rider visiting to say thank you for an act of kindness – has turned into something else. I watch her close the blue door which was slammed on me only a couple of weeks ago, giving me a little wave first. The brass number 40, the trees along the street. I am standing on virtually the same spot as when her husband called me back. But a whole lot of other things feel very, very different.

Goran is already asleep when I get back to Cecil Court, his wrestling videos playing on endlessly to no audience. I go quietly into his room, gather up his phone – his password is my birthday, like mine is his – and press stop. Going back across the hall and lying on the mattress, I know straight away that it will be more difficult than usual to sleep. *Is there a way I could see you again?* I think about her eyes widening a little as she asked the question, as if she had taken herself by surprise. The glimpse of the tattoo through the waves of hair at the back of her neck. I was with her for probably no more than twenty minutes, but it feels in my memory like my entire work shift was twenty minutes and the time at Decca's was the rest of the day.

I want to get my phone out of the wall and send her a message. Just to say I enjoyed it; to say thank you for having me over. But it feels like another step into something I do not understand, into water of uncertain depth.

It is strange to think how cautious I was; how sending a WhatsApp felt like a line I could not cross. The only line that really mattered was the one separating me from her house, separating rider from customer. Once I stepped across that line, everything that followed was always going to happen.

*

A thousand pounds! When I wake up to the quacks, part of me wants to dance around the kitchen like the Norwegian family who won the lottery twice. I slip out to the café where I bought Decca's card and, when Goran opens his eyes, I am standing over his mattress.

'Christ, why were you so late back? You get laid?'

I feel the briefest shift in my stomach at the question. 'Please accept this complimentary coffee and croissant.' Around his bed there is nowhere to rest the cup and the pastry bag; clothes, headphones, food wrappers – more mess than it should be possible to generate for one man who hardly owns anything.

'What, are we too good for normal coffee?'

'Why don't we find out?' The glee of the reveal has taken me over. 'Monday, we finish at six p.m. I have a mission for us.'

'Mission, what mission?' Goran stretches a long leg out of the blanket to kick me in the thigh. 'What are you talking about?'

'I want us to do a big food shop. Go to an actual supermarket, load up on stuff. Somewhere where they haven't had rats recently. And then I want us to go for a drink, not in the Cork or at Mario's, in a . . . a nice actual bar.'

'A shop where they haven't had rats! An *actual bar!*' Goran rubs his hands. 'Have we gone up in the world? What is your deal? You sold a song to Adele, or a kidney or something?'

'Yeah, both of those. She was having a hard time writing and couldn't find a donor.' It is too much to hold back; I open the app, get into My Jobs. 'Have a look at the tip there.'

The noise that comes out of Goran is hard to transcribe. If you could do it in letters, it would be something like WAAAAAAAAAHHHHHH-HAAAAAAAAA-HAAAAAAAAA. It is maybe close to when Mum threw a bucket of cold water over him at a barbecue, years ago; one of her last parties.

'Are you fucking with me?'

'Well, was the coffee real or not, and are we going to have yoghurt in the fridge later or not? You decide.'

'And you're sure it isn't a mistake, someone . . .'

'I've checked with the woman. It's real.'

'So the woman is, who, the Queen of England?'

'It was a crazy rich person.'

Goran has taken the phone and is looking at it intently, like a customs guy inspecting a passport. When he sees the pickup details, the burger place, he does another mad laugh. 'A thousand bucks tip off an eight-pound meal! She could have bought a whole farm! *Ajme!* She must be insane, man.

You need to be her personal food chauffeur! One drop a week, the rest of the time sit with your balls out!'

He leaps out of his bed, completely naked, and starts to sing a song called *'Kad Čujem Tambure'*: 'When I Hear the Tambourines'. This is something you would hear around the campfire if you came to Croatia, and then only if your companions were eighty years old; he is singing it because it is stupid, the same as us having this money out of nowhere is stupid, and Goran loves it when things take a stupid turn. 'OI!' He thumps down the toilet seat and cackles, repeating out loud the amount of the mad tip, Decca's tip. 'A thousand pounds! Mary Christ!' It makes me grin, all this; it is what I have imagined ever since I first saw the big number on my screen.

But deep in my chest there is something else, too. The tipper is not just a crazy stranger. She is a person I went to see last night, and will see again next Friday. She has already messaged me: *hope I wasn't too forward last night. It was a lot of fun.* I have begun, and deleted, three replies already. I do not know how to feel about Decca, yet. About this tip. I just know that things are more complicated than they were even twenty-four hours ago. And if I do go through with this, if I do go to her house again in a week's time, they are certainly not going to get any simpler.

6

Down the Ilford Road, a motorbike at lazy speed and a cyclist going full pelt; big backpacks on as usual. But we are not wearing our delivery jackets. And the backpacks are for us, not them.

For a while we just wander around the huge, shiny building, as Petra and I used to when we were taken to the toy superstore in Zagreb. We take in the smell of hams and cheeses and the bright colours of the fruit. Of course we can see and smell these things at the market, or the Turkish store, and they would probably be fresher, better, there. But it is about the experience. It is like seeing a film in a multiplex cinema, instead of on your phone.

We have set a limit of £100 for this historic shop. This seems like the sort of money Louis XIV would spend on entertaining, but it is soon obvious that you can spend it very quickly in a supermarket this size. 'Seven pounds for that chorizo,' says Goran, rubbing his eyes at the meat counter, like a pensioner finding out what his childhood home is worth now. 'I don't care if you hang it up like we're in Spain, seven pounds, *ajme*, fuck my life.' We browse, laughing, like tourists. A ready-made lasagne, for ten times what the ingredients would cost us, because the packet has a chef's name and a drawing of Venice. Tomatoes still on the vine. Ice cream in flavours which sound like a poet has written them: 'A touch of mango', 'Viennese patisserie swirl'.

But, of course, there are also bargains you can get here, if you can justify the time it takes to come – which we normally cannot. There are big packets of goods which, on our street, we would have to buy in single tins or boxes that say NOT TO BE SOLD SEPARATELY. We load up on as many of these as we believe will fit in our backpacks. Canned vegetables, pasta, rice, tortillas: food for many weeks of meals to come. Kitchen roll and toilet paper – together in our flat for the first time. Goran keeps track of our spend on his phone, messing up the button-presses as usual and getting the math wrong.

'Thirteen bucks plus three ninety-nine plus one seventy-nine – wait, how are we at twenty-four?'

'We aren't, Gogo. Just let me do it in my head, will you? Eighteen seventy-eight.'

'What do you want, a badge?'

'Doing stuff in your head is good, it's good for Alzheimer's.'

'You are twenty-eight, you weirdo. If you're worrying about that, you already have vegetables growing in your brain.'

We get strange looks from people who are trying to say:

the supermarket is not meant to be fun, what is the matter with you? But to be here, now, with Goran, is the greatest fun of all. We grant ourselves a large case of beers, which can go on the back of the Empress, and some luxury items like mayonnaise, stuffed olives, grapes. At the checkout the bill comes in at £99.40. Goran runs off, comes back with three bananas, and we watch the till creep up to £99.82.

'You have anything for eighteen pence?' I ask, in English. 'There is a budget.' The woman at the till smirks; she can sense this is some sort of private joke. She points to a selection of kids' lollipops by the side of the counter. We find one for twenty pence; I enter my PIN – Goran's birthday digits, 1212 – and £100.02 disappears by magic from my phone. When I get to the other side, where Goran is packing, the woman hands me a two-pence coin from the cash register with a 'don't tell' finger to the lips. All this clowning, this playing with money simply because you know you have it. It is disconcerting, but a voice in my head says that I could get used to it.

We roar and pedal back home and drop our prizes at Cecil Court, quickly throwing the cold items into our tiny fridge which – for the first time – looks almost uncomfortably well stocked. Then, the tube station. Part two of the adventure I have planned. The strange names on the map; although we have lived in London a while now, we never go to the famous parts. Charing Cross. Islington. Camden, where bands play that I would listen to when I first took the guitar on, up in my bedroom, starting to learn English from the *NME*. The many coloured lines of the tube – pink, different blues, red, black; each one a different set of possibilities.

'Where – like, if you could go *anywhere* – do you want to see?'

'Anywhere?' Goran's entire face is a smile.

We change to the Northern Line and get out at London Bridge, walk towards the tallest building in the whole city. Goran has told me about this bar before. He was invited there, not long after arriving, by a Croatian acquaintance who worked in finance. Goran could hardly speak English, and could not afford anything. He panicked, claimed to be allergic to alcohol, and spent the evening trying to cover this lie in more and more difficult ways, while the guy's boss kept calling him 'Gordon'. But he remembered being up in the clouds, where he loved to be – planes, mountains, even just the hill we used to race up on our bikes. He wanted to go back.

To reach the bar, we have to take an elevator with a security guard stationed outside it. The guy takes a couple of long looks at us – even without the jackets, our vibe is not the usual one of customers here – and then nods us past. Inside, it is almost too dark to see each other properly, and the cocktail prices feel like the prices of paintings in a gallery.

'This is psycho to even be here,' says Goran. 'We don't have to drink here, I just wanted to see it, you know? We can just go down and go to a normal bar, or—'

'*Ko ovo more platit*,' I say, that phrase: 'Who could pay for this?'

The whole building is a window, London below. Outside, skyscrapers are lit up like a movie; trains go by; a helicopter passes just overhead. Goran's eyes glitter. Views like this are for people who own the city: guys like us are there to help them. That is all fine and we understand it. But tonight it is not like that, and I think about Marjan, about the day he told me he was leaving, and how far we have come since then.

'We *do* have to drink here,' I say. 'One drink.'

'I love you, man,' says Goran, and we do not even bother to undermine the idea with humour.

★

The next night, the Tuesday, I summon Dad and Petra for a special Zoom. I show them an Amazon confirmation, a pair of items on its way to them. A second-hand projector and a large screen. I have photoshopped a clown's face onto the screenshot to hide the price of this, which was just over three hundred pounds. It would have been worth this price just to hear the gasp and yell that both of them produce.

'Dami, you idiot, how can you afford this? *Can* you afford it?' Dad is wriggling around in his orthopaedic chair and Petra keeps clapping her hands together and screaming.

'Of course I can, or I wouldn't do it. Work has been going well, like I told you, so . . .'

'Petra, go and tell Bogdan!'

'I'm on it,' called my sister, already leaving the room. 'I'm going to tell everyone on the street! I don't care if they're in bed! Get up, assholes! We have a cinema now!'

It is a rash use of money, of course, but I know what would happen if I just sent cash: they would spend it on food, on fixing the boiler. And the cinema is my family's favourite thing. When Mum was alive, we would go to the beach at Bačvice, to the open-air showings. People in chairs on the sand, cocktails from the bar. The wild sound of the seabirds, the way the sun sets on the water and looks like it has been swallowed up, turning the sea red. I still have dreams where we are all there, the four of us, and wake up feeling cheated. Of course, that cannot happen again, and anyway Dad cannot easily go as far as the beach now. So when his back started to be a big problem, we used to joke about building a movie theatre around him, turning the home into one.

The equipment I have got online is very likely not high quality. Dad will not be hosting a film festival, showing Keira Knightley where the bathroom is (top of the stairs, cannot miss it). But it is something that could not have happened without me. The feeling reminds me of when I had been here for six months and pulled together enough money to send them a Nespresso coffee machine, and Dad acted like I had got him a space rocket, demonstrating its use to everyone who came within a mile, including a bailiff who came round about an unpaid gas bill and ended up staying for a cappuccino.

It is not that Dad and Petra would starve without me, but

things have not been easy for a while. Even without his grief for Mum, Dad is now in poor shape for a man only in his mid-sixties. The shipyard where he worked for twenty years was bought by a multinational company who 'stripped down the workforce for strategic reasons'. The payoff did not at all reflect the sweat he gave the company, and the work had wrecked his back and shoulders; plus, at sixty-five you cannot easily show up to the Job Centre and say, 'So, what have we got?' Petra, meanwhile, is held back from career success by her two great loves: marijuana, and not working.

If I had stayed in Split, maybe I would have been able to support them, but I would have been worn down by now, even if I had found something better than the record shop. And I would not have been able to get treats, like this; Dad would have been too anxious that I was wasting money on him. Since I have been over here, he has had almost no idea what is going on with me. I keep topping him up with positivity, with the notion that anything is possible here, that Goran and I are not just having fun but making good. The first part of that is true; now, thanks to Decca, the second part is too – at least in this moment, even if a moment is all it is.

Lying on my mattress, I am seized again by the temptation to message her. I want her to see that the tip has made two people happy in a part of the world she might never have visited – quite apart from Goran and me. Every kind act has multiple consequences: that is the sort of thing you see on Instagram posts but maybe do not internalize. I want her to feel it. Or maybe I just wanted to text her all along, and this is the opportunity. I attach the screenshot of the Amazon confirmation, and then of Dad and Petra's excited faces through Zoom. *You did this!* I write. My fingers dance over the screen, I delete, rewrite, and finally send.

It is late, and I imagine she is with her husband, or – who knows? – at the theatre, already asleep, doing any number of things. But the caption 'typing' comes up immediately, and I feel myself holding my breath.

This is amazing. I didn't know whether you would text again or whether I should message or whether I'd sort of imagined the whole thing.

I have saved you on my phone under the name Female Customer.

(Typing. Typing. Typing. It is not quite like the funny irritation of waiting for Goran to spell something out. There is a suspense to it. I can visualize her dark eyes, the way they darted around the kitchen when she was working up to saying something.)

I have been thinking of you literally since the moment you shut the front door and left, she writes. I start to reply, not knowing quite what to say, but she is writing again. *Did you mean it when you said you would like to come again on Friday? Would you like me to cook something? Sorry if that's too forward. AGAIN.*

By the time I digest this, she has added yet another message:

I'm a pretty shit cook, by the way, if that lowers the stakes.

'Would you like me to cook something?' How has it happened that this is now a dinner invitation? I think of her hair, all the great curls and waves of it, and the loud, delighted way she laughs. She is not mine to think of in this way, or to sit and have dinner with. I should not be going back to her house like this, surely. But, in a way, admitting this to myself is enough. I have always done what I 'should' do. I am a nice guy who picks up Goran's coat when he leaves it on the floor, lets other people past on the cycle lane, sends money back home to the family. Maybe it is not surprising that my old girlfriend dumped me pretending she wanted to be single, or that – while Goran has a woman from Manchester who sometimes sleeps with him when she comes down here on business – I have not had any attention like that since I first stepped off the plane. The person who always does what he 'should' is not exciting company.

I would like that a lot. Thank you.

'Send'. The ticks go blue to show that she has read the message. I wait for a response, but nothing comes. Has she changed her mind? Is she just asleep? Goran's wrestling videos come screaming from across the hall, as usual. *'Well, will you look at THAT!'* The real-time of WhatsApp, the 'typing' and the 'seen' notifications seem like a curse now, making me stare at the screen to see whether it will come to life. Whether her fingers will spark into action again, a couple of kilometres away in Laurel Gardens. I see our neighbourhood from above like a shot in a movie; her in her expensive house, me lying on my thin mattress, this invisible thread snaking between the phone screens, between us.

Decca Bevan, @jessicachloebevan: she is easy enough to find on Instagram. Three thousand followers; it feels like a lot. Her profile picture shows her clinging to a zip-wire, a big red helmet, her face frozen in a kind of horrified delight, mouth wide open like she is shouting. I like that it is not a particularly glamorous photo, certainly not a posed one like so many on the website; she just looks as if she is having the best time of her life. Other pictures show her on a beach; in a stadium, maybe a music gig, arm around the teenager; raising a cocktail to the camera with two similar-aged friends. There are no pictures of the husband, the bean-waster, in the first ten or so that I look at. It feels like a good sign.

But come on, Damir. This is madness, however fun it might be. I make myself get up and plug the phone in on the other side of the room, safely out of reach and face-down so I will not be tempted if I see it light up. There is another day of riding ahead; I am tired, I need to sleep. But sleep will not come for a while and, even when it does, I feel on some level that I am still watchful, not really resting at all. The way you sleep when you are expecting to snap awake at any time; when danger is near.

7

'This is absolute bullshit, man.' Mario is sitting on his motorbike, sweat from the already hot morning sparkling on his forehead. His massive hand is on the shoulder of Bartosz, who is shaking his head and gnawing his fingernails and looks like he might be about to cry, which is not something we do a lot of.

'What's up?' I ask, or Goran does; sometimes, like twins, it feels like he says the exact same thing I was thinking, and I almost question whether it *was* me who vocalized it.

'They took elite off me,' Bartosz mutters.

'Jesus. What?'

Mario explains. A couple of weeks ago, Bartosz got Covid – even though he still always wears a mask, and has been more careful about it than any of the rest of us. A customer came out coughing, looking ill, took the bag right out of Bartosz's hand. Maybe a coincidence, but he got sick forty-eight hours later and, because he respects the rules, missed out on a week of earning. He used the app's 'feedback' function – a little icon with a man talking through a megaphone – to say, hey, we should be better protected from this kind of thing; customers should be subject to a code of conduct like we are. The company said they would investigate it, which we know normally means as much as saying Santa Claus will sort it out; it is like us 'contacting Caroline'. But what Bartosz was not prepared for was that, mysteriously, his 'elite' rating has vanished. Fewer good drops, no bonuses. No official communication from the company. His little star – which takes you, minimum, two years to earn – is just gone.

'It is nuclear level bullshit,' Mario reiterates. 'Should be illegal.'

'I'll be fine.' Bartosz's face is as red as the diagrams of lava we studied in school. He does not want this attention; it is making him more self-conscious. 'I'm going to sign up for one of the other ones, do both, it's what everyone is doing.' We nod, wisely; lots of riders do shuttle between different services now, switching jackets like the guy in Dubrovnik who does quick-change shows in the town centre. But we all know there is no real likelihood a different company would treat us differently. If anything, we are the lucky ones. There was a guy working for the biggest delivery firm in the UK who did not get paid because of some minor offence, could not make his rent, was found dead. We all know these stories. We look after ourselves and, as far as we can, we look after each other.

'OK,' says Mario, 'everyone's coming round to ours tonight, like late, after ten. Karel's in town.'

Goran and I say the right things: *awesome, Karel, we'll be there!* Like this is a guy who never fails to get the party going, when in fact we hardly know him from Pol Pot. 'We'll be there half ten or something,' says Goran as we all part. I high-five him, and give Bartosz's shoulder a little squeeze, but there is a curious feeling in my stomach. I am going to have to use an excuse – oh, I got a drop far away, I am exhausted, not feeling so great, something like this. The secret suddenly feels bigger than it ever was.

I have not been lying to Goran, just not given him the whole truth about Decca. But those things feel like the same proposition now. We are on a footing we have never been on before.

Come on, Damir. Every second counts. I pick up a large breakfast order from a place that sells overpriced baked goods and I drop it at a place called Escape Studios just off Roundwood Road, the long spine of this postcode. I have done drops here many times – it is a wonder they get any music recorded, the amount of time they spend with their mouths full of croissants – and I always wonder who might be in there, what they are working on, and try to get a little look inside when the door opens. As usual, though, the cool guy in a sweater takes the brown bag as if from a robot waiter, and all I can glimpse is the big framed Arctic Monkeys record print hanging in the lobby. Still, the sight brings a Monkeys song into my head and, as I ride, I play with the tune, re-arrange things, shift a chord in and out so it is not quite their music but mine, and matching lyrics come into my head.

ONE MINUTE AWAY

Sometimes you wake up and you think you know the day
But then when you live it, it goes a different way

You have to hear it with the tune. The tune takes on more layers from the beat of my feet on the pedals, the sound of my own breath in my head, wild shouts from market traders as I head out towards another drop. Where I felt uneasy a little while ago, there is now a kind of dizzy energy in my legs. After delivering, I sip water and check my phone. There is chatter on the WhatsApp group about tonight's meetup, but none of it quite seems real, because of my own plans for the evening.

I have walked through a door – the blue door – into a different world, like the kids who go through the wardrobe and find the lion, a man who is a fawn, et cetera. And tonight I will walk through it again.

*

At just after seven, I pick up from a dark kitchen, in a little street around the back of the cinema. 'Dark kitchen' is not the official term, of course, and in fact the existence of these places is not official. But when you order takeaway from a particular well-known Indian place, the food is not prepared at the restaurant but at one of these kitchens, by people who have never been to the place itself. It would make sense if you thought about it – how could it possibly be with you in forty minutes, if it was coming from the main restaurant, almost ten miles away? – but our app removes the need to think too much, as I have already said. In these kitchens, the guys work ten-hour shifts for low money preparing meals to the exact recipes of the popular franchise, handing them over a little hatch when we produce our bag numbers. The man who lifts the bag to me looks like he has not slept for a week. Bartosz is approaching as I zip the bag into my backpack; we do a high-five. These are familiar scenes; it could be any Friday night, the last three years. But what I am planning now is outside our shared experience. Is not something I could easily explain to him.

The drop is done by twenty to eight – your order has been delivered by Damir – and I do not want to seem like a super-keen teenager knocking on the door at one second past eight o'clock. I hop off my bike and linger for a little while at the end of Laurel Gardens. For once, I see one of the other residents. An old man in a traditional shirt and collar is in a little deckchair on his front path, talking to someone on the phone. I get my own phone out and look as if I am busy on it, in case it seems I am mooching around for dishonest reasons. For me to be here as a delivery guy, with my backpack: it is so familiar it is hardly noticed, I am invisible. Now I feel very visible, in a way I am not used to at all.

My heart is heavy and loud to me as she opens the door. I am hit by the smell of cooking, a smell which makes me feel crazed with hunger in an instant, like my body is remembering all the times I have been hungry since I started this job and piled them all on top of one another.

ONE MINUTE AWAY

'Hi.'

'Hello.'

'You can put the bike in the conservatory, but you mustn't look at the state of the place.'

I am wheeling the Silver Fox towards the big glass doors, past the coffee table with its books of what to do before death. There is a bike in the conservatory already, cherry red: like her phone case, like her toenails. The Silver Fox slots next to it, and they stand there awkwardly like people who have just met at a party. I have a little of that feeling myself. How am I meant to behave, what do people say for conversation? There is a world outside of people sweating and grafting over grills and ovens, straining their muscles to get up hills with backpacks on, and normally that is my world. But in here – the chopping boards, the cookbook propped open, the delicious smell – food is just about pleasure, about having your Friday night the way you want.

'Are you hungry? I don't know if this will be any good.'

'Really hungry. But if it isn't, I will pretend it is.'

'Now you've said that, I'll be paranoid that you're pretending.'

'You would know,' I said. 'I do not pretend about things very much.' This sounds like sub-standard English, and I abort the attempt. 'I think it will be delicious; anything would be delicious.'

Decca's big front teeth chew on her lip. She is wearing a black vest-top, lipstick, silk pyjama trousers: it looks like she is not sure whether she is leaving the house or going to bed. She puts down her wooden spoon, glances at her phone, picks up her wine-glass. 'Sorry, I have to use a recipe *and* the internet because I don't trust myself not to fuck it up. Did you want a beer?' But she can see I am looking at the glass. 'Or a wine? We've got lots of nice wines, I've got a subscription to these guys who send you – I've never got round to cancelling it.'

'It might be wasted on me.' I have drunk wine only a few times in my life and have no real idea what it is meant to taste like. At home we only ever had beer, with one famous exception: Mum and Dad had a couple of ancient bottles of spirits which they brought back from their travels in the Black Sea before we were born. One night Goran and I, already drunk, cracked open one of these bottles and ended up on a roof we had no right to be on, and the hangover lasted three days.

She turns and walks towards a wooden rack in which there are easily twenty bottles. My breath is a little short as she bends to pick a bottle out.

'I was home all day,' she says, 'and I wondered – I thought about whether you were delivering nearby. Whether you were nearby sometimes.'

'Today, not really.' I attempt to sip the wine, but jerk it back way too far; it is not a sip but a big, greedy gulp. The sensation is so intense that I choke a little and splutter, and Decca in a concerned way turns off the oven heat. I raise a hand and smile to show that I am OK; she reaches out to touch me on the arm, then withdraws the hand. All this in a few seconds.

'Earlier this week, though, I was really close to here. Coldharbour, two minutes away.'

'What dictates it, where you go and when? Is it just fastest finger first?'

'Fastest finger?'

'Oh! Sorry. *Who Wants to Be* . . . it was a TV show. What I mean is, is it just whoever gets there first gets the job?'

'The algorithm decides a lot of it. We are "elites" so we get more jobs. Goran has a motorbike so gets further ones. If you have a better rating, you get more. Other times you don't get a lot. You stand by a wall, you earn six pounds in a morning.'

The algorithm is like a sort of god, it occurs to me in this moment: it sends you gifts if it is pleased with you, it messes with you if it thinks you have done wrong, or it just does what the hell it likes to you for no reason it ever has to explain.

'And, I mean, how do you cope when that happens?'

'Maybe one of you made more money in the day, so he pays for something instead of the other one. You know. We're a team.'

She gives a different kind of laugh and turns back towards the hobs. 'I remember being in a team, once. Feeling like we were on the same team.'

I cannot know exactly what this means, but it feels like some sort of hint, or invitation, or at the very least like we are in a space where the rules are not fixed or certain. I take a few paces forward, as if someone was pushing me, and I am standing right behind her. She looks over her shoulder, the dark eyes glittering in a humorous kind of way.

'I'm going to be forward again. If you were thinking of touching me, it would definitely be worth going for it.'

Her back is still to me. My hand is on the waistband of her pyjamas. Everything from here happens with a momentum which feels out of our control. She steps out of the pyjamas, muttering 'oh God'. On her right buttock is a tattoo of three roses in a triangle, and this secret detail fills me with even more need. Her breathing is loud and ragged. I turn her to face me, kiss her on the neck. She whispers, 'Through here, through here.' She is guiding me into the living area, with the yellow sofa, but I am also guiding her. I am sitting on the sofa with her naked on top of me. It is the maddest and best moment of my life so far.

★

Afterwards we sit without saying a thing for several minutes. Just the breathing, and the night outside. The TV is in standby mode – the word flashes in the corner – and it is getting darker out of the window. I stare at the coffee table, think how beautifully made it is, how sharp and precise, its edges like blades. Decca feels warm and wet like me.

'Do you want me off you?'

'What?'

'Am I not heavy?'

'No, you are the exact right . . .' I cannot work out how to finish this sentence, so I swerve into something else that is in my head. 'You smell of – you smell like . . .'

'Oh God, like what?' She wriggles a little bit on my knees and I pull her gently back to me. 'Garlic, I bet.'

'No. It is in a swimming pool.'

'Oh! Chlorine!'

'I love the smell. You are amazing.'

She leans into my face and kisses me on the lips, hard, like an attack. Her breath is kind of stale with wine, like mine also must be, and I find this excites me again. All the things she does not mean to be sexy are sexy, because they are things I have not done before, and thought before.

'It's just stupid insecurities,' says Decca. 'It's what happens when you start to feel over the hill.'

'Over . . .?' I am looking around for my phone to note it down, but it is still in the kitchen.

'Put it this way. It doesn't seem *hugely* likely that a . . . what are you, thirty?'

'Yes. Well, twenty-nine next month.'

'OK, it doesn't feel overwhelmingly likely that a good-looking guy fifteen years younger would think these things about me.'

'Well, I definitely have come here and I definitely have made love to you,' I say, 'and I already want more, and also the roses on your bottom is the sexiest thing I have seen in the world so far, so.'

'My God,' says Decca, 'this is . . .'

This time, she is the one who does not seem to know the word. I nod and say quietly, yes, yes it is. And we look at the moon outside through the conservatory glass.

8

Sometimes you wake up and you think you know the day
But then when you live it, it goes a different way
A message arrives and your life is not the same
You thought you knew the rules but it's now a different game

(You have to hear it with the tune.)

So tell me . . .

'Jesus and the whole Christ family,' says Goran. 'It's a surge, man, you can't be lying around with your dick out.'

'I'm working on a song. Get out of my room, you weirdo.'

'Great, well Adele will be really happy, but just until her payment clears, is it maybe time to think about some clothes and getting on your bike? Come on, fifteen minutes. I'll make you a coffee. Oh, by the way, I think the hole in the kitchen is getting bigger maybe?'

Through the weekend, into Monday, into the week, we text, text, text. She says how wonderful it was, that she wanted me to stay longer, that she cannot stop thinking about the night we had. There are a couple of very positive reviews of my penis which I delete straight away because it feels dangerous somehow even to carry them around. As I pedal through Monday the song is thumping around me; every turn of the wheel is a note. I am cycling faster than Tadej Pogačar, faster than Lance Armstrong when he was cheating with massive amounts of drugs. I cruise past lights one second before they change, my timing perfect. Your order is delivered by Damir. Every drop, I know there is a good chance a new message is waiting. 'F Customer'.

How is your day? Any 'tippers' do you think?

No, everyone miserable. One place, a dog jumped like it wanted to kill me. The guy laughed like the dog was cute. How are you?

Axel was a pain in the arse getting to college. Filthy mood, hungover.

She's the kid?

Yeah. Actually goes by 'they', not 'she', now. I'm behind the times with this stuff – pronouns – but making a valiant effort to keep up. By the way, what would you have out of flying and invisibility? It's just come up on the radio.

Flying because I could come and see you much quicker.

I avoid saying that I already have invisibility.

Sometimes this chatter turns to more personal things pretty fast. On the Wednesday morning I wake up to find two messages from 'F Customer' and I jab at the screen, unable to open them fast enough. The first is a picture message and it sends an electrical current through me. She is standing in a bathroom and has taken the photo in the mirror, looking over her own shoulder. It shows her ass with the trilogy of roses. I immediately grab myself and do not see the second one for a little while. It says *the longer this picture goes unacknowledged, the more I have the heebies that I (an ageing woman with a hefty arse) sent it to you. Please reply.*

I tell her straight away that the photo made me have to do things to myself, even though it is frightening to write this. She asks if I want to see her other tattoo. *Yes yes yes.* Again, the back of her in the mirror, but very zoomed-in. It is on her neck, high up. A small star in black ink. Something else I did not know about; ownership of another tiny piece of her.

Wednesday is a quiet day, the kind when you have to hope for a big hour to make up for each empty one. I am leaning on one of my usual walls, near Orchid Chinese, complaining back and forth with Goran. He is in a temper because he has had to stop for fuel and two jobs got away in a minute. *At least you are seeing orders come in,* I say, *everyone in this area seems to have died.* We bicker back and forth a little, and then it comes into my head to message Decca.

Hey, you hungry? Nobody is ordering a damn thing and I know you are a 'female customer' of a food delivery service.

It feels weird to say this, because it is kind of playing, but it could also be serious. If she put in an order at a place we agreed, it would be a legitimate job – just one with a quick kiss at the end of it. But that thought is problematic. She would be, in a sense, paying to see me. Still, when her reply comes, it removes the problem.

Just got out of the pool. Hey, what if you were doing a pickup and I just happened to see you for a second?

If you were on the main street I could tell you if I get one?

I'll just get showered and I can set up with my laptop round there. Haha is this nuts!?

Even thinking that she is taking off her costume and standing naked in the shower, with all the hair getting flattened against her skin, and the tattoos, I feel like the wall is going to fall down behind me and send me flying backwards.

About an hour later there is a notification. *Bloop-bloop-BLOOP. I-want-YOU.* I swipe to grab the job – ting! – and head for the burger place, and text Decca. Wait for my order number, shifting from foot to foot. When I come out with the bag zipped into my backpack, there is Decca, leaning on the fence, where I have been a thousand times. She is wearing a black tracksuit and her hair is tied up in a massive curly bunch. She has glasses on and no makeup.

'Sorry, am I in your way?' she says.

'No, it is fine, thank you,' I say. We are undercover agents or Cold War operatives for a moment. Then, quietly and only half-looking, she says:

'Come and stay over on Friday?'

'Stay . . .?'

'Niall and Axel are going to Norfolk; he's got a pretty much unbearable brother there. It'll just be me. Stay the night with me. If you'd like.'

ONE MINUTE AWAY

'If it's not too . . .?'

'Forward, yes.'

Our eyes meet in amusement for a second. My heart is beating as hard as if I had just done a drop at the top of Forest Way, the hill which is the enemy of the delivery rider.

'Yes, I will definitely come.'

'That's settled, then. Have a good day.'

The whole thing is under twenty seconds. If you had seen it from the wall, if you were one of the other riders, you would think maybe she was asking me for the time. She walks, with her gym bag over her shoulder, through the market stalls.

The clock is ticking on my order. The app will already have told the customer that 'Damir is on his way'. But it is not quite true. I am just standing there, with the crazy guy playing his loud music, with the shouts of the market traders, like I have just appeared from Outer Space, and have no idea what my next move is.

9

This time, there is no way of concealing from Goran that something unusual is happening. There is no possible reason I would not be sleeping at ours, as I have done for the past thousand nights. What else can I say: I have gone on a mini-break to Paris? (Anyway, he knows that if this did happen, I would take him with me.) Besides, this secret has been in my stomach for long enough now.

'Hey, so tonight I am not going to be at home.'

Goran's face twists into a naughty grin.

'You're seeing someone, right?'

'Yeah.'

He pulls out one of his delighted noises, HAAAAAAAYEEEAH! 'So this is what it was about the other night too, right? When you "had too many drops" to come for a beer even though it was like a zombie wasteland out there?'

I nod. 'There's . . . someone.'

'Croatian, English?'

'English.'

'Holy *shit*. You snake, how have you managed to meet someone? I haven't had any action since Noah was building his fucking boat.'

'What about Hannah?'

'She hasn't been here for like two months. My dick might as well be in the lockup. Come on then, who is she, tell me everything literally now.'

'Well – remember the tip?'

Goran does a satirical mime, screwing up his face like he is searching for the memory. 'Let me think, *tip* . . . oh, wait, yeah, I do remember it because it was *the biggest event of all time.*'

'So it's – it's her.'

He frowns and chews the information like it was food.

'I thought you said it was a crazy old rich lady.'

'Not an *old lady*. She's a bit older than us, yeah.'

'How much older?'

'Forty-four.'

'Forty-four!' Goran repeats this like I have said I am having sex with Joan of Arc.

'She's married, but I don't think their marriage is . . . the guy is an asshole, she kind of admits it herself, and she's unhappy . . .'

'Married.' Goran rubs the side of his long face. 'Dam, seriously?'

'What, are you the Pope now?'

'I don't mean it like that, I just . . .' He shakes his head. There is a strange little pause and we hear a motorbike growl by outside. Someone like us already on his way to pick up an order; someone who has got a head-start on us while we sit and talk. 'I don't know, that seems kind of dangerous, doesn't it?'

'Well, yeah. But, I don't know, it's *her* who's married, and if she thinks . . .'

'No, not that either.' Goran's voice is almost impatient, a tone which does not fit him. I find I am looking at the coffee cup in my hand, instead of into his face. 'Just – who we are.' He gestures across the room, but because there is so much mess, it takes a moment to see what he is actually pointing at: the jacket – my uniform – crumpled on the floor. 'If something went wrong, someone complained about you. The elite rating goes, or even – they kick you off. We don't have protection from that, you know? There's a reason people like us don't do this shit.'

'I guess I'll have to hope nothing goes wrong,' I say.

'OK, lover-boy.' He rolls off his mattress and starts digging through the pile of clothes. 'Well, you know I trust you. I mean, you're the only one I *do*. It's not you that's the problem, it's everyone else in this city. Now, we better get out there, or it doesn't even matter because we might as well be fucking retired anyway.'

★

End Shift. I go into the Travelodge bathrooms to change out of my sweaty clothes into a plain T-shirt and jeans. The receptionist blinks as I pass, but unlike the burger bastard she does not try to stop me. When I come out in plain clothes she smiles understandingly. Probably she thinks I am going to another job.

The evening is warm and the sky is still blue like it was in the middle of the day. The front doors of Laurel Gardens, blue and yellow and white in the creamy sunshine. The smell of a barbecue. Someone is playing music in a back garden, a heavy bass over soaring synths and strings, and for a minute I think I have been inspired to write a tune; actually, my brain just wants to steal *this* tune. Still, even to be thinking this way is progress, would not have happened a few weeks ago. Something in me is waking up.

The hesitancy of our previous hellos does not carry over into this evening's meeting. Decca grabs my arm, her fingernails are on my elbow; she rolls up my T-shirt and plants one kiss on my chest. She is wearing a yellow dress with sunflowers. She leads me out to the garden. On a table is a large bucket and a bottle of wine.

'You like fizz?'

'I don't know.'

Decca laughs, showing me all her teeth. For a mad moment I want to reach out and touch the teeth. Her foot stretches out to play with mine. 'It's not a trick question – do you like bubbly?'

'I am more of a beer guy, we know this.'

'You are properly, properly adorable. We know *that*.' She says it quietly, almost like she is shy – which feels funny to me, in her own big garden, serving expensive wine to someone who only recently got changed out of a jacket which smelled of curry. The bubbles of the wine rise in a very neat line right up the middle of the glass, almost too good to be true, like a computer animation. I feel, as the sun shines right through the glass and turns the liquid almost white, like I am seeing things for the first time.

'It's delicious. Can you say delicious for a drink, or is it just food?'

'You can say about it food, or drink, or – I'd say – any sensory pleasure, really, like for example Damir Kovač . . . Kovačević.' She attempts the surname the way British people often say words in other languages: as if all the accents on the letters were just there as decoration.

'Ko-VATCH-eh-vitch. Say it with me.'

'It's such a lovely name.

'To me, Decca is, too.' This sounds silly as soon as it is out of my mouth, but I am OK with the silliness; I am enjoying myself, already feel somehow light-headed.

'It's daft. I went for it in my twenties, doubled down, got stuck with it. See also: my marriage.'

I am not sure how to react to that, so I look closely at the wine-glass sitting in front of me and see a logo which is familiar and surprising. 'You have been to Wimbledon?'

'We always go, we – well, one of our partner companies has debentures.'

'Sorry to be the stupid kid in the class, but I have to ask you what *debentures* means, too.' I do not feel stupid, though.

I can sense that there is knowledge I have which is missing from *her* life, too. That perhaps, despite the big house and the tickets to sports games, it has been a while since she felt something like Goran and I felt observing London from the skyscraper bar.

'Oh, it just means you can go to any match. It must be coming up, actually; they're back to doing it this year, aren't they?' My face must change as I try to imagine that somebody could have a ticket to 'any match' of a world-famous tournament, an event many of us would give one or both bollocks to attend even for a day. 'You like tennis?'

'Yes. All sports. There was a time I did not like tennis because my girlfriend left me for a guy who played, but . . .'

Decca shakes her head. 'Imagine leaving you.'

'Oh, it was never a big thing. I am over it. Just occasionally I google to see how he's playing. He played last week in Bratislava, lost in the first round.'

This time, she laughs loudly enough that I glance up, towards the back windows of other big houses, and for the first time think about what this would look like to a neighbour. Surely if anyone who knew Decca glanced down to see her sitting and laughing with a man who is definitely not her husband, it would be something to talk about. But maybe all these windows are too far away, or maybe when people have this much space, they hardly know each other at all.

'What is it – your "partner company"? What is your business?'

Decca tops up our glasses, although I have hardly started to drink from mine, and wipes her hands on her knees. Watching this action, I think about what is under the dress and remember the weight of her on top of me, her hard breathing. The thought makes something happen to the back of my neck and I pull her hand towards me and kiss it. A weird thing to do with all this lust, like a gentleman in a black-and-white movie, but she makes a little noise and I can see her having to drag her mind back to the question.

'We . . . the short answer is, it's property. Niall owns property.'

'You are landlords?'

'He is a landlord. He has a *portfolio*.' Yet another new word, and she speaks it in an ironic kind of way, like it is a phrase you would not be proud of. I think of our landlord, Caroline. Since she is unseen by us, and never answers our messages, I have come to picture her as someone who lives on a different planet, or in some kind of castle. Now it occurs to me that she could be living on a street like this, very close to Cecil Court: I could have cycled past the person we pay all this money to, looked her in the face. I could have delivered her dinner. 'Niall spends half his life sizing up properties, or going to conferences for developers. My job is basically PA to him, propping up what he does, which is essentially printing money. Sorry, you probably don't want to hear about – he's definitely not coming back, if you're worried about that. I have pictorial evidence they're in Norfolk. We're safe.'

Two things now happen which come together to make a strange coincidence. The word 'safe' tightens something in my heart, because it reminds me of my mother. When I was a young boy, sometimes kids in the school playground would play games about bombings and shellings like it was sport. I did not like these games because Goran did not join in, and I would sit up in bed after nightmares which had something to do with war, with explosions or disappearances. Every time, Mum would sit by the bed and say, 'We are safe here. Completely safe.' *Ovdje smo sigurni.* Back to sleep I would go, with those words in my ears. After she died – even though I was an adult by then, and nobody was likely to bomb the record shop, except maybe Josip himself – I sometimes thought about the words in my head, knowing I could never hear them again for real.

In the few moments it takes to be surprised by the memory of these thoughts, I see an ant which is doing its thing, scuttling by a large flowerpot, next to the swinging chair, and I take a few paces over.

'What are you looking at down there?'

I beckon her, I say: hey, can you see the ant, down there?

A frown, her eyebrows low and expressive. 'Bastard things. I use stuff to kill them off but at this time of year, they . . .'

'They are not bastards. They are hard-working guys and they're just getting on with life. Three or four years. However long they are lucky.'

She is pressed up against me, making me prickle. 'Are you lecturing me on an ant's life expectancy, Professor Kovačević?'

'They think, actually, ants can get to twenty, but it is not easy to track because, well, pretty hard to tell which ant is which.'

'Yes, I suppose they don't have birth certificates.'

'When I was a kid, I had an interest in ants and insects and stuff and did a – what is it called at school when you study a tiny thing like this, make a book of it.'

'A project, maybe. A school project.'

'Yes. I did a *school project* for ants. So, hey, how many can you see?'

'How many ants? There's only that one.'

'OK. Watch with me. Look really hard at the ant, right. Just concentrate on nothing except the little ant. Focus on him, nothing else. What can you see?'

'There are loads!' says Decca, with a kind of wonder and horror in the same voice. 'God, hundreds!'

'My mum taught me this thing on a camping trip,' I explain. 'It is about how there are always more things happening than you know – well, you *do* know them, your eye is seeing them, but often we don't listen to our senses. Or something, I am not talking about it well. Anyway, not being like a Buddhist, but she died a few years ago – and, well, for a second I felt like she sent the ant. I always feel like this when I look at them.'

'It's gorgeous, you're gorgeous.' Decca kisses me right on the mouth. I am hard for her. I am here with someone whose life is not like mine, who says English words I do not know, has a 'portfolio', goes to Wimbledon. What am I doing in her garden, my heart speeding up with how much I want to put my hands on her? 'I bet your mum would be proud of you.'

'For what, for being a food delivery guy?' Maybe the wine makes me say this, because it is more negative than I intended. She has taken me by the hand, her fingernails biting into my skin a little, and we go towards the swinging chair. She gestures to me that I should sit on her lap. Laughing a little, shaking a little, I put my weight against her.

'What *do* you want, then? Like, what's the dream?'

It is almost a whisper, and I try to whisper back, but my voice comes out louder than I aimed for. 'That is a secret. That is for when I am a little more drunk.'

'We can work on that,' says Decca. Her hands are on my face; I put the painted fingers in my mouth, one by one. The sun is still high in the sky. Soon we are doing things which cannot have happened many times in a swinging chair, not even in rich people's gardens.

10

Falling on top of her, reaching for her underwear, burying my face in her. 'I've wanted you in my bed. Since the first time I heard your voice. Out there,' she says, in a series of little breaths. The sweat of our bodies together, a vase of yellow roses by the bedside, birds outside the open window, the wine on our breaths, the muscular way she yells at the end. It is a set of messages from brain to body, back to brain, a series of spots of blinding light.

The bathroom is three or four times the size of ours in the flat, with a huge bathtub like a hazelnut. I glimpse myself in the shower glass; a razor and aftershave sit on a small shelf above the toilet. When I am lying next to Decca again, she reaches across to take my hand in hers, which is warm as it always seems to be.

'Do I get to hear your dream job yet?'

The question appeals to me now. Under this sheet, secrets are another kind of sex.

'OK, I write songs.'

'Oh. Amazing.'

'Not amazing, I can tell you that. Just normal stuff, rock.'

'Oh,' says Decca, her eyes mischievous, excited, in the low light from the bedroom window. 'Sing me one of your songs. What is it in *Titanic?*: *Draw me like one of your French girls*. But with a song and with a chunky personal assistant instead of Kate Winslet.'

'I haven't seen *Titanic*.'

'I suppose you were about three when it came out. Jesus.'

'I can't just sing something of mine. It will sound shit. You need the production.'

'Even to be talking like that, you must be good. Or maybe I'm just completely agog at whatever you say.' *Agog* is another addition; I am going to be busy with my iPhone note tomorrow. 'You should hire a studio – lay some tracks down! My God, that's the lamest phrase to ever come out of someone's mouth.' I am stroking the side of her face. 'Isn't there a place round here, sort of behind the leisure centre?'

'Yes, I deliver there sometimes. They like pastry, those guys.'

I add the second part because the first sounds a little sad. Although it was not deliberate, I have made it pretty clear that I cannot afford to get a studio, hire an engineer to record my work; my job is to ride my bike and bring a bag of snacks to the people who do. To remove this idea from the air, I change the subject. 'What about you? What job would you most want?'

Decca laughs, puffing out her cheeks a little sadly. 'I'm probably a bit old to be going in to see the careers adviser.

My degree was in history of art. It turned out not to be a money-spinner.'

We kiss again. The phrase *money-spinner* feels as if it was made for me. I like to think I am an ant, but I am also like a spider, scuttling across London, my bike spinning a web in which I catch five pounds here, five pounds there. 'I reviewed exhibitions – also books; all sorts of arts journalism really. This was in the days when you could make money out of journalism. One day I was at an opening; the artist was a friend of mine. This guy appears, buys one of her paintings off the peg, five grand.'

'Five thousand pounds?'

'Yeah. My friend, Vicky, almost died on the spot. She'd never sold anything quite like that before. And he was handsome. We got drunk with them. He was kind of bashful about the money.' (I guess that this means aggressive, from the word 'bash', but from the context soon realize it is the opposite; typical English.) 'Said, oh, I just made a bit of cash recently. We were pissed enough to stick our noses in: how? Property, he said. He'd bought two places in Hackney almost straight out of university, and now ten years later sold them for a fortune.' She laughs, softly. 'I . . . sorry, is this boring?'

'No. You do not need to ask things like that.' Her voice alone has a particular power over me. Nobody talks to me this way: who would? I am hard just listening to her; she could be reading out a council tax letter and it would probably have the same effect.

'Well, looking back he only *had* the money to do that

because he'd inherited from a rich granddad. But still, at the time – I don't know, I'd not met anyone like that. Me and Vicky and pretty much everyone we knew were a shambles in our late twenties. This guy knew what he wanted, he wanted to make money. It was sort of impressive, a bit Eighties throwback. But he wasn't flash about it, he didn't come across Thatcherite.' (Again, I am piecing together the meaning of this as well as I can.) 'That came a bit later, I guess.'

She pauses her story and I take a strand of her hair and curl it between my fingers. She sighs. 'If you're going to do that, I soon won't be able to maintain polite conversation.'

'Good. I mean, I like the conversation. But still, good.'

'That night . . .' Decca is looking off into the corners of the room, like their relationship history is written across the walls. I do not mind; it is good, in fact, to have the back story. To understand. 'Vicky seemed quite weird, quite off with me, as we were going home – and this is after, like, the greatest night of her career. I said, what's up? She said: he fancies you. And you fancy him back. Admit it.'

'I texted him. Sent an SMS. 15p well spent.' She is looking up at the ceiling now. 'I did keep the writing going for a long time, the reviewing, whatever else. But then you're raising a three-year-old and your husband's business is skyrocketing. My mum gave me a bit of "tough love". That's her phrase when she wants to massively undermine you in some way. She said, darling, would it not just be better if you assisted Niall? If you *have* to have a job.'

A little silence after this. This place can be silent in a way ours, at Cecil Court, never could. There is always a vehicle making the windows judder; when the guys downstairs raise their voices at each other, they sound so close that occasionally, when half-asleep, my brain convinces me they have wandered in to our flat to have their argument there. But here at the back of this big house there is just us, our breathing, the quiet creaks of the mattress springs as they track our movements. The call of a bird outside, a siren very far off. My mind is playing with a word, one moment among the torrent of unfamiliar phrases.

'Do you . . . do you *"fancy"* me?'

'This isn't fancying.' She pulls me back towards her. 'That's for kids. This is something I didn't know existed. Is that too much?'

'Too much what?'

'I don't know. Emotion.'

I answer her with my body. The sun is only just leaving the sky outside, the clouds turning purple. My phone is face-down on the floor, not even charging.

*

She falls asleep before me and I watch her breathing, her shoulders rising and falling; listen to her snore gently and shuffle onto her side. I think about the fact that I have never seen a face as beautiful before – the eyelashes, the big lips, the little flush of red in the cheeks when she speaks.

My life and Decca's are roads that should never have joined

up, even when I came to London. I could have delivered to her door ten more times, cycled past her on her way to swim fifty more times, and never shared more than a 'have a good day', 'enjoy your food'. But instead things have gone in this direction, and even though all the details are strange to me, I feel like I understand the main story. She is a person who feels a little lost about where life has brought her; who is struggling for a purpose, maybe. That was me, too, before Goran brought me here.

My pillows are so big and fat that I have to drop one of them over the side of the bed because I feel like I am hanging from a crane. The bed itself is so high, compared with the mattress on the floor I am used to. And when it gets dark, it is darker than my room ever could be, and this makes things even stranger. I text Goran and say, yes, things have been very good. He replies, of course, with aubergine emojis and other obscenities. I gaze up at the ceiling and rewind the tape to our conversation.

Of course, I understand what he meant, that there are plenty of reasons I should not be here. My dad's jaw would drop so low you could get your fist in it, if he knew. An *affair* with a *married woman*. It is against morals, it is dangerous; it could blow up in my face, for sure. When we see characters act like this on our hacked Netflix, it is rare the moral of the story is 'and that was a very wise thing to do, with absolutely no serious consequences'. I am not an idiot: I accept the majority verdict would be that I should not be lying in another man's bed here.

And Goran was probably right that they would always take a customer's side. That we have no real protection; that I can be replaced as easily as, back home, Goran's friends could throw a fish back in the sea and cast the net for another one. In fact, they would not even *need* another fish; someone would take my place instantly, the way skin cells regenerate. Guys like us have no status here. We do not live on Laurel Gardens. In some senses we do not live in London at all: we do not vote, we are not sitting in the West End theatres, we do not have gym memberships. The city would not notice us if we disappeared tomorrow; it does not notice us as we feed it, keep it moving.

But what is in my head as I lie there, listening to Decca's breath, is: what if I do not want to be 'guys like us' any more? Decca asked me here. She is excited to have me in her house. I make her laugh; I have made her come twice tonight. This is a relationship between adults, who have made their own decisions. Delivery riders do not date customers: true. But I am not a 'delivery rider' for ever. I did not come out of my mother on a bike. I came to London to build a future, sure, but maybe that future is beginning now, and it can be more interesting than just picking up Chinese food from one address and taking it to another address.

I am becoming a new type of person; that is how I feel as I lie here tonight. I do not know the word for the feeling, even in Croatian. Or maybe there is not a word for it yet. Maybe we are inventing it.

PART TWO:

INSIDE

11

It was never official that Mum was going to die, that she had a particular amount of time left. She would not go into a hospice or anything like that. So, in a strange way, life went on almost as normal into her final weeks. There were just a series of events which we quietly knew, but did not acknowledge, were the last of their kind. One evening Mum got Dad to help her onto the piano stool and he held her shoulders steady while she played. We had a party with family and friends, everyone drinking beer in the garden, singing songs, playing a traditional game where you throw stones at an ever-smaller target. There were little clues, reminders that things were not really normal at all; that we were coming to the end of something. Petra, Goran and I tried to help clear the backyard when everyone had gone home, for example, and Dad would not let us. *Moram nešto učiniti*, he kept saying: I have to do something, I need to do something. The sight of him shuffling with his head low back towards the house, eight beer bottles in each hand, is one that I still see sometimes at night.

In her final couple of days, although by now her breathing was bad and the drugs were making her go in and out of sleep, she gave us a series of instructions as if we were kids again and planning a family weekend. You have to have the best birthday party of your life so far, she said to me – I was turning twenty-four the next week; it was the time of year we are talking about in this story. I want you both to travel, see the world; it's a big world (this was in my head when I finally made the move to London). And make the most of every moment, because even though you *think* you know life is short, it is even shorter than that.

Near the very end – although there were lots of false ends – she said *vidimo si uskoro*, see you in a bit. Yes, yes, my darling, said Dad, we will see each other soon. *Pomalo*, said Goran, the traditional Dalmatian phrase: it means take it easy, have a good time, but also goodbye. After that, there was no talking; 'see you soon' turned out to be the end. There was no dramatic final breath, no one moment; just an awareness which crept over us all at the same time.

When it was over, there was a kind of peace, but it was impossible to know what to do. Dad would not leave Mum's side; Petra went into the garden and lit cigarettes, staring off into space. Goran said: come on, you need to get out of here, just for a bit. I have a plan. We rode side by side on our bikes. People were out in their yards, drinking and laughing; I thought about how, every time we had been having a good afternoon, someone just down the street might have lost a mother, brother, daughter. We pedalled

ONE MINUTE AWAY

all the way to the beach and went out to our favourite bit, where a mossy shelf of rock made a natural diving board. We stripped to our underwear, jumped in, clambered out; did it again and again with no thoughts except hitting the water, until it was starting to get dark.

One thing that bothered me in the months that followed, although I kept it secret, was that in all her advice and wisdom for the future, Mum never said anything about my guitar playing – although she had come to see me a few times in small clubs, and always seemed pleased that one of her kids had carried on her musical interests. Of course, it was a stupid thing to have taken away from the occasion. My mother was dying; she was not giving a PowerPoint presentation. She was not saying 'one final thought: your music is shit, give it up'. But in the mischievous part of the brain where these things can happen, that is how the conversation was archived. For my final few months in Josip's shop, I hardly picked up the guitar at all, and every time I have made any serious progress with songs over here, it has felt a little foolish even to try.

But now I am quietly playing with it; now I am working out chord sequences, using GarageBand to build bass and drum parts. On Tuesday morning, my door swings open and Goran catches me singing quietly into my voice-note app, trying out my lyrics about how one day can change so many things.

'What was that? That was good.'

'Nothing. You heard nothing. Go and get on with burning the toast so you can start making the new toast.'

'Why are you hiding from me? You are literally naked.'

'You can hear it when it's done, when it's recorded,' I tell him. Goran sighs and slopes away and a moment later I hear the shower and a cry of 'motherfucker!' as he receives the electric shock.

Of course, 'when it is recorded' does not mean anything. The other night I did a very brief Google search on the studio down the road, the one with the Arctic Monkeys print, and it is as I thought: for the money they charge, I could just about afford to go in, introduce myself to the engineer, drink a glass of water and leave again. Sure, I could do what some people do and just video myself, put it on Instagram or the new one, TikTok. But most of those videos sound like they were recorded in a toilet, and might as well have been put down it afterwards. I know I am only a wannabe, same as any of these dudes with pink hair who are 'influenced by Ed Sheeran' and make songs identical to Ed Sheeran's. But I know what good music sounds like; I do not want to put something into the world which is less than what it deserves to be.

All these thoughts are silly, pretentious, when I am sitting here with no fans, no money spare to get my songs produced properly, and indeed – as Goran has pointed out – no clothes on at this stage. No, I will not be in a recording session anytime soon. Still, even to be thinking this way, to be playing with music again, represents change.

The lockup has not been secured, once more; the open padlock is hanging from the door. 'Joseph Christ and the disciples,' mutters Goran, 'which one of them is taking the piss?' There is a moment in which we look at each other and share the unspoken thought: we both know it is probably Mario, and we are both scared to talk to him about it. Then I glance down to see my phone, and there is 'Female Customer'. *Why haven't you texted me yet today, am I abandoned?*

After my first drop of the day, looking down at my phone for a new notification, it is impossible to resist looking at WhatsApp. As soon as I bring up her profile – the picture is now the zip-wire one, because I said I liked it – *typing* appears on the screen. I feel not just that I have made it happen, but that we are in a sort of psychic connection, knowing instinctively what the other one needs. This is a crazy thing to think about someone I have known for such a short time, and anyway I do not believe in psychic connections: where will this end? Am I becoming one of these people who thinks they see Jesus in a piece of toast, or ask an animal to predict the football by moving its paw, et cetera?

> *Tell me what have you done with my mind*
> *Feels like I've left the old me behind*

(You need to hear it with the tune.)

The lyrics bounce up at me. 'Mind' is in the squeak of the brakes as an old lady wanders into the cycle lane like she is on her holidays. 'Behind' comes from my two-part breath in my own ears, as I accelerate to ensure your delivery, by Damir Kovačević (4.72 stars), arrives on time. When the bloops come to offer another job, I hear: *I-want-YOU. I-need-YOU.* Yes, my mind has been stolen, for sure, but I do not want it back.

The 'old me' was a guy who slogged around the streets making sure that nobody was waiting too long for pizza. Anybody who took a moment to watch me today – anyone who could pick me out from that bar at the top of the tower – would see pretty much the same person. But that is not the person I feel like. The smell of fried food from the low-quality café next door; the cars cutting in front of me; the endless sirens making me jump out of the way. All of this has more of a shape now; feels like part of a story I can read. Even though my movements around the city still are almost random, it feels like there is a plan. Not a 'plan' like Goran claims to have whenever he has come up with a whimsical idea; no, a real purpose. That every turn of the wheel is taking me back towards her again, towards this other world, where this reinvented Damir can live.

*

Outside the burger joint, green and orange and purple backpacks, lightweight jackets. There has been a notification that this is a hub right now; multiple orders. Everyone's phone is in their hand ready to go; we are like a bunch of ducks waiting on a lake for someone to throw bread. I scan the little square with my sharpened senses. The sky is a heavy grey, rain on its way. Once again the guy is dancing to his old-fashioned stereo, reggae music, shouting words that make no sense. All of these things were going on around me all the time, but the volume has been turned up.

England are close to making the final of the football, which is a popular conversational topic on the WhatsApp group and in front of the restaurant. 'It's going to be a madhouse, Sunday night,' says Mario, swigging from his water bottle and throwing it into the bin like a basketball player. He pauses with a look on his face like we should be applauding him, although it was not even the recycling bin. 'Come round ours Friday,' he orders, 'plan for the war.' Of course, Friday nights are not so convenient for me any more; I cannot just do what Mario says. And this thought leads to wondering if I should be brave and say something about the lockup. Somebody has to do it, and I am not normally the 'somebody' in these situations, but I have not felt this confident since I first came to London.

'Hey . . .'

'What?'

But I glance down at the phone, to minimize the difficulty of this conversation, and the magic is happening again: *typing*.

I can see you.

It feels exposing, as if Mario or anyone else could see the message, but he has lost interest in the conversation even before it began, and is swiping to take a new drop. I look over my shoulder at the dancing man, and at the market stalls and gym in the other direction. My eyes follow Mario into the burger place. And there she is. A white T-shirt, short-sleeved, her magnificent arms. Khaki trousers. Almost close enough to Mario that she could reach out and tap him on the shoulder. Our eyes meet through the window.

Did you come here just in case I got a drop!?

I see her glance at her phone and grin. She puts her fingers in her mouth and licks them clean.

How dare you. I am a loyal patron of whichever establishment this is.

She is holding the phone a little closer to her eyes, concentrating on the writing; I imagine pressing my face against the back of her neck, the dampness of her skin.

I'm lining my stomach, going out with the girls tonight.

Lining the stomach?

A plate of food emoji and a wine emoji in response. My phone shudders: *bloop-bloop-BLOOP.* Swipe right; Accept Job. Ting.

I have a drop. I have to come in.

Her fingers on the keyboard, her serious eyes. There is something magical about knowing I am on her screen while also watching her through this pane of glass, and that no other customer would dream of guessing all this; nobody would think, one of those guys in their coloured jackets, one of the city's ghosts, is texting back and forth with that beautiful woman.

You'll have to pretend you don't know me. Walk right past me. Stew over it all day.

ONE MINUTE AWAY

The phrase 'stew over it' is a new one, another one for the iPhone note; she almost needs her own folder, like the hidden photos folder in which I hoard naked pictures of her in case someone takes my phone. But it feels like all these words – greedy, delicious, stewing – tell a story about her body and mine, a story of hunger and appetites. And with every new food smell, in the waiting area of every restaurant, I think about it a little more, about her a little more.

12

Riding in the rain is tough; it is the only time part of me, the traitor part, wishes that I had an e-bike. Back home, summer rain is often a welcome break from the heat, but here it always seems more like payback: like we are being punished for the good weather that came before. On wet roads, the thighs feel like they are doing extra work, as if the roads are made of grass, have actually got heavier. I get blisters on the area below the buttocks, feel like I am sitting on little stones that are pressing into me. Most of it is the body's response to stress, because London on a rainy night is Stress City. Normal strangers become bastards, and bastards become super-bastards. Pedestrians hurry across the road in bizarre places, with no notice; taxi drivers get in an even worse mood than they normally are; traffic gets worse by magic. By nine o'clock, the orders are thinning out. I go into a chain restaurant to pee; there is no code for the bathrooms here. I am about to message Goran, who is complaining it has been a quiet night, but the breath is knocked out of me by 'F Customer'.

ONE MINUTE AWAY

This message was deleted.
This message was deleted.
I want you in my arms, is there any chance of that?

'In my arms': nobody has ever spoken to me this way. Of course not; Téa and I would have laughed at each other if we started messaging like we were Romeo and Juliet. But coming from Decca – from someone who has lived, travelled, seen things – it feels right. The weariness in my bones now feels like a good thing, like the sensation I used to get lying in bed after a long ride with Goran; before it was work, when it was exercise and we could sleep in the next day. Yes, I want to be 'in someone's arms'; I want to be going home to somebody. Of course, 40 Laurel Gardens is not my home. Worse, it is another man's home. But it is getting easier and easier not to think about that.

I can be there in thirty minutes.

Not long ago, even weeks ago, I would have felt guilt about this, finishing an hour or ninety minutes before the jobs have completely dried up. I have never let Goran pay more of the rent than me, even though he has the Empress and can take on better drops; I have never, since the beginning, sold him short, and I will not this week, either. But that extra hour or ninety minutes is ten pounds, could be even less. I am not a robot, even though some customers believe I am, and even though in ten years' time, delivery riders probably *will* be. This is what I was thinking about in her bed the other night. I deserve some of my time to be about more than just dispatching my duties; about more than 'your order is with Damir, your order is one minute away'.

AMAZING. Can I make a couple of requests?

Yes.

This is ridiculous, but it's been so long since the burger, and I ended up not having food tonight for reasons I will go into . . . could you pick us up something!? I'll pay you back.

I can probably find a takeaway place, I know a little bit about them.

A different person might add a 'laughing' emoji here, but I do not want to seem like I am trying to be funny; it feels as if she understands the tone without a stupid face with tears coming out of the eyes.

What is the other request?

Typing. Typing. Typing. Although the rain has stopped now, the air is still cool; lights are dancing in the puddles. Come on, lady, I say to myself, half in impatience and half in enjoyment.

I'll tell you that one when it's dark, she says.

At the counter in the Thai place, the girl looks at my jacket and asks me for an order number. A moment passes before I realize I have to explain: I am not here to collect. I am a customer, like everyone else.

★

The trees stand very still all along Laurel Gardens. Lights are on in windows; a door contains a beautiful stained-glass panel.

Now that I have been inside number 40, I understand more of what is behind these doors. The houses are so much larger than you could ever think from the street. They are heaving with long coffee tables, books about how to spend your life, framed vintage movie posters, mountain bikes, electronic goods. The people inside them can have, more or less, what they want, and it can be brought to them as quickly as they want.

I have taken off my backpack and unzipped it and am holding out the bag, just as I would outside any house. In a spirit of fun, I slam the knocker harder than needed. Decca's hair is pinned up and she has makeup on, dark eyeliner, a lipstick, an emerald green cocktail dress. I say the name of my delivery app. 'Enjoy your food, have a nice night.'

'You were so quick!' She kisses me on the lips, then reaches out to wipe the lipstick off me. I can smell chlorine on her fingers, and alcohol on her breath, and I want to be naked with her.

I am pushing the bike through the hall – the old map of London, with ancient spellings; the Andy Warhol spoof with four versions of Kermit the Frog. 'I go as fast as I can when I am delivering, but it turns out I can go even faster if . . .'

'If what?'

'If there is something special to get to,' I say over my shoulder, wheeling the Fox to the conservatory. My own comment makes me cringe; it sounds like a *line*, like I believe I am being charming and actually stink of aftershave. But she makes a happy noise.

There are three bikes leaning where normally there is

only one, and this is a small shock, but she must know what she is doing: if the other family members were at home, it seems unlikely she would have invited me. The TV is on, some famous chef cooking on an open stove in front of a river in India. 'And what's truly remarkable about the way they prepare this fish . . .' There is a nearly empty bottle of red wine on the long glass table, a glass with her lipstick stain on the rim. Decca has already put the food out on plates, with another bottle of wine, and the smell makes my stomach twist in anticipation.

'God, last time you saw me I was cramming a burger into my face, and now I'm going to eat a mountain of dim sum. Classy.'

'Well, at least you don't stink of fourteen types of takeaway.' I remove my jacket and hang it neatly over the back of the sofa. She kisses me on the neck.

'We were meant to be having dinner, me and the girls.' Decca laughs in a short sad way. 'Fucking washout.'

'They didn't want to eat?'

She seems to hesitate. 'Promise me you won't look down on me if I tell you something embarrassing.'

'Of course I promise.'

Decca leans down with her lighter and sets a white candle burning on the table in front of us. The smell reminds me of her usual fragrance, and I shuffle up even closer to her, our thighs resting together. I am so consumed by her that, somehow, I cannot believe only a few weeks ago I knocked on her front door having never seen her before.

ONE MINUTE AWAY

'I was meant to go out with Roz and Sapna who are my two besties, supposed besties. That was the plan as of when I saw you. Niall is away at some fucking junket in France, Axel is staying with her – sorry, their college friend. Their. Sapna flakes on me mid-afternoon; she's not feeling too well. This is her thing. She's a hypochondriac. She googles every time she stubs her toe; she has a cancer scare once a fortnight. I love her, but seriously.' This is a lot of information, and she is speaking at the speed of a slightly drunk person; I am going to have to look up several terms in the morning, I tell myself. My hand is on her knee, moving up; my other hand moving chicken and rice up to my mouth. It is incredible to be behaving like this, just taking what I want, everything at once: am I a Roman emperor now; have I fallen down some portal?

'So, fine, just me and Roz, and I get myself dolled up because Roz is stunning and I was all up for chatting about you – I've told her I've started seeing someone and she's like, I'm dying to hear about this. In a way actually *better* with just the two of us because Sapna – I love her – she can be a bit judgey, you know? And I'm literally on my way to the pub, done up like a dog's dinner, and Roz texts: her fucking coercive-controller of a husband has booked them cinema tickets, by a massive coincidence, and she's caved in. And that's that: I've been, basically, stood up twice in the space of a few hours. By my actual best friends.'

'That sucks,' I say, and I find myself leaning in and touching her face. It is a more intimate action than I intended.

She gives a little sigh and opens her mouth and my finger is in there for a second. She says 'oh!', quietly, but not in a surprised way; it feels like this is something we have been doing for months.

'It's just a bit . . .' Decca waves at her phone, in its red case, on the table in front of us. 'I don't know, it gets lonely. He's away a lot. My mates are either working till midnight in Sapna's case – she's a lawyer – or in Roz's case, believes she's in a happy marriage with this guy who will hardly let her go to Tesco without texting him every five minutes. I mean, I do have other friends. I don't want to come off like a loser.'

'I was not going to say you were a loser.'

'It's just a weird time of life. I thought this would be where we all started to party again, I guess. But we're all just in our own separate little cells. Too busy with this, too tired from whatever.' She gets up from the table, goes to the wine rack for another bottle. There is always wine here, always food in the fridge. They are not going to the Turkish shop at ten p.m. The way our kitchen was after our crazy supermarket spree: that is just what they expect.

I am not sure how to respond to everything she has said. Having a teenage kid, I cannot really imagine, although I would like to one day; the problem of having too much time but nobody to spend it with does not chime with my own life, either. Above all I feel sad for her, want to stop her feeling lonely, but this feels like it carries the risk of pitying her. I touch her elbow as she opens the wine, and wonder how quickly this will go to my head, and what will happen tonight.

'So, you were going to tell your friend about me? Really?'

'Yes! Why not?' She frowns, her eyebrows comically low for a moment, like when we had that first conversation outside her house. 'You don't mind?'

'No, of course not. It feels nice. That it is something serious enough to do that.' The phrase feels awkwardly constructed, but in a way the awkwardness is just adding to the attraction, to the tension, because it is on both sides.

'Of course it's serious enough. I know it's new, but – that first morning after you were here – I sent her like fifty WhatsApps. *Oh my God I've just met the greatest man ever.* I sent her a photo of you in the swing chair and she said, fuck off, he's gorgeous, are you serious!? She's no fan of Niall, so . . .'

Although his shadow has been over every meeting we have had – his aftershave in the bathroom, his money in the bricks and mortar of his place, the memory of his abuse on the doorstep – it is still strange to be talking about Niall, the husband. My face probably changes as I picture him sitting here, right where I am, maybe as recently as yesterday. Decca brushes her hand against mine. 'Sorry, should I not – you probably don't want to hear about him.'

'It is not exactly that.' I am not sure, myself, what it *is* that I want to hear. It is just that, now he has come into the conversation, it will not be possible to get him out of the door again. I feel a need to understand what the rules are, and the risks: what is really happening here. 'I just . . . I don't really get what things are like between you and him. Why you are doing this with me.'

'It's complicated. He's not a bad guy. I know you must think he is.'

'I never said he was a bad guy.' This is technically true, if saying things in our heads does not count.

'You didn't get off to the greatest start.'

'No, I guess I will not be invited to his birthday.'

Decca's tongue plays around her lips. The candle burns on, and it feels dark in the room now. She tops up our wineglasses. I am not used to drinking at this speed, not even beer. All the tight springs that carry me on my bike seem to be loosening, and my brain feels like it is softening, the way butter does on a warm surface.

'I don't know. There are still things I like. Things I could almost say I love. But: well, I don't think he would call me beautiful any more. I haven't felt desirable for a long time. All this stuff – beyond a certain point, you sort of come to accept it. I mean, I've got a lovely house – houses. Don't want for anything. My kid is doing well.' She rubs at her face, the eyeliner coming away on her fingers. 'A lot of people I know are in this situation. Drifting.'

'You definitely are beautiful,' I say. 'I never stop looking at pictures of you, I always want more.'

Her hand tightens on mine. 'See, I didn't know *this* was an option. I didn't know you – or someone like you – could be out there. How would I know that?'

It feels as if she is justifying herself, and I want to say that there is no need to do this: neither of us is innocent. I am also not meant to be here. It is a complicated thought, and before I have excavated it, Decca's phone is in her hand, the red phone case with the bluebirds.

'What do I owe you?'

'What?'

'For the food.'

This time it is me laughing: partly because it seems funny, partly uncomfortable. 'You paid me a thousand pounds because your husband threw edamame beans in the trash.'

'Sure, but . . .' She plays with her phone, reads a message, looks up at me with a tired kind of smile. 'Sorry – Roz is being all grovelling now, of course she is. Look, we both know it's fine for me to get it. Just put your bank details in there. Do it.'

Holding the phone is strange: it feels so different from mine. Of course, it is a new model, bigger screen, better condition, but that is not the reason. This phone has been with her in bed, when she texts me at midnight; has rested on the sink, looking at her, while she stands in the shower. I am almost convinced I can feel it beating in my hand, like a heart. Again, I wonder if my brain has been hijacked by aliens, like in Goran's grandmother's fantasies: this is an iPhone 12, not something found in Hogwarts.

'Thank you.'

'You can find a different way to *recompense* me.' She says this word with deliberate emphasis; the unfamiliarity of it is a treat. 'Remember what I said about waiting till we were in the dark?'

'Yes.'

'I've got something I'd like to try, while I'm drunk enough to suggest it. Come on. Bring my phone.'

★

Lying on the bed, on the beautiful white sheets, I wonder what I might be signing up for. There are people who like to be whipped or tied up or attacked by someone dressed as a giant rabbit. Back in Croatia, Goran was once with a very attractive girl who could only enjoy sex if he sang Michael Jackson songs to her; he learned the words to 'Earth Song' especially for this. Decca slides into the bed beside me and snaps off the bedside light, swearing as she fumbles her phone onto the floor and then almost knocks over her glass of water trying to put the light back on. When she speaks in my ear it is more breath than words.

'Look, do you feel annoyed that I – we – live like this? Have money, and you have to . . . well, you just deliver to us?'

'I don't – it is not an important thing for me.' My hand is on her hair, I am pulling her closer for a kiss.

'OK, but imagine if it was. Would you – like, could you judge me? Tell me that it's disgusting?'

I begin to understand.

'That is what you would like?'

ONE MINUTE AWAY

'That's what I would like, Damir.'

I am on top of her, her broad body, her stomach underneath me, my hands on her sides. 'You are – you don't deserve to have your money,' I say, uncertainly. 'You are landlords.'

It feels very unconvincing, but I can feel the shudder go through her body. 'Talk to me about that. Say more about it.'

'You have whatever you need, just delivered to you whenever you want it. You don't have any worries. There is a whole world of people just doing whatever you need and you pay for.' I cannot really be sure, as these words come out, whether I mean them a little, or absolutely, or not at all. They are for her, and her body is squirming beneath me.

'Can you do it in Croatian?'

'You want me to talk to you – like, harshly, in Croatian?'

'Yes, Kovačević.' She has mastered the pronunciation, now.

'*Odvratan si, gadiš mi se.*' I can feel our bodies responding to each other, sweat starting to glue me to her.

'What was that?'

'I said: you are disgusting, you make me sick.'

She groans. 'Tell me I'm bad, tell me I should be ashamed.'

You should be ashamed. *Trebaš se sramiti.* The sound of the word 'shame' is not so different from English, and I dissociate it from its meaning. I do not care what I am saying: I just care that Decca moans happily and bites my shoulder. I am ecstatic to turn her on like this, and the turn-on comes back to me; we are mirrors for each other. It is not that we each have something the other person wants; it is that we are what the other person wants. Her phone falls to the floor with a little thud, and after that there are no more sounds to hear, just Decca and me and the night.

13

'You coming to Bartosz's for beers, or going to the fuck-house again tonight?'

Goran is kneeling over the toilet seat, and from a distance you would think he is throwing up. Actually, he is – for the third time this year – tightening the seat with our ancient screwdriver. The shower is dribbling feebly onto my head and shoulders; one of them downstairs must have got in ahead of me. I think of Decca's en suite, the powerful frothy jet, the silver buttons.

'The fuck-house, although it doesn't say that on the door.'

'Fine, whatever, *bro*. Soon you will forget I am even here. I'll start waking you up by saying *hello, my name's Goran Jurič*, we met some time ago in Split.' He gets up and grins. 'There, the seat is fixed, help yourself. All thanks to Caroline.'

After the sex game, the harsh words, on Tuesday night, I wondered if it would be complicated to talk about – if she would have regrets, or if I would – but in fact, it seems to have unlocked a new level of intensity. I now have a video of her touching herself, in the bed right where I lay. It was followed immediately by the usual messages of remorse: *awful video, delete it*. We have also started to talk more and more about other things, about life, constantly, through the day, giving me something to look forward to each time I stop. Axel has an 'attitude problem' and does not always show up for college, where they are studying business. Axel fairly recently changed their name from Alice. Decca finds the whole thing difficult to adjust to, like the pronouns.

All these little pieces of chat happen while I am refilling my water, or waiting outside the burger place as my colleague-rivals swill down their energy drinks, or leaning on the hatch at the dark kitchen. She asks me questions about the work day. Is it a good one for orders? (No, a little bit slow.) Do I feel annoyed if Goran is having a better day than me? (Yes, but not really.) Who are the biggest assholes, or 'arseholes', I have served – except her husband? (Oh, how long do you have?) What is the scariest thing about cycling around London? (Everyone else in London.) But you will be safe, won't you? (So safe that I am not even looking at the screen as I type this, just the road.)

I offer small pieces of news I can – the streets are quiet today, the pubs are full of football flags. I observe that it has been very wet this summer, and Decca replies: *weather chat! We'll get you British citizenship quicker than you think.* Although this is only light-hearted, like most of what we say away from sex, it gives me an image of a future I can half-imagine.

Sitting with her in the garden of a little house, maybe near here, maybe some other area. Goran down the road, or next door. It does not have to be a grand house like 40 Laurel Gardens, or even a third of that size. I do not need a chair that swings, or a SMEG fridge the size of a wardrobe, or a wet room. Just a little shed outside to play guitar, a spare room for Goran to sleep in, a table where we can all have dinner together.

There are many details missing from the vision, of course. Are we still out on the bikes, delivering? Would she even be rich any more? Maybe Niall could cut her out of their business. Maybe he would make both of our lives hell, graffiti the walls, send dogshit in the mail, as crazy people do to TV actors if they cannot tell the difference between life and fiction, et cetera. Probably, a guy with his money and status could take far worse revenge than that; things I cannot imagine yet. And, of course, it is all so unlikely – that she starts her life again, with a delivery guy – that it should not be worth imagining, not even in this abstract way. But one month ago, what we have *now* was just as unlikely. Fairy tales are not real, sure, but they can have real things in them.

Send me a picture of your beautiful face or breasts or ass, your choice.

I wait for 'typing', but it will not come. When I am only down the road from Orchid Chinese, the *bloop-bloop-BLOOP* floats out of the phone and I hear it as *where-are-YOU*, and because of this little mental digression and the fact I am distracted by wanting to hear from her, I am too slow; somebody else swipes for the job. If I hung around here I would even see him show up, grab the bag that should be in my backpack, top up his app with money that should be mine. Come on, Damir, I mutter to myself. This adventure with Decca is a little holiday from the job; it has not taken over *from* the job.

Maybe she has gone swimming, or to the gym, but she always tells me these sort of plans in case we can stage one of our coincidental encounters, and if she were swimming I would normally expect a picture of her naked from the changing cubicle. I try to tear my thoughts away from what she might be doing, and whom she is possibly doing it with. Two hours, three hours: this is no time at all to be waiting to hear from someone. There were entire days after Goran came to London when we did not exchange a message. And that was Goran, the greatest buddy in the history of civilization, not a married woman I am pining for like a puppy. Every second counts. Get on the bike. Deliver.

The trouble is Sod's Law, a phrase I learned when a restaurant had a power cut on Christmas Eve and all the diners were outside in the street, looking like they had been smacked in the face. Sod's Law on this Friday means that at the very time I need orders to distract me, they dry up. There are only three notifications in half an hour, and all of them are gone before I can jump on them. Every second, right now, does *not* count, and it is almost impossible to stop myself going to Decca's WhatsApp profile, the small version of that picture of her on the zip-wire. On one occasion 'online' comes into view for twenty seconds, thirty, but it vanishes again. What is she doing that I am not the first thing on her mind? And – once again – how can I be thinking, more and more automatically, in this silly teenage way. *What have you done with my mind.* I am reaching for a chorus, another verse, but the song feels stuck, like everything else does.

At last a drop comes in, but even then it is an annoying one: a bunch of freshly squeezed fruit juices which have to go upright in the compartment, forcing me to pedal slowly. The address is one I do not recognize, a business area of some kind: it begins 'Unit 8B', and 'unit' is never a word which, for the delivery rider, means party time. Sure enough, as we approach the 'finish line' marked on my GPS, the magic blue dot starts to wobble around the screen: sorry, Dam, I am not sure about this one. The building seems to have four different groups of units, but none of them has the right name, DEMON DESIGNS, and there is no sign of an 8B. I have to call the customer through the app, and he emerges looking impatient. 'It's over there, mate, we're over there,' he says, pointing at the door like it is one of the great London landmarks. He takes the bag without thanks and walks back to his Aladdin's cave without further words.

It is a job on the board, at least, but a minor one, and when I look at the phone I experience a flip of the heart and then a plummet. F Customer.

Bad news. Niall has got us tickets to the football final on Sunday (he turned them down before but now England are in it, as you know). So he's back from here till then and I'm stuck with him. I'm sorry.

It's cool, I message back at once, *just text me when you can. I will.*

A heart emoji. That is all I am getting instead of what I had imagined: the real, beating heart next to me in bed, the warmth of her skin, her voice, her sweat. Although I have known about Niall all this time, of course I have, it is different hearing that he is definitely going to be in the house with her. 'He got us tickets' to the football. Will it be a date night for them, with an expensive dinner beforehand? Even tonight, will she play the lovely wife? Will they climb under those soft white sheets together, and laugh and play as we do? It seems impossible to believe they would, because if they had that sort of arrangement, Decca and I would surely not have got to the place we are in. But I do not really have the right to ask her, and it will only do harm to ask myself.

As I pedal down Roundwood Street and back again, each time passing within sixty seconds of Laurel Gardens, muscle memory almost persuades me that I *am* still spending the evening with her; almost convinces me to turn down her street without being able to stop. Not long after, a second run from Superior Pizzas – a dreadful place, superior to absolutely nothing – back to almost the same street again. Even more Sod's Law here; now that I am in a bad mood and do not really want to do deliveries, the orders are coming in like I am Amazon. This time I literally ride past the turning for Laurel Gardens and, gazing down towards the house for ten seconds, I let my momentum take me so close up behind a pedestrian that he shouts and has to swerve out of the way. 'Stupid fucking prick!' he shouts, and even though he was the one walking in the road, I do not completely disagree. Enough is enough. I will select End Shift, take the Silver Fox home, and then surprise Goran by showing up for the drinks at Bartosz's place.

Bumping the bike up the stairs feels like more effort than usual. There is an argument happening in the downstairs flat. I think about how we all live in Cecil Court – clawing money together from other people's desires – and feel tired in my legs for a moment. I remember Decca asking, in bed, whether I felt resentment at that situation.

The honest answer – away from the sex play – is, no, there is no point in thinking like that. Goran and I are not slaves. We came here to carry out a plan, to make money, and if enough people are mad enough that they will *pay* money instead of walk to a takeaway place, we have a deal. It is a pity that someone can own our home, and does not have to answer our messages, but what is the point in me getting annoyed that some of the world is richer than the rest of it? You would have to get angry that their relatives made money three hundred years ago, or they inherited money like Niall and bought property, or they went to a university you could not afford and then straight into an

£80,000-a-year job. And of course, anyone is within their rights to get angry about all that, but it would take a lot more energy than just getting out of the door and on the bike. It is just that tonight, with the blister just below my buttocks, with the fatigue in my thighs, my energy feels low, and the person who has been recharging me is not mine to claim.

'Who's that?'

Goran's voice, startled, from his bedroom. I laugh, even though I understand it: when it comes down to it, we do not really know who else might have keys to this place, who might have lived here and owed someone money. Other people on the WhatsApp group have had break-ins and not even called the cops because, although we have the legal right to live here, the UK at the moment does not feel like it is desperate to keep hold of us.

'It's Caroline. I heard you had a problem with your bathroom and your kitchen floor?'

'Fuck off, Dama.' He is lying on his mattress, in just his underpants, a bowl of pasta almost finished on the floor. The wrestling commentators yell on his phone. 'You're meant to be staying at hers!'

'*You* are meant to be at Mario's with everyone.'

'Sure,' says Goran, 'well, guess what, without you, I can't be bothered.'

It is difficult to know what to say to that: it is a little pleasing and a little embarrassing. I go to the fridge for beers. We are almost out of the ones we bought on Supermarket

Night. Soon, back to the ones brewed in some garage in Moldova.

'Why didn't you go?' he asks.

'The husband is there.'

Goran nods. 'That sucks. But, I mean, not for me.'

'I . . .' How do we get into this? We have never been bad at expressing affection, but still: I feel like I am about to give him one of those Valentine's cards where two pigs are embracing with a heart over their heads. 'I'm sorry if I've not been around as much, you know, with Decca – with everything.'

'Don't be stupid.' Goran stretches his long body and gives a melodramatic yawn. 'I couldn't be less interested in hanging out with you. I only live with you because you're tidy and bring in the rent. But I do think you should introduce me to her pretty soon, if this is going to be a thing.'

'I would love that. We could go to the pub. I think you'll like her.'

'If you do, I will. But probably not as much as you do. I prefer women who were born after the invention of TV.'

I launch myself at him and unbalance him, push his head into the pillow, like we are seventeen years old again. When I finally leave his room and put my phone in the wall, there are five messages from F Customer. *I wish things weren't this way. They won't be, for ever.*

I curl into a ball, facing away from the window with the bright streetlights, as usual: towards the hall, towards Goran. I can tell from the tone of his snores that he is facing me also. Really, we are like a married couple ourselves, I think to myself – in fact, the flat is so small that we probably sleep in closer proximity *than* some married couples.

Things 'will not be this way for ever'. The fact is, most things could be this way for ever, and I would be happy. Only a couple of things need to change. It is not completely within my hands to change them, but it is within my and Decca's hands together. The phone lights up at one minute to midnight and I get out of bed and go over to the wall, because it can only be her; she has sent three hearts, like the three roses on her bottom. I cannot take the phone off charge and curl up with the image, and so I settle back in bed with the memory of it. And I wonder if I will dream about a time when we look back on this as just the beginning of the story.

*

Pomalo, says Goran, when we go our separate ways at eleven on the morning of the football final. The take-it-easy word is even more of a joke than usual. This will not be a day when we stop and smell the flowers. It is a day to grab the flowers, take them where the app commands, go back for more flowers. We know it is going to be a day where the notifications build and build, and continue until we are almost falling asleep in the saddle. The city is a sea of riders; at the traffic lights I glance back over my shoulder and see nothing but people like me, lined up like Formula One cars on a grid. This is the final level of the video game. Big points, big prizes. The phone almost melting from the notifications. In the hour before the game begins, I make three separate trips to Superior Pizzas, one of them at an address so close to the place that whoever ordered it will virtually have been able to smell it as it was cooking. I see people walking past carrying slabs of beers on their back, like labourers on a building site; twice, people ask in the 'special instructions' if there is any way of me bringing them alcohol, even though the place they are ordering from does not offer it. We are about three years away from an app where Damir just appears and pours beer straight down your throat, I think to myself. Clears up the cans, washes up, tucks you in for the night.

The match starts, and I cannot resist watching the first couple of minutes through the window of the Cork. England score a goal straight away; beer gets thrown around; people dressed as King Arthur's knights embrace. As the evening goes on, we piece the events together across the WhatsApp group: Mario has watched two minutes outside a restaurant, his friend is watching clips online, *his* friend is at home with the game on TV. The game is going to finish in a draw, which will mean a penalty shoot-out. I tie up my bike outside the burger place, where I can see Bartosz sitting on the wall, the backpack off his back and parked on the floor, his phone turned horizontal in his hands. This is a rare moment. Not everyone watches football, for sure, but pretty much everyone up to the Queen and her little dogs will be paying some sort of attention for a couple of minutes; the phones will be quiet. I perch next to Bartosz and watch as he flicks through three, four Wi-Fi networks nearby, the images on the screen freezing and re-animating. Finally the host is looking into the camera. 'So, worrying scenes around the stadium, but we're going to concentrate on the football . . .'

'What does he mean, worrying scenes?'

Bartosz shrugs, takes a mouthful of Coke. 'Some fighting or something. People trying to get in the stadium. English fans. You know.' He glances across, into my face. 'Why?'

'Is anyone hurt?'

He frowns in an amused way, his face paler than usual in the half-light from the phone screen. 'You know someone there?'

'Yeah.'

'Like, a . . . you have a girlfriend?'

'Is it that obvious?'

'It is, man.' Bartosz's eyes are large and serious. 'Just the way your face went. It must be someone you really care about, right?'

This is not the sort of conversation we usually have outside restaurants. But it is impossible not to say something as I feel the tightness in my chest, picturing her in the stadium, in the middle of some battle, flares being thrown, whatever the hell else might be happening. I do not have proof any of this is going on at Wembley – all we have is 'worrying scenes' – but everyone has seen things of that kind happen at football; everyone knows the history.

ONE MINUTE AWAY

The first player steps forward to take a penalty and I find myself screwing my eyes up, trying to pick out individual members of the crowd, a ridiculous task.

'It is, it is someone who – who I . . . really care about, yeah.'

'Are you in love?'

In the moment, it seems surprisingly easy to say it, although I cannot meet his look. 'Yeah. I would say so, yeah.'

'*Is* it a girlfriend?'

'What?'

'If it was a guy, you know it wouldn't matter.' Bartosz's eyes flick between the screen, the tense footballers, and my face, making me shift my position slightly on the wall. 'I don't want you thinking I'm the same as Mario, the way he talks about stuff. That's all.'

'It's a girl – a woman.' I am almost ready to tell him more, to tell him about Female Customer and the fact she is just around the corner when we are doing our deliveries. That she could be sitting in the burger place, if she chooses, when he is standing by the grill waiting for the number to be read out. But then: *bloop-bloop-BLOOP* in stereo. *There-are-TWO.* A notification is crawling across his screen, blocking out the footballers, and an identical one is on my screen too. So much for getting a break to watch the penalties. We look at our phones and at each other. This kind of thing happens a lot, of course, but not usually in the middle of a heart-to-heart, and if we hesitate for five more seconds, neither of us will get it.

Bartosz rotates the phone, his fingers are on the screen, his phone tings to confirm he is on his way; all done. He gets to his feet, which means I may as well do the same.

'Nothing personal, man. It's just, I'd get there faster, you know?'

'Of course nothing personal, idiot. See you soon.'

He touches the pedal of his e-bike and glides effortlessly away, taking the phone with him – taking Decca with him, or that is how it feels to me. I stand in the drizzle and wait for the next notification; I do not even know who is going to win the trophy. People like Decca are watching it in the stadium, ten kilometres away, and everyone else is watching it in pubs, in their homes. I am one of the ghosts. I wait in the shadows for my instructions.

*

Nearly midnight. My battery is down to 10 per cent as I lie on the mattress, but I cannot put it in the wall; cannot settle at all. I have heard nothing. No texts. No 'online', never mind 'typing'. Naturally, I have looked up what happened at the stadium: a mob trying to break in, clashes with police, injuries. It does not sound likely Decca could have been caught up in this, but still: mad thoughts go through my head. What if she *is* one of the injured people, she cannot come out for a while, he stays at home to look after her? What if it is a bad injury? My brain spirals: imagine if something terrible happened to her – if not this, something else – and

ONE MINUTE AWAY

I would have no claim to speak to her, no official right even to be upset.

This mental avenue is unbearable, and although it seems like a long shot, I open Instagram. @jessicachloebevan posted only hours ago. The sight of it hits me in the middle, first because of how beautiful she is, and then because I feel that beauty being taken away from me. The photo shows her and Niall in the stadium. She has a kind of England football shirt made by a fashion label; Niall is holding her arm and punching the air with excitement. They look like they have always been in love, and could be in a different universe from me, in this tiny flat, staring at their faces.

Incredible to be here with @niallbevan at the big game! So lucky to have tickets (thanks to @BaxtersLets). An emoji of an England flag.

I put the phone onto silent, plug it into the wall, lie on my mattress.

The worst thing is that, of course, absolutely nothing is wrong with the picture, which swims in my brain as if I had been looking at it for ten hours. He is her husband. I am the one that is wrong. I am an aberration: that is what anyone would say if they knew the story. They are the real people and I am someone who cannot exist, who is not meant to exist.

I have been living in the moment with this adventure. But the trouble with that is obvious. One day you run out of moments. It has been a thrill to ride along, not looking at the scenery, not looking out of the windows at all. With one moment like this post, though, I become like a cartoon character who is going fast, fast, fast, and then goes over a cliff. There is the moment a big question mark appears over their head. Then the fall.

14

In the morning, Decca messages as if I had dreamed what I saw last night. *It was a good night,* she says, *just a shame about the result, poor old Gareth, they did so well!!* We could go on like this, but I am not in the mood. I say: I want to see you. She offers to come again to the burger place or to some other hub, but I say no: I would like to talk to you where it is just us. I tell her I will come over when the algorithm sends me that way. Maybe today, maybe tomorrow.

Of course, it is a big effort not to pretend that the app calls me to her straight away. I could invent a job near Laurel Gardens; I would be able to kiss her again and hold her face. But I have to hold on to the little bit of power I have. I make it through the day and she starts to message a lot, saying that she wants me very badly and needs to feel me close and has missed me. I wonder how she can say all this when last night she was standing next to her husband, and he had her arm, and they looked happy enough to put it on the internet for seventy-one people to click 'like'.

Obviously, he is not with her anymore, but that itself is an empty feeling. Am I just here as a fun alternative when the main guy is not available? It is fun to have sex with me on free weekends, but she can forget about it when J. D. Rockefeller returns to town with his free tickets for the big game?

These thoughts chip away at me. I am grumpy all evening, especially when the app sends me to Superior, the hopeless pizza place, and the Tokyo Kyoto: the Japanese place from that very first night. Just like on that occasion, the bag is not ready for pickup, and I mutter 'fucking hell, man' at the sweaty guy behind the counter. It is not completely his fault; it seems like the chef here does not know which end of the frying pan to hold. And everyone, as always, is lying a bit. But right now I feel tired of being part of a lie. Late at night I force myself not to reply to her usual flirts; I put the phone out of reach and think of other things. Really, though, what else is there to think about?

On Tuesday lunchtime there is a drop which is close enough to Laurel Gardens that I can justify the decision. It seems a long time since I saw her. I message to say I am ten minutes away. That adrenalin rush, as always, when 'typing' appears on the screen. *I'm doing yoga,* she says, *but I've been watching the phone all morning. Give me twenty minutes to get showered?*

Does she not understand, by now, how my life works, every second counting? Does she think I have time to unroll a mat and do twenty minutes of vinyasa, while she applies shower products to herself and the notifications come and go like banknotes blowing out of the window?

Needs to be straight away. Work.

Decca greets me at the door with her hair piled up on her head and her cheeks a little red. She is wearing a grey vest-top and black sweatpants. She pulls the door shut behind us. I leave the bike leaning in the hall. I am ready with the little speech I have practised on my way: why do you say one thing and then publish a picture which says another? Do you really care for me, or is this a hobby? But before I am able to start this, she is guiding me by the hand to the mustard sofa. 'Look, I need to ask you about something.'

'OK.'

'The other night – when we were in bed, when we were doing the thing I asked you to do. I . . . I loved it, and everything, but I hope you didn't think I was too serious. I know that if you look us up, there are people saying things . . . Niall has people who—'

I hear an unpleasant laugh come out of me.

'So, you have hurt me by putting up a picture of how you are in love with your husband and how happy you are to be at the football, but the thing you want to say most of all is, make sure you do not look into what we do?'

There is a silence and I wonder if I have been too strong.

'Listen,' she says. 'I had to do the Insta thing because – we have these letting partners who—'

'I don't care about the Instagram – post what you want.

I care whether you lied to me about how your marriage is. Whether you really like me, or are just playing.'

She looks away from me, down onto the ground. 'Just playing? You think? Really?'

'Well, I don't know, do I. You are bored with your husband for sex, we know this, but. You could be doing this with other people, with any amount of . . .'

'With any amount of people? With any amount of amazing men who just happen to knock on my door?'

The way she says this begins as anger, or sarcasm, but her voice snags on the second half of the question and her shoulders heave as she starts to cry. I think to myself that I have never seen anyone more beautiful, and it is impossible not to take her hand and swivel her towards me.

'I think anyone would want you.'

'You're stupid,' says Decca, biting her lip.

'That is a little offensive in my country.'

She snort-laughs and wipes her eyes, then with her free hand gestures at herself, her face and hair, her body. 'Like. I answer the door to you like *this*. Sweaty pig. I'm in my forties. I look at myself – Facebook memories keeps showing me ten years ago, twelve years ago, and I cringe.'

'I didn't know you then, though, so I don't care. All I see is right now, you have an incredibly nice face, you know lots of words, you are funny. I am excited when I can see you typing to me, and you are kind. And it's good we didn't know each other then, because – well ten years ago, I was wearing tie-dyes and these really bad pants.' This time she laughs the usual way, loud and generous, and I kiss her on the cheek. 'Also, you smell nice and it is amazing to have sex with you.'

'Oh, God, I want you to do it to me now. Please. Just here.' She can see me hesitate; there have been two or three *bloop-bloops* even while we have held this conversation. 'I know you're on the clock, I know you have to – it's up to you. You've already done me a favour by coming here. I'm sorry about the game, the Instagram thing. That's not real. *This* is real, Damir.'

As soon as I am on top of her, the rest of the world does not need to exist. No orders, no customers, no GPS to read, no rain falling on my screen. There is just the warm feeling of her beneath me, her moaning, my own loud breathing. Then the silence. Two or three minutes as if we were in the sea, or in space: perfect peace, nothingness. When a new notification comes in, for just a second it is as if I cannot think what it is, what it means. As if I had never owned a phone, never used the app. Then reality re-dawns, as if my brain was knocking on the inside of my skull: come on, Damir, you maniac! What are you doing, looking at yourself naked in an expensive mirror in the middle of the day, while Goran is out on the Empress, while Bartosz and Mario are racking up the dollars!

'I need to get going.'

'When can I have you again? Can you come on Friday?'

I cannot resist a little joke as I am stepping into my underwear. 'Just us? Or will Niall be here – we play cards or something?'

She smiles, in a pained way. 'He's in Barcelona and he's taking Axel. You can stay over. If you'd like.'

'I would like.'

'I love you coming here,' says Decca. 'I love you, in fact.'

Nobody has spoken these words to me in English before, and it is surprising how hard they hit. My legs feel strange, unsteady, as I mount the Silver Fox. I swipe to take a job, but for sixty seconds I do not start pedalling. They can wait an extra sixty seconds; they will not starve without their ham baguettes. I breathe in and out, hear the birds calling from the tall trees of Laurel Gardens. Then, a push to the pedals, the chain cranks, the wheels turn beneath me, and I am the bike again.

*

Petra and Dad have set the projector up in the backyard and invited half the street round to watch his favourite film, *It Happened One Night*. On the Zoom call they chatter excitedly about it, my father rubbing his hands together. Tomislaw brought a bottle of vodka and everyone got nicely baked. Ludmila – with whom Dad plays chess online – came from three neighbourhoods across. People have been talking about it, in the butcher's, in the hardware store. The projector only froze once, says Petra, and they restarted it easily. 'His back is killing him now,' she says, 'but it was worth it.'

'What is this, I'm so old you have to talk for me, like a nurse?' They laugh and play-fight a little. 'Get me a whisky, then, slip it onto the ward.'

It is the liveliest I have seen Petra on the screen for some time. It makes me think maybe I could afford to go back, just for a day, surprise them. I ask about her job in the pizza place: yes, all going great, she says. It is a perfect little moment in time, in which all three of us are happy; I want to capture it somehow, the way you screenshot an image, and beam it to Mum wherever she is watching us from now.

'And what's new in London?' asks Dad. 'Sorry, I know it's annoying how I always ask.'

I cannot help it: I want to see his face change, pay him back for the times I have had nothing fun to talk about. And perhaps I am chasing the same feeling I had when I told Bartosz the other night: each time I disclose it out loud, it feels a little more real, less like something that is happening in a series of dreams.

'I've been seeing someone.'

Petra, who I thought had left the room, does her kissing-the-hand thing in the background. I make a filthy gesture at her, laughing. Dad is clapping his hands together.

'Who is she? An English girl?'

Not quite a girl, no: a married woman, considerably older than me, who sends me money and then asks to be punished for having it. I will not be giving Dad *all* these details.

'Her name's Decca.'

'Decca.' He tries it out, nodding, like a sip of drink. 'That's an English name?

'Not a common one. It's like a nickname or something.'

'And she makes you happy?'

'I'm really happy, Dad.'

This is what he wants to hear, what he has always wanted to hear. It is what Mum wants to hear, wherever she is: happiness was the assignment she set us. And, saying it in the moment, it feels true. Saying goodnight to Goran with a beer, hearing his wrestling nonsense, thinking of the day ahead; lying in bed, checking my app, a couple of small but nice tips, a little more money from the past week than I expected. All these familiar, pleasant components of life have a new sparkle on them, because I can look back to what we did this afternoon, and look ahead to the Friday. The swing chair, the taste of wine, the taste of her. This definitely is what happiness feels like, just like when I am in a bike race with Goran, or on the beach back home.

But it is a strange form of happiness. A heightened place, where the view is spectacular, like the one from Marjan. I cannot always live on a mountaintop. What would be real happiness would be to feel this way in my own home, every day, not to wait until I am invited in and be ready to disappear if the time is not right.

★

Nine per cent battery. Sometimes I am convinced that the phone is losing charge more quickly, or the mobile charger is becoming less effective – either of these things could easily happen with age. But buying a new mobile charger is a day's money; getting a new phone is a week's money, *and* time, and a conversation with a 21-year-old trying to trick me into a contract while the jobs come and go.

Hope I didn't freak you out with the 'I love you'. I definitely AM in love with you but maybe it's challenging to hear that. Anyway: everything I said was true. I'd got used to being lonely, I guess. Maybe not even acknowledging it as loneliness, but it was/is. Friends flaky, or moved out of London, or in servitude to kids. Husband broadly uninterested. And now this, this wonderful thing. And I just have to believe it's actually happening, follow it where it's going. All right, enough from Decca. Can't wait for the weekend. I'll do a slow-cooked lamb. Text me back when you wake up. Xxx

'I am in love with you' feels even more of a hit than what she said at the house. It is like a sledgehammer, and for a few minutes I think I will not even get to my feet. Just stay where it knocked me out, let it send me falling into sleep.

I play, in my head, with lyrics: *nobody talks to me the way that you do. I didn't know there was a person like you.* That second line is similar to something she said to *me*. It is true for both of us. We were not realistic future possibilities for each other. But we are no longer living in the world of hopes or predictions. We have built our own reality, and I go into dreams still singing these words in my head as if she were here to hear them. One kilometre away, maybe she is dreaming about me too.

15

High-five outside the lockup, which has been properly secured again – this problem seems to have gone away without my having to talk to Mario or do anything, which is my favourite way of solving a problem.

'Fuck-house Friday?'

'You know it.'

'Well, let me know as soon as there's a wedding day. I'll have to hire a suit. Can you hire suits?' Goran sits astride the Empress, gives it one of his loving pats. He came early yesterday to polish it; the red and green paintwork gleams like Christmas lights. The bike could be brand new today, like the day he proudly sent that first photo, rather than having been ridden through mud and puddles and across bad roads every day of its life.

'It depends if we invite you, I guess.'

Bloop-bloop-BLOOP. See-you-SOON. Goran is off, swiping with his fingerless gloves, then raising his hand to me in an obscene gesture. I watch him to the end of the street, as always. Soon, yes, but it does feel strange that it will be tomorrow morning, not tonight. I have not really thought about what it might be like for him, sleeping on his own. There are the other guys to go for a beer with, but last week I caught him not even doing this. *Without you, I can't be bothered.* The memory of this sentence whispers a little guilt into my ears. Soon, I have to introduce Goran to Decca, join everything up. At the moment they do not fit together in my brain: trying to picture them hanging out is like visualizing Marge Simpson walking into the *South Park* world. But until it happens, there will be this strange feeling of something we are not saying, and of a part of my life he cannot access, which is not a situation we have ever been in before.

Decca sends a photo of a huge rack of lamb, onions, tomatoes, sitting on one of her big wooden chopping boards. *Prep underway.* Even the picture is enough to make my stomach growl; it is a demanding day. I have heard riders predict that as the lockdowns recede into the past and people come out more, there will be less and less need for us – that we have lived through a kind of gold rush. But even though things are getting to be normal now, there is not much sign of the work drying up. Either people are still reluctant to mix like they used to; or maybe ordering things to your door, relying on the invisible couriers like me, is now part of people's nature. Cities have evolved that way for good. At the traffic lights, there are not just food riders with our different-coloured backpacks, not just Amazon, but also motorbikes with supermarket deliveries on the back, guys riding little trailers with boxes of wine, new logos appearing every single week.

The only problem is that there are also more new competitors riding every week. I see people on scooters with 'L' plates who are so wobbly they look as if they should not even be riding a kid's tricycle. They go up on pavements and nearly run people down; they dodge through gaps that make me want to hide my eyes. E-bikes are far, far more common than even when I arrived, and sometimes when they speed off ahead of me – like Bartosz, the other day – I do wonder if I should upgrade. But a good e-bike is well over a thousand pounds. If you are a slow cyclist, the upgrade would soon pay for itself. I, however, am not a slow cyclist, despite what Goran says. That is the point. I have the legs to match these guys on their funny electric toys.

Nobody talks to me the way that you do
I didn't know there was a person like you

I am starting to hear it with the words, bass, whole tune together. I could record it tomorrow if I had the equipment. Down Roundwood Street, only two hours before I am due at Laurel Gardens; kids squealing in the playground. I glance down towards her house, feeling like I can already smell the meal, and feel her skin against mine. When I get a water break, between drops, there are four messages from F Customer. Because of what happened before, my empty stomach cramps briefly with the fear that it will be cancelled again, that the bastard is back, taking her to Céline Dion in

Vegas or on a fucking safari. But no: she is just looking forward to the evening.

I thought we could watch a movie.

I need you to kiss me all over my body.

Sorry, I know you're on the bike, I'm just skipping around the kitchen and I can't stop messaging you.

These messages make my heart lift up, but elsewhere on the phone screen things are not looking so good. My battery is into the red zone, 19 per cent. I have had it charging from the portable power pack as I ride, but there is now no mistaking it: the power pack is not working like it used to. It needs replacing. It is a worry, but also a good excuse to End Shift a little earlier than I was going to; no point in going below 10 per cent, it could almost be dead in a single drop. When I knock on the door of number 40, I can hear her, faintly, crying out in delight.

Red lipstick, a Rolling Stones T-shirt with the sticking-out-tongue logo, flared blue jeans. Her breasts heave beneath the top; I cannot resist putting my head in them.

'Oh, biker boy, you look tired.'

'I am, but good tired. I need to charge my phone and pee.'

'I can do *one* of those for you, give it here. Hey, so can you smell the lamb cooking?'

'I think so,' I say, uncertainly, because the usual rich smell is not in the air as I perch the Silver Fox in its home-from-home. Tonight, a full house of three bikes. As always, the sight of them digs me in the ribs; but he is in Barcelona, she said. To hell with thinking about him, anyway; fuck him for a game of soldiers.

'No, no you can't.' She calls along the hall. 'The thing is, it turns out I didn't take the *slow* bit of slow-cooked lamb seriously enough. Long story short, by the time I got it started, it wouldn't have been ready till about Halloween. So: well, what do you fancy?' Standing back next to her, holding her, as I have waited to do all day, I am unable to stop my stomach from rumbling at the news, and her eyes go big in mock-horror. 'Oh no! You're starving and your girlfriend has failed to provide! Quick!' The red phone in her hand. 'Indian, Chinese? I'll have whatever.'

For some reason it is hard to say what I actually want. Even though handling and smelling all these different deliveries provokes bursts of hunger, by the end of the day they have all kind of blurred into one. The reason Goran and I eat simply is not just economy: it is also that after ten hours of food bags, the brain just does not want to spend any more time on it. Really Decca could lead me blindfold to the table and serve something of her choice, as I have read they do in a restaurant somewhere in London, and I would be happy. With choices in front of me, I suddenly feel like even the smallest decision is too much.

'I can't think.'

'Hey.' She is waving the phone in front of me. 'Want to hear my idea?'

'Yes, unless it is a threesome or something. Just because I'm a little tired and I don't have experience of that.'

ONE MINUTE AWAY

'Ha, no. It's scary enough being seen naked by *one* person when you're my age.'

'Are you going to talk about your age for ever? You are not seventy.' I do not say this because it bothers me, but because I want better for her than to be feeling this way. 'What is the point of fucking a guy off a bike if you don't get to feel younger?'

'Point taken. What I was going to say was – I mean, maybe it's not possible, but what if we got Goran to deliver? Like, found out where he was nearby and just ordered from there?'

'Goran?'

'Yeah, I'd love to meet him. And I mean, obviously we'll organize something properly, but it feels strange we haven't met at all. When he's as important to you as he is.'

'Yeah, it could work. He will still be out, for sure.' I am walking over to my phone, already back up to half-full battery; she has a fancy charger, one of those they supply if you buy your phone on the high street. *How's the night? Where are you?*

Outside Donburi. Quite a good day, busy.

Same. Love you, man.

I give the name of the restaurant to Decca. 'It's Japanese, better than the shitty one which made your husband angry.' Even now, I notice I do not like to say his name; it makes him more of a real character in my mind, whereas 'the husband' is just a pantomime bad-guy. 'Goran hangs out there waiting for orders because there is a girl he likes. If you get an order in straight away . . .'

She is flicking through the app already. 'God, the font is tiny, it might as well be *in* Japanese. I'm going to click on a bunch of things. Go go go!'

She completes her order and there is a moment of funny tension as we wait for the confirmation. Then: 'yes!'

Your order will be delivered by Goran.

It is strange to see him on her screen – the photo from near the time he first arrived here, almost clean-shaven instead of the messy stubble he has now. Next to his face, the 4.87 rating and the little 'elite' badge. We are doing it: combining the worlds. Decca takes my arm, leading me into the lounge, the way she likes to do.

There is that smell of chlorine; no perfume today. My breathing accelerates. I can hear the song in my brain, like we are creating it jointly. If I am thinking about the Goran situation, it is not in much detail. My brain does not go any deeper than the idea that it would be good to see him. I want them to meet, and now they will. The tip does not need to be a big deal; it is just her, a rich person, spending money to make her boyfriend's best friend happy. A small amount to her, a great boost for him. We have fancy beers in the fridge; he gets a new pair of leathers.

Your order is one minute away.

It is only when the knock comes at the door that I start to have misgivings; without being able to tell myself why, I feel in my guts that this was not a great idea after all. Of course, far too late now. I am at the door with Decca just behind me, laughing and clapping her hands. It is strange: I have never heard Goran knock on a customer's door in all this time, never been this side of it, and yet I feel I would have known it was him even if his face was not grinning out of a box on my girlfriend's phone.

The Empress is standing out on the pavement, her engine purring. Goran is standing a few paces back, a *respectful distance* as it says in our guidelines, his helmet on, the bag held out. He removes his helmet and scratches at his hair. Rain is falling, like it always is, this summer.

'Dam?'

'Surprise!'

By now I am 95 per cent sure I should not have assisted with this plan. The vibe is just not right. We should not be on either side of a threshold like this, looking at each other like customer and server. This was not what Decca and I intended, but Goran is smiling in a kind of good-natured way like the victim on a prank TV show. Decca is right behind me now with her arms around my waist, and I can see it as my friend is seeing it: we are somehow now a well-off couple like all the other ones on this street, using the phone like a toy.

'Ha, so – so this is the house, this is where . . .'

He puts the bag down in front of me; somehow to hand it to me would be even worse, even more of a reversal.

'I've heard so much about you,' says Decca, in a tone which is bright and friendly but also sounds too much like what you might say at a dinner party, at a reception she would attend with her husband: somewhere, anyway, we would not be found.

'Oh – cool.' Goran shifts weight from one foot to another; looks back at the motorbike. 'Yeah, it is really nice to meet you.'

'Do you have time for a drink?' she asks. 'I know you're on the clock.'

Goran looks pained. I am not sure he has understood her phrase, but he certainly is thinking about time, at the very least. There is sweat in the small of my back, a different kind of sweat from the usual slickness of pedalling. A prickly type, like when Dad brought a load of middle-aged friends to see me play in a club called Ritam, and I was playing my songs about fucking on the beach or being drunk on a roof when they were hoping for cover versions of 'Here Comes the Sun'. This is the same thing: everyone trying, but nobody quite in the right position.

'I should . . . busy night,' says Goran, nodding towards the Empress. 'I should be back, work, a bit.' He is choosing his words as well as he can, because of the language, but also because he does not want to seem like he is criticizing my own workload. Still, here we are: he is slogging around the streets and I am in a three-storey house with a glass of wine waiting for me. It is, as I heard someone say about the drunken dancing man, *not a good look*.

'Another time,' says Decca, her own voice showing that she also has come to regret this stunt. Her arms are marginally tenser and tighter against me, moving up towards my ribcage, as if she fears I will also run away. 'And thanks for the . . . for the delivery! I hear there is a tip function on the app!' Straight away this sounds like it is digging us even deeper into the hole and she follows it with a terrible awkward laugh. Goran is laughing in a strained way, too, and the whole scene has been like something from a comedy improv show which went on too long.

'I guess we're *definitely* not having that threesome, then,' says Decca, as we stand in the doorway, the heavy bag of food still on the drive in front of us. It is a funny joke, and we manage to laugh. But the sight of Goran receding from view, roaring away back to work, is a little different from the many, many other times I have seen it.

16

The strangeness of the little meeting hangs over the meal, and I do not even finish all the edamame beans, which Decca was particularly proud of having ordered. She says I am sorry; it was a silly idea; he was offended. I stroke her knee and tell her not to worry. That if it is anyone's fault, it was mine, as the person in the middle of this situation. But the price of this counter-apology, especially after some wine, is that I start to feel something pretty much brand new in my life: irritation with my best friend.

Could he not have laughed, come in for a beer, taken half an hour – to meet someone who is now so important to me? Did he have to make it weird, when all she meant was fun? When she is in the bathroom, I text him to say 'sorry if that was strange, she just wanted to meet you' and Goran just sends back: 'all good'. I think once more about him saying that 'they' are not like us, that this relationship is not something the real world supports. It feels like maybe that is what he *wants* to believe. But this is reality. I am here, next to her, feeling good about myself.

Decca's fingernails are newly painted black, like she is a teenager. I watch as her hands play with one of three remote controls, shuffling through a menu of shows and channels which never seems to end. Netflix, Apple TV. Sky Sports, BT Sports. Disney. 'I never know which show is where, these days,' she mutters. 'Axel has all sorts of shortcuts, she . . . they have to show me half the time. Sorry, is there something in particular you want to watch?'

'Yes, I want to watch *you* trying to use the TV.'

'Shut your face.'

'You know, one time I would like to watch the dancing show.'

'*Strictly?*' She laughs. 'Really?'

'Yes. Why is it called that?'

'It's – yeah, it is weird. It's *Strictly Come Dancing*, but that itself is a stupid title, based on *Strictly Ballroom*, I guess, but now people just use the short version and it means nothing at all. Language is strange, isn't it?'

'Yours is, yes.'

It is like being a couple, more than we have been before so far: takeaway boxes by our feet, stupid show on while we sit on the sofa, and still the prospect of the whole night together, her lovely body, then the soft thick mattress under my weary bones. We watch an idiotic thing on Netflix where two people have to buy a house without having met first.

Of course, it goes wrong, and at the end a voiceover says that they sold the house and had decided not to see each other again, so the entire hour was a waste of time. She changes channel and gives a hoot of laughter; it is a sex show, contestants deciding whether to date based on glimpses of each other's genitals. It amuses and surprises me to think that for every one of these shows, there must be enough people just sitting around with the time and inclination to watch. So much you can be doing, if you are not working until late every evening, I think to myself. And if you have someone like this to do it with.

'We did sort of say we'd watch a film,' says Decca. 'What if we got into pyjamas and did that?'

'I don't have *pyjamas*, do I.'

'No, so you'll have to be naked. Oh well. Hey, what about a Croatian one?'

'A Croatian movie?'

'Yeah. There's bound to be something on here if we search. We've got a whole channel with, like, a thousand European films that we probably pay for and have never used in our lives. You can be my subtitles guy.'

We skip past something called *Što Je Muškarak Bez Bukova?*, which I explain means 'What Is a Man Without a Moustache?' and does not sound like one of cinema's great classics. I spot something called *Mali*, about a drug dealer fighting for custody of his son. This was successful at home and Dad went with Petra to see it not long after I came to London. I remember being jealous, homesick, at the idea. He enjoyed it and Petra said it was boring, but she says this about any film in which a car has not blown up by the time the titles have ended. Decca selects it and we watch the screen go dark. Everything is dark: the curtains are drawn; she blows out the candle and we smell the trail of smoke together. She is in blue silk pyjamas, and I am completely naked, and it could be my house, it could so very nearly be my life.

'So this guy – his name is Franjo – he has just come out of prison. These guys are . . . what do you call it, his wife's parents.'

'The in-laws. My in-laws live in Hong Kong. Once a year we have to go over to them and Niall's dad talks about horse-racing and addresses me as if I'm basically the home help, and his mum hints that it's weird we haven't had any more kids, despite the fact I quite obviously shut the shop a while back. Anyway. Yep. So they don't want him to have the child?'

'That's right, they say he is . . . they are calling him *klošar*, which is like – it's the word for a drunk, for a guy who is always outside the village shop with his beer in the paper bag.'

'Wow, they sound more and more like my in-laws. Are you sure you don't mind doing a running commentary? There must be subtitles, if we—'

'No, I like it. I like being your guide.'

'I like it, too. It's super-hot that you can speak two languages this well, have I mentioned?'

'Well, everyone can speak English because you kind of

have to. Some people try harder than others, I guess. Goran still does not read or understand it as well as me. But all of us can do it a bit because you guys used to run the world and the Americans now do. In your schools you probably do not have Croatian in the first lesson every morning.'

'Not at the moment.' Decca pours more wine. 'But that'll all change when *What Is a Man Without a Moustache?* becomes part of the canon.'

When it is over, she takes me upstairs to the en suite, runs the taps, lights a series of little white candles along the sideboard. How many candles are there in this house? The smell of them feels as if it has always meant her; as if the association has been there for ever. The water hammers out of the taps like the Magical Water Mill of Rastoke, where Mum almost took Goran's head off his shoulders for trying to push Petra in. Decca laughs as I watch her emptying a jar of what looks like orange gravel into the tub.

'What, you don't have aromatherapy crystals at yours?'

'No, we can never agree on which kind to buy.'

She laughs. A long deep sigh comes out of me as I get under the line of the water and feel it fold me up. It has been so long – years, I guess – since I was immersed in this way. The feeling is of a different time, and it lands on me with such a lovely heaviness that I mutter *ajme* and close my eyes.

'What was that, what did that mean?'

'What?'

'The word you said there.' Decca tries to repeat it.

'Oh. *Ajme*. It's like – well, it doesn't have an exact meaning, it kind of has many meanings. It can mean, fucking hell, this is awful, or kind of the opposite.' My eyes are closed as I talk; I feel like I have never delivered a pizza in my life. 'Goran used to get me to go swimming with him – not at Bačvice, but places with not so many people around. We would jump off rocks into the water, or go walking in deeper and deeper. Sometimes it would be way too cold but Goran is a maniac; he would lead you into the Grand Canyon. So, I was not scared of actually jumping off the rocks, of it being too high, not really. But that moment when the water hits you and it kind of knocks your breath away. Goran said, what you have to do is shout this word, *ajme!* It gives you the adrenalin and you just push through.'

She tops up my glass of wine.

'Is it . . . what's the name of the beach you said? Bac . . .'

'Bačvice, yes.'

'Is it really beautiful?'

'It's a great beach, yeah. I would love to take you there. It was number thirty-eight in the Top One Hundred Beaches of the World that someone did online.' I think to myself that maybe this sounds too low, makes my hometown unimpressive, and promote it a little way. 'Actually maybe it was more like twenty-eight. What I really love, though – it's just to be in water, to swim. Anywhere. This is as good as a beach for me.'

'I tell you what you would love.' Decca is standing behind me now, her hands in my hair like a barber's. 'Isn't it your birthday soon?'

'Two weeks. I don't think about birthdays so much as a big thing, because my mother died like almost the same date. Goran and me, we usually have a bike race, just up by the marshes; he borrows someone's bike. He always wins, even though it is my day.'

'What if I took you to a spa?'

'A spa?'

'Just for the day. You could swim around as much as you liked while I admired your dick in your trunks. There's one I go to. Sauna, steam room – I bet you like a steam room.'

'Not too many of them on my usual routes,' I say. 'I probably only go to a sauna two or three times a week on average.'

'Oh, it would be so fun.' Decca's hands are on my shoulders, the back of my neck, and under the waterline I am struggling to control my desire. 'Can I book it? Like, could you just take that day off work? Or is that stupid, do you not get to do things like that? I'm sorry, I don't know what I'm doing, except wanting to treat you.'

The water is so warm. I imagine being immersed all day, feeling my skin go pink and shrivelled. Goran is on the fringe of this daydream, of course he is, his eyes good-humoured with something troubled in them, like earlier: have you stopped working completely, bro? Is this who you are, now? I do not have to answer to imaginary-Goran right now, but it is difficult to think of my birthday without thinking of the person I have always spent it with.

'The only thing is, I definitely still have to do the bike race with Goran.'

ONE MINUTE AWAY

'Of course. Well, what if we did the spa, I drove you back, you could have your race and we could maybe even have a drink together? Make it normal. Or I'll just get out of the way.'

My head is fuzzy from the drink and the water is making my body anticipate the bedsheets. The feeling of her fingernails tracing lines down my back sends a thrill through my whole body. Again: why should I not live like this? To be the kind of guy who goes to a spa for a birthday treat. Would Mum want me to have miserable birthdays for ever because of the memory of her passing, of how empty everything felt, how helpless Dad looked? She would be delighted if she could see me now, although maybe not right now, because Decca is fetching one of the large fluffy towels from the rail where it has been heating, and blowing out the candles, and it is straight from the bathroom to the bedroom, because in her world that is just how everything connects.

★

We lie on our backs, breathing in sync and around one another like a drummer and a bassist.

'What are you thinking about?' asks Decca.

'That it was the best sex I have had in my life. That is, kind of, the short answer.'

'It's been the best of my life every time so far. Hey, question.'

'Yes, how can I help?'

'Might you play me a song?' she asks, touching my face.

She is sitting up cross-legged, and the bedsheets are hanging off the end of the bed. 'Are we at that stage? Do we live in that world yet?'

'Play you a song on what?'

She gets out of bed, the roses tattoo bared to me for a few lovely moments. I can hear her walking around upstairs; an entire level of the house I have never visited, the area from which I was seen by Axel on that night I relieved myself in the lane. If that had never happened, almost certainly I would not be in this bed, with this life, right now. I would be one of the guys on the bikes outside, passing the house, never suspecting.

Decca is back, laughing, holding a guitar which has been painted black and has stickers all over it. I take it in my hands, sitting up against the pillows, and try the tuning: it is a little out, has probably not been touched in a while.

'I will play you a song that we both know, if you can sing it.' I try to think of what I can definitely pull off, in this very unusual concert. 'Do you know this? It's your kind of time in history.'

'*Time in history*, fuck me, what is it? "Greensleeves"?'

I pick tentatively at the strings and she squeals in recognition of the song. Tracy Chapman. Immediately she is singing the first line, the right key, a confident voice. I mess up the chords straight away and have to start again.

'Sorry, I do not normally play with no clothes on.'

'You're not playing it with your cock. Although you probably *could*, knowing what I now know about it.'

We go through the first verse, the chorus. C major, G, E minor. It is not – as they say here – a picnic, but this is a song I have listened to a lot in my life.

'Absolute banger,' says Decca.

'It used to play in the music store. I always liked it because of the tune. It's an amazing tune, obviously, but when I had been there for, like, too long, when I was feeling like I had to get away, and Goran was over here already – then I would hear the lyrics and feel kind of sad and desperate to be in the fast car. The whole thing about leaving tonight or you just carry on the same way till you die.'

She pulls the covers over us and I tell her about Goran sending me the picture of the motorbike, about how this place was a new adventure for both of us. Talking nonsense, gazing up in the dark towards the big lampshade that is like a full moon, I feel like I am being reminded of an earlier time: of being a student, a kid, sleeping under the stars at a festival, falling in love, feeling the size of the universe, seeing it all for the first time with a new person. But, although there were small moments like this in my past, none of it was like this. The real thing has begun.

17

For the first few moments I cannot work out where I am. In my dreams I was in New York, playing the guitar while Decca sang; not a big performance, just in the street with yellow taxis going past. It was confusing to work out how we had got there from here, and the reality is less fun. I realize, as I stop the quacking, that I failed to put the phone into her wall: it has been ticking away all night for nothing, the precious charge draining slowly away. It is on 28 per cent; I will have to juice it up here in her house before it is worth going out, because the power pack is so slow these days. This means a late start, which means I will not see Goran at the lockup. I am annoyed with myself, my head is sore, and it is so dark in this bedroom that it is hard to believe it can be morning. I have to use the torchlight from my phone and crouch down to find Decca's charger, and then pick my way through to the en suite where my clothes are lying on the floor where we left them. The candles still lined up along the bath. The fierce jet of the shower. Decca is still half-asleep, mumbling and muttering, the sheet half-off the outline of her body. I plant a gentle kiss where the roses are, and whisper to her to stay asleep.

The wooden floorboards under my feet, the uplighters in the corridor, the big photography books in little alcoves like exhibits in a museum. A huge painting above the stairs, the figures smudged and blocky: four women dressed in red and, nearer to the viewer, a bigger one dressed in blue, with the body language of someone who is being left out, does not belong. I am trying to get ahead of myself mentally, to catch up the time I have already lost by planning the next steps: make a coffee, drink it down, maybe even make a piece of toast, although that would still feel strange on my own in her kitchen. Go back up, say goodbye, retrieve my phone, Begin Shift. Maybe these thoughts prevent me from fully registering what is happening around me, or maybe it is just the hangover. Because when I look back later, I will feel like I remember hearing a cough, some movement. But it would not have mattered even if I had heard it, because I still have to go into the conservatory for my bike.

Lying flat on their back with bare feet up on the arm of the sofa, sucking a smoothie through a straw, is a person I feel I have met before, although you could hardly call it a meeting when they banged on the glass that night. Axel.

We look at each other. Axel has on a black T-shirt which says OBEY, smudged eyeshadow, and short hair which is bleached almost white with dark streaks in it. My heart is beating hard; I feel like a burglar. Axel's face cracks into a sort of ironic grin.

'Well, nice to meet you, I guess. Jesus.'

'I thought you were not here,' is all I can say, which naturally makes me look and feel ten times as guilty.

'I guess not.' Axel's voice is a lot like Decca's, but with some different shade in it, slightly American-sounding, like something they have picked up from TV. 'I mean, forgive me for assuming that you're not *actually* delivering to the house. It's just not even Mum would have breakfast delivered to the bedroom, I don't think.' Axel takes a slurp of the drink and scratches the back of their head, lazily. 'Sorry, I could be talking shit, the fucking idiot I was meant to be staying with disappeared, I've been out all night and I'm absolutely hanging out of my arse.'

The speed and rhythm of the sentences, and the sense I have of having to keep up, adapt: all of it reminds me of Axel's mother. But with Decca, I always feel like I know what to say. Here, what am I meant to say? I am standing in this person's house, in my rider uniform, having very clearly spent the evening with Axel's mother while their father is away. And it must be fairly obvious that this is not the first time, either.

'I-I know this must be kind of strange, and I want to tell you that I do not mean any harm to your – your family. I . . .'

But Axel is hardly listening to my moving speech. They suck their drink noisily again and peer at me. 'So is this you out, now, like you just get on your bike and start your day and see who orders food?'

'Basically yes.' I walk past the sofa, towards the conservatory. 'I wait for notifications and I go where it sends me.' As I am saying this out loud, it hits me again how we are controlled by invisible hands. Even my hero the worker ant does the jobs he chooses: he forages for food; he builds the nest. He is not just waiting for the Queen to say, OK champ, I want you to walk but I will not tell you where you are going.

'And so how did you – I mean, you can see why I'd be curious, and I'm not even really judging because fuck knows Dad's got his secrets too, but . . . like, how did this start?'

I can sense, in the surprisingly casual attitude, Axel's desire to act like this is all normal, part of everyday experience. That young-adult wish to be above whatever is happening, to have seen it before, which I remember from the way Petra talked about boys and drugs when she was hardly old enough to have been out to the cinema with her buddies.

'Well, it started when – I mean, you saw it – when I had to take a pee in the street. After your dad had shouted at me for the order being late.'

Axel puts the smoothie down, slowly, on the coffee table. Finally I have said something that made an impression.

'Wait, what. You were that guy? You were both those guys? The guy who fucked up the order *and* the man pissing in the lane?'

'I did not actually fuck up the order. The restaurant gave me the wrong bag.'

'And that – Mum coming out to investigate – *that* was your meet cute?'

'Our what?'

'A meet cute is, in a romcom, where the two lovers first see each other. You know. She drops a schoolbook, he picks it up. Whatever.'

'So – yeah. Outside your house was the meet cute. And now . . . now we are seeing each other a lot. Messaging a lot.'

Even that seems a large thing to admit to, standing in Axel's home, with the sunshine streaming unpleasantly through the bay windows. For a minute, now there is another character in the mix, the reality of my situation feels like it is slapping me in the face. What is my bike doing here with the bikes of the family? How can it be that I have had extra-marital sex right here, in this person's living room, in fact on the spot where they are now reclining? Everything that seems so wild and blurry by night is over-exposed here.

'Well.' A shake of the head from Axel, and the cynical half-smile again. 'I mean, their relationship is pretty fucking dysfunctional, but now I really have seen everything.' This seems to me like a funny thing to say from someone who, in reality, cannot have seen that many things at all, not compared with Decca, or even me. But I am certainly not going to undermine Axel: with a slight alarm I see their fingers wander towards their phone. Axel clocks the change in my face and laughs.

'Don't worry, I'm not going to snitch.' (I make a mental

note to look this word up, add it to my phone note; the thought relieves the tension a little bit.) 'I have as little to do with them as possible, to be fair. I'm sure he'll find a way of doing a fucking Alan Muse on you if he wants to, but that's between you guys.' I have no idea what that phrase means, but it does not seem especially like I would want to know, either. Axel looks me up and down. 'When are you actually – I mean when do you start getting delivery orders? So does your phone start going off soon, or?'

'My phone is upstairs, charging.' Again it rings strangely in the air, because it is a reminder to Axel that I stayed the night here. 'In a minute I will get it, then I choose to begin my shift, and I go out on the bike and that is me.'

'It's wild, seeing it in action, the gig economy.' Axel pronounces this a little like Decca once pronounced 'portfolio'. There is a sense with both of them, I think to myself, that they want to stand aside from things which they find a little shameful or distasteful, but also enjoy whatever benefits are brought by them. 'Do you just keep going all day basically?'

'Yes, kind of. There are times when the app says, you have to end your shift now, if there are too many riders, not enough drops. But this does not happen to me and my mate Goran because we are elites, which means your rating is high. Which is why I did not like it when your dad was threatening me, about a bad review.'

'Yeah. Dad's got a temper. I don't know – be careful, I guess. Or something, whatever.'

Axel takes a final slurp of the drink, looks down at the phone. The conversation seems to be over, suddenly. It is difficult to say what they might be thinking, but it feels as if I should not push my luck any further than this.

'I should go get my phone.' I go to the conservatory for the Fox, prop it up under the Kermit the Frog picture.

'See you around,' says Axel, with a dry little wave of the hand. It is not clear whether this is meant as a joke – again, perhaps Axel does not know either. My legs feel heavy and unsteady as I climb back up the stairs.

Decca is awake, sitting up very straight, her hair knotted from where I clutched it in the night, from where it tangled behind her as we made love.

'Fuck, fuck. What did they say? I'm so sorry, I didn't . . .'

'It's fine. Did not really say that much. Didn't stay with their friend, stayed out all night, came home early.'

'But about *us*?'

'Not that much, either.' I kiss Decca on the top of the head. 'You know, if we are going to do this, do it properly, people have to know one day.'

She considers this, seems to feel the weight of it.

'I know, but she . . . they shouldn't have found out this way. I need to have a conversation with them, sit down with them.'

'Sure. I know it is not easy.'

'But I'll get there,' she says. 'I will, Damir.'

We kiss on the lips, this time, and agree to text each other, to find a way to be together before Friday rolls around again.

She slides out of bed and we go together down the wide flight of stairs, past the paintings and the bookshelves and the big house plants which sit in the corners. I go straight into the hall, leaving her to go in and talk to Axel. The house is theirs again, not mine.

On the way out of the door, I replay mentally the last thing I said, and I am happy I said it. It feels strange and exposing that a new person knows our secret – somebody so close to Decca, somebody who lives under the same roof as Niall. But I do not want to be a secret for ever. I do not have much to lose, I tell myself, and there is so much to win.

As I look back now, it is strange that I convinced myself there was not much to lose.

18

Riding hungover, my legs feel like they are full of clay. The situation is of my own making, but I become more and more grumpy with everyone else, blaming them for it. A couple of girls, hand in hand, ambling along the bike lane, ignore my pleading dings of the bell. Somebody else has to nudge them and say: hey, get out of the way. The girls have little earphones in, it turns out; the taller one loses one of hers on the path, bends down to collect it, and I have to brake all over again. They stand there howling with laughter; they have nothing to worry about, I guess, nowhere to be. Good for them. Good, also, for the motorbikes who power past me while all this nonsense is going on, on their way to jobs I cannot compete for. When am I going to graduate onto a motorbike, I ask myself in a tetchy way. Goran took a few months to get his, and here I still am slamming the pedals to the ground, putting aside these tiny little chunks of money. And from this thought my brain even turns in annoyance on Goran. He has not even messaged me today;

he is still being weird about the joke-that-went-wrong last night. I am unsettled, scratching around for things to be annoyed by, and soon there is a perfect one.

Leaning against the wall of Orchid Chinese, checking the phone, I see I am down to 30 per cent – this morning's charge was almost back up to full power, but not quite, and these inches make a difference on the road. I slide the power pack out of its compartment, put the two of them together, wait for the reassuring noise and the icon of my phone drinking from the well. But nothing. The lights do not come on. I take the wire out, reconnect. Again nothing. Several more attempts and I have to admit it: the power pack has gone from weak to dead.

Ajme!

The situation needs dealing with straight away. There is a shop on the high street, two minutes from Orchid, which sells pretty much everything in the world – Beyoncé T-shirts, beach towels, tennis racquets – but it is all arranged in total chaos, as if Goran had been given the stuff to put out on the shelves. The guy behind the counter is chatting on his phone as I approach, a language I do not know; he raises his eyebrows a millimetre to acknowledge I am there. *Power pack*, I say, *battery pack? iPhone.* The shopkeeper spreads his hands helplessly, gestures around as if to say: point at what you want. I cannot see it, though, and all this is taking time. I fish the deceased object out of my rucksack, show it to him. Still with his own phone tucked under his chin, he rummages around in a cabinet and takes out something which looks like his kid made it for a technology project at school.

'Fifty.'

'Fifty pounds!?'

He taps the amount into his own phone, holds it up, in case I did not understand the number. I now feel insulted as well as frustrated. A day's money for this piece of shit, which has no manufacturer's mark on it, and could stop working ten minutes after I get it out of the shop.

'I will give you twenty.'

The guy is not interested in haggling. He shrugs, is already pointing at a new customer. Muttering and swearing, I take myself back out of the shop and text Goran: *where are you, can I borrow your charger?* I can see that he has read the message, is online, but no response comes. Everything is digging into me; everything feels slightly wrong. The sun has come out from behind the clouds. A man in a suit walks past eating an ice cream. Even working people are having a good time, I think to myself, but not me. Sweat in my armpits, sweat on my back. When Goran's answer comes, it deepens my bad mood.

Running around a lot at the moment, 6 k from our patch.

No *bro*, no chat, none of the usual fun in the tone. Maybe I am being oversensitive but it feels, for sure, like he is pissed off with me, and this feeling is an almost unknown one. I try Bartosz; better luck, he is nearby, and shows up almost straight away. *Any time, my friend*, he messages: typical of the man. Bartosz's face is flushed as usual; there is a bottle of water sticking out of his jacket pocket. His uniform always seems in good condition, I think, like he has taken care of it, even ironed it. He looks at me with his keen eyes.

'Hey, we didn't see you again last night?'

'No, I stayed with my – with this woman. My girlfriend.'

'Whoa.' Bartosz grabs my elbow playfully. 'Goran *said* it was getting serious.'

'He talked to you about it?'

'Just to say you were always over there.' Bartosz looks at his phone; mine is lapping up power from his device. Maybe for this reason, or just because things have been weird today, I feel an impulse to tell him more.

'She wants to take me to a spa for my birthday in a couple of weeks.'

'A spa! Like – what? Fucking . . . Lourdes?'

'No no, not healing waters. Just a place where you get, you know, a sauna, and swim.'

'Yeah, you love to swim, right? What about Goran, though?'

'Oh, we are still going for a bike ride, and then we will take Goran for a drink. You and Mario should come too.' Bartosz is nodding, thoughtfully.

'So you just won't work that day?'

'No, and I'll make sure Goran doesn't work the evening either.' I can feel, in the silence, the need to justify myself. 'You know, you've got to have *some* time to just actually live your life, right?'

Bartosz nods slowly. 'Yeah, I guess so. I'm jealous. I wish I could do that, and I wish I had love, or sex, or something.'

'You will. Maybe not with a customer, I admit.'

Finally home, sitting in one of our chairs, a bowl of pasta and a Kosovan beer on the other one. I am texting Decca, exchanging rude photos, when the key rattles in the lock. There is a little thump and I hear him use a disgraceful Dalmatian word. When it is hot like this, the door expands a little bit in the frame – because it is cheap, like everything – and it sometimes takes two or three attempts and a shove before it gives way. Goran shuts it sharply behind him. He comes in with his jacket slung over his shoulder, throws it down on the floor; I bend and pick it up, put it over the chair, hand him a beer. He has also had a tough day; it is obvious from the droop of his shoulders. I have moved my bowl and can into my lap, so the chair is free for him, but he stays on his feet.

'Seriously, what a load of shit.' Goran drains half the bottle of beer in one shot. 'This guy in a van backs towards me so close he is in my fucking eyeballs, man. Then honks his horn like *I* am doing something wrong by existing. Christ.'

I drape an arm around his back. The heat of the pavements, the way his shirt is stuck to his skin. Our grandfathers used to come home this tired and sweaty from working on shipyards; we are them, now, but instead of building things which last for decades, we deliver goods which are gone in less than the time it took us to pick them up and drop them off.

With the aim of changing the mood by giving him

something else to think about, something beyond the fact we will do the same once again when the quacks go off tomorrow, I introduce a topic which – with hindsight – is not the right fit for the moment.

'Hey, so for my birthday. Decca wants to take me to a spa for the day, well, half the day, like go for a swim and that kind of thing. And then she was thinking, what if we had the bike race after that, and then we could go for a drink: like, you could get to meet her properly, not like last night, which I realize was a bit stupid.'

Goran wipes his hand slowly across his lips, swallowing a couple of times as if something is wrong with the beer. 'You are going to a spa with her?'

'Yes, Gor. I still want to go out on the bikes, obviously.'

'Sure.' He seems like he decides against adding something, and that is enough to make me chase a confrontation.

'Sure, what?'

'I don't know, man, it's just not quite the same as what we usually do, is it? Like, usually we would get up and do the race in the morning, chill, have a bit of breakfast, whatever. If it's this way round, I am going to be kind of fucked from the day at work, and you will be so chilled out you will hardly remember which end of the bike is which.' I try to interrupt – are you kidding, I am not going to be a zombie after a few hours in the water – but he continues. 'And, so you're saying we do it when you come back, and we have a drink after that, so . . . for the whole evening, like, neither of us is working at all?'

I feel like I can hear judgement in this phrase, and it bothers me: have I not kept up my half of the rent since I first got here, first with savings which took time to put aside, and then by riding so fast and hard that I earn more or less as much on my trusty old bike as he does on his dream machine? And another kind of judgement too, maybe, the broader one which keeps sneaking into view: he does not really and truly believe this can be a real relationship, and so it is just a waste of time that could be spent in the saddle. When is he going to get over this?

'Gor, the rent won't be an issue.'

'Yeah, I guess it won't.'

Goran ruffles my hair, like Dad used to do, and goes across the hall. The conversation does not quite feel finished to me, and I get up and follow him, but he goes into the bathroom and closes the door behind him. The action is so unusual between us, and the two or three seconds as our eyes meet feel so strange and sad, that I make a weird little noise, like a child.

After a few moments, I hear a curse from the electric shock – honestly, it is hardly right to call them shocks these days; there must be an expression more like 'regular appointment'. Once I have had this thought, I want to share it with Decca, want to see her big lips curl into a smile, hear her noisy laugh. But she is not here, and Goran is somehow not, either. I am caught between two worlds and, right now, it is as if I have fallen down a crack where the two of them meet.

ONE MINUTE AWAY

I have to sleep, but it will not come easily. If I am lucky, Decca will text me, there will be sexy goodnights. But when she falls asleep, or is called away by her husband, or whatever happens to her, I will just lie there. The night often seems very short when you are as exhausted as we get, but this one – with the bright streetlight glow outside – is going to seem long. I am back to that feeling of being a ghost: not out on the street, this time, but in my own life, my own home.

The exchange of comments runs through my head. A heavy vehicle heaves its way down our street, the windows rattle. The sky is not really dark, I think as I glance at the blinds; just a sort of grey smudge, a soup of all the lights. The phone screen is the same, as I lie on my back, staring at it: a confusion of lights, thoughts, pictures.

The rent won't be an issue. I guess it won't. I know what he is saying: that I seem to have entered a world where the rules are different, and that is strange for him. In my head, though, it makes sense, because I want to bring him there too. I want this magical thing to be for both of us; we are Dama and Gogo, after all.

There is just the whisper in my head that if I saw the whole truth, I would not like it; that he senses something I do not. There are hints in the way Decca talks about shame, about them having done bad things; that thing Axel said, 'he could do an Alan Muse on you'. All these codes, this language I can understand, speak, but not really get inside. The phone stares back at me, daring me to open a search engine, dig a little deeper. But soon enough it will be light again. People will need things to be brought to them. I have to try and rest. I drag myself up and put the phone in the wall.

19

A week later, first thing in the morning, the phone is going crazy. Buzz, thump. Buzz, thump. I wipe sleep from my eyes, sit up sweaty from the sheets. The phone is still going. What is wrong? Up from the bed, across the room. The first rays of sun glaring in through the paper blind.

H
A
P
P
Y
B
I
R
T
H
D
A
Y

G
O
R
G
E
O
U
S

Twenty-one separate messages, and then party poppers and hearts. The tiredness clears in front of my eyes and I laugh out loud. Nobody has ever done anything as stupid as this for me. *See you at 10! Excited!* There is a picture of her, naked in her kitchen, holding a cupcake with a single candle. *This wasn't as sexy as I hoped it would be, but you CAN have the cake xx.*

I feel the image working on my skin, in my blood, and have to turn the phone quickly face-down and pull the sheet over my lower body as Goran barges through the door, a takeaway coffee cup and a napkin in his hand. He holds it out like a waiter.

'Happy birthday, bro. This is your present. It comes with a napkin.'

I make a big performance of raising it to my mouth, drinking a mouthful as if it is a fine wine, and as if I knew what fine wine tasted like. '*Buonissimo.*'

'Is there something wrong with your eyes?' asks Goran, leaning over me with a concerned expression.

'No, why? Do they look . . .?'

'Well, I just wondered if you couldn't see clearly or maybe you had lost the ability to read.'

He gestures impatiently at the napkin and I see for the first time his handwriting on it: an awful scrawl, like he has written it in a rowboat on a choppy sea.

Dva sata snimanja u Escape Studios sa audio inženjerima. 'Two-hour session at Escape Studios with professional engineers.'

'What the fuck!'

'You have a year to use it,' he says, 'but don't take a year. Record your songs, man. Get them out there, let's do it.'

I picture myself, guitar over my shoulder, walking through those doors – the Arctic Monkeys print, the receptionist in his neat wool jumper failing to recognize me without my rider jacket on. In honesty, the vision is more terrifying than anything else. I imagine struggling to play a single chord, my hands unsteady. It has been so long since anyone saw me play, if we do not count Decca in bed, and that was not exactly a gig. But my face feels like it is going to split with how widely I am grinning.

'How did you afford this, you idiot?'

'I bid online,' Goran says proudly, slurping his own coffee in what is probably a deliberately disgusting way. 'Now, I'm going to get ready. Some of us work around here. Enjoy your babies' paddling pool thing, and get ready for pain later.'

★

To get here, we have had to do some work over the past week. Goran and I made up easily after our strange little conversation in the kitchen, for the same reason we have repaired any other little nicks and grazes in the friendship. What else are we going to do: fall out, after twenty-five years? The next morning it was *di si*, back in the bathroom together, burning toast and punching the screaming alarm (him) and re-making the toast (me), walking to the lockup. Even so, it was eating at my mind that something was wrong, off balance. Whether it was about the feeling that I had gone mad, gone over to the side of the privileged; or whether it was just being pushed out for this new woman he could connect with, it was there in the gaps between our sentences.

Last week, though, Decca messaged in the middle of the day, asking to meet at the burger place. There is still something about these moments that feels like espionage, like when we were first snatching meetings and pretending to be strangers. It would still be strange for me to be seen in a couple by any rider other than Goran or Bartosz. But it is also exciting to me that Decca herself does not seem to be working under these considerations. Either she does not think it is possible that she could be caught here by her husband, by any of his friends – if he has friends – or, and this is the possibility I hope for, she just does not care. Even wants to be caught. Certainly, when I showed up in response to Decca's text, it was the opposite of secrecy: she was sitting with two trays of food in front of her, one for me.

ONE MINUTE AWAY

'I thought maybe you'd like lunch. There's a bacon burger, chips – sorry, *New York-style fries* – and I don't know if you like milkshakes, but this is a vanilla one and you can have the rest of it. It's too much for me; even looking at it is about two hundred calories. Or I can get you a different drink, or—'

'No, this is . . . are you sure? This is so kind.'

'I think we're past being "kind", don't you?' she asked, curling her foot around mine under the table.

Once again she had opened the magical door that separates me from them, separates the line of riders waiting outside in the heat from the people sitting in the wooden booths with their red vinyl backrests. I glanced behind the grill, where the usual man was perspiring, shouting out his endless register of orders behind him – 'two patties, cheese, onions' – and the numbers for customers, for the bikers in their jackets and helmets. 'Seventy-one! Seventy-one!' Despite all the urgency, despite the fact this whole game is set up because customers need their food this second and we want their money as fast as we can get it, bag seventy-one sat there for three or four minutes, and the worker had to shout the number again and again, until it started to sound meaningless. Meanwhile, I thought about how everything else in the restaurant was designed to make you feel you are on holiday: movie memorabilia, Beach Boys music, photos on the walls of customers having a birthday party. On the next table, a man was watching *Drag Race* on his phone, taking a huge carton of chips one at a time, mayo leaving flecks on his chin as he studied the screen as if he was reading a police report on a serious matter.

'So I've been thinking about this Goran thing, about the way I've basically just barged in.' She grabbed my elbow gently as I started to defend her from her own accusation. 'No, you don't need to say anything, and your mouth is full.' It was true: the big juicy burger, coming as a surprise in the middle of the day, had turned me into a wild creature. Goran and I were out of bread, pretty much out of all foods; we had broken a cereal bar in half and neither of us wanted to take the bigger one.

'I totally get why he feels strange about me; it would be weird if he *didn't*. I was just thinking about what you said: for these races Goran normally borrows someone's bike, right?'

'Yes, because his is a motorbike, as you know, and it would not exactly be a fair fight.'

'OK, so I don't know if this would make a difference, but . . . have you ever properly seen Axel's bike?'

'Not really.' I tried not to think about the trio of bicycles in the conservatory, the family memories they might represent, the long weekends.

I hosed half a gallon of milkshake into my mouth. It was so thick I had to remove the straw and suck out the remnants before the straw was good to go again. Decca watched this with what looked like relish. Her legs, in cut-off denim shorts, brushed against mine. I thought about being close to her, all day, in the water, just the thinnest of fabrics between our bodies.

'Well, their bike is a super-expensive racing one, because Axel had, sort of, a week of enthusiasm for cycling when we were in Provence one time, and Niall being Niall immediately bought them a bike like you'd have if you were about to enter the Tour de France.' I thought of Tadej Pogačar, our cycling hero, bombing up the mountain to the sound of cheers and cowbells. I could guess where her suggestion was going, of course and, in my mind's eye, Tadej's face turned into Goran's. In his heart, Goran is still the athlete he was when he left Split: a man whose feet blur on the pedals, who carves through a city centre like a knife, leaves challengers for dead in the sweat and pain of a steep climb. That version of him has been replaced over here by a man on a machine, his skills automated to make money as efficiently as possible. But that is still who he is.

'You're saying Goran could borrow *that* bike?'

'I think we could get away with it for a night; it's not like she, they, do anything with it most of the time, to be honest. And I know he's a mad keen cyclist and – look, I took a pic so you could send it to him. If you wanted. Just – I thought it might make him more enthusiastic about the whole birthday thing, and also, you know. Make him feel like I'm on your side, not a threat, or whatever.'

'He doesn't think you're a threat,' I say, without dwelling mentally on whether that was true.

'But it's weird. Of course it's weird. A girlfriend he can't properly meet – well, hasn't until now – and who's old enough that it's questionable whether you can even say *girlfriend*. Suddenly taking up your Friday nights, and whatever else she can get. And then planning your birthday. I don't mean to be in the way. I just love you, and I would like him to like me, or trust me, at least.'

'He will freak out if he gets to ride this bike. Trust me.'

'Yeah? You'd like the bike?' Decca motioned to me to lay my hand flat on the table, spacing the fingers out. She moved the fork into each gap in turn, bringing it down hard onto the tabletop, hard enough it would make me scream if she hit bone. Bang! Bang! 'If you'd *like* the *bike*, watch out for the *spike*.' She laughs at my face, the way I flinch. 'Don't worry, Roz taught me to do this. It's not always popular in restaurants, I admit.'

'Have you . . .' It was strange to bring it up, but also felt important. 'Have you talked to Axel about it? About what happened?'

'No.' Decca's face clouded for a moment. 'But they've been completely nice and normal. I think things are OK. You don't need to worry about that. That's on me to sort out. Like I said, I'll get there.'

'I am allowed to worry about your stuff,' I said, noticing I no longer waited to empty my mouth before talking to her now. The politeness, the caution of our early meetings had become strange to look back on. It did not even feel strange any more to be sitting together in public.

When I glanced at my phone next, knowing I should be

back on the road despite how much I want to stay in the spot with her all day, Goran had already replied to the picture of the bike with a dozen exclamation marks, and I knew we had made a breakthrough; we had hit him where he felt it the most, in his itchy feet.

*

And now here we are, with a destination on the in-car GPS which I could probably not pedal to if I had all day. After less than twenty minutes' driving, we are further away from my neighbourhood than I have been in the whole time since I came to London. I have not even been in a car for more than three years. There is a box of tissues in the glove compartment, a sporty rucksack on the back seat; the windows are down and the radio is on, blasting Eighties songs across the lanes of traffic.

'Oh my God, I love this. *WOAH-OH-OH*,' Decca sing-shouts. '"Love Is a Battlefield". Do you know this?'

'I think so? Maybe.'

'I taped this off the radio, onto a C90. Same sort of time as "Fast Car". Me and my mates used to make mixtapes with only women singers on. Sisters!' Her painted fingers drum on the steering wheel. We wait at a roundabout. It is a release to be the passenger, not to be making any decisions. A courier bike buzzes like a bee around us, the eyes under the helmet locked in concentration. I know what it is like to be exposed to the air like that, one tiny error away from being on the pavement. The inside of this car, as a contrast, seems impossibly spacious, the boot a long, long way back from where we are sitting. You can hardly feel the road at all.

THE LEAZE GOLF CLUB AND SPA RESORT. Decca swings the car onto a long drive which goes on and on, past golf lawns, stone lions, until a series of timbered buildings appears and then a big white house. I smile imagining trying to deliver here: the blue GPS dot circling the screen like a drunkard, giving up. Inside the reception area, everything is soft and white and smells of herbs, and the incidental music is 'The Shape of My Heart' by Sting, without the vocals and some of the notes. Decca checks us in; the woman instructs us where to go, hands us towels, offers a glass of Prosecco.

'I shouldn't, but he will,' says Decca. 'It's his birthday.'

The receptionist wishes me a happy birthday, asks if we have been here before: I am beginning to say no, but Decca says 'yes, yes, thanks!' and takes my arm, leading me like she sometimes does at Laurel Gardens, straight into an accessible toilet cubicle. Here, she puts each pair of the swimming shorts on me in turn, takes each one off, kissing my dick in between the changes. I am backed up against the wall and worried about setting off the hand-dryer.

'What if someone . . .?'

'I don't care,' she whispers. 'I don't care who sees us, I don't care if we see someone I know.' Her hands on me. 'I've thought about it all. I know what I want.'

The swimming pool is very blue under the pale lights and

there are chairs and beds down both sides. We glide up and down, pretending we are not racing, but both of us glancing to the side to see who is in front. She pushes off hard from the side, her legs kicking behind her, and I make extra strokes as we approach the other end, trying to sneak ahead. The feeling of weighing nothing is so different from any other day, and the silence: padded footsteps and the occasional conversation in murmurs between people on loungers. It is hard to notice how much noise there is everywhere, including in the brain, until it stops. Here I can hear every flick of my limbs or hers against the water, every breath.

I hold Decca in the water. Her skin does not smell of the chlorine today. Maybe they do not put it in a pool like this. Or it could be that I do not pick it up because I smell the same: I am becoming more like her, more a part of her.

*

Decca seems to know our waiter. After we have ordered, she uses a phrase I do not quite catch and we are taken to a different table, in its own little corner, looking out onto the huge garden. My hand goes to my pocket to take a picture, and it is only then I think about the fact I have not seen my phone since I shut it in the locker, which is four hours ago. Easily the longest separation from my phone since I came to London. My dining partner clocks the movement of my hand, the glance, and smiles.

'Do you wish you were getting all your birthday texts?'

'No. I don't wish for anything different from this.'

The Spanish waiter returns to check how we are enjoying the food. I allow myself to imagine that we are in Spain, in some plaza in the sunshine, and the waiter is one of those guys who come round the tables to play romantic tunes or sell flowers. Giving the guy a tip and borrowing his guitar to serenade Decca (it is a dick move, an ego trip, but if it stays in my imagination, nobody gets hurt). Going back to a hotel room, one with a balcony, coffee in the morning, our naked bodies.

'Is it nice?'

'It's really good.'

Chicken and mango salad with rice noodles: when did I last have a lunch like this, in the middle of the week? I turn it over in my mouth, milking all the flavour of it: the soy sauce marinade, the delicious slipperiness of the noodles.

'What are you thinking, then?'

I sip my Prosecco. It is my birthday, and so much has changed since the last one. Last year, after our bike ride in the morning, we worked all day and then Goran said, 'I am taking you out for dinner.' What he meant was a bag of Chinese food and beers in the street outside Cecil Court. I talked to Dad and Petra in the evening; they raised a glass to the camera. It was an enjoyable evening and I felt happy, naturally. But this is something else, a new world. The beautifully cut grass, the light reflecting off glass, a fountain, an old couple walking along holding hands, the gardener with his wheelbarrow. It is all so pretty, but through a window, it could just be a painting, a screen-saver. Just like the day the tip landed in my account, I need to know this is real.

'I mean: this is incredible, this is one of the best days of my life. Every time I have been with you it is in the top twenty things of my life, probably, if I am making a . . . I don't know what the word is.'

'Maybe a chart?' Decca bites her lip gently. 'We used to call them the pop charts. Anyway. Go on. Please.'

'Yeah, so if I am making a chart, you are just everywhere on it. These nights at your house, amazing. Even just sitting and eating a burger with you, it is off the scale. It's like my life has been kind of here . . .' – I move my hand in a horizontal line, like a graph moving gently along – 'and now it is like this.' The hand diagonal now, arching towards the ceiling. The waiter glances over with a slight smile and I wonder whether I am talking too loudly. Most of the other people at tables are not talking at all, just sitting in fluffy white dressing gowns, clinking their knives and forks on their plates. Some of them are probably staying here all day. 'The graph is off the piece of paper, the scientist making it is going crazy, calling his scientist friends to check the math.'

'Or *her* scientist friends,' says Decca, her dark eyes shining at me. 'Also, we say maths, not math. But continue.'

'Or *her* scientist friends. So, that's where we are, and it is amazing, but it is only these little moments, and – you know – it does not have to be. Right now it does, because you are hiding it from your husband. And I know a lot of things would need to happen, for you to stop hiding it. I just want to say, that life – a different life – is possible, and we could be happier than we both are now. Even if you just lived in my room for a while. Or we rented some shitty place. Well, I know *I* would be happy. And I feel like you would, too.'

Decca runs her hand over her face and her eyes look very tired for a moment. There are things in that expression which I think I understand (she is in a relationship without much love; she feels trapped), and aspects of it which I only part-understand. Maybe it is naïve to think that I could make these problems go away if I woke up with Decca every morning. But what is the alternative: for her to go on living a half-life, dressing up as the wife for public occasions? Feeling almost as much like a ghost, in her own way, as I am on the bike? We could both do better: we both deserve better.

'This has all been so quick,' says Decca, 'and so overwhelming. I think the first couple of times, maybe I thought – this is the adventure I haven't had. This is what's missing from my life, why not see where it leads. To be desired. To be . . . all of it. By someone like *you*. It was that, at the start. Ego, weakness, whatever. You know on the continent – well, you're *from* the continent . . .'

'Europe?'

'Yeah. In lots of parts of Europe, or I guess in lots of parts of the world, people don't flinch at this kind of thing. An affair, someone being a mistress or a – whatever the word for you is. Marriages go stale, the sex side of it isn't working: you just find it somewhere else. It can just be – don't ask, don't tell. In my head it all sort of made sense. Told myself

I was a lady of leisure in, I don't know, a Jean-Luc Godard film. But then, well.'

'Then, what?'

'Well, I said I was seeing where it led. And it's led here, to me being really deeply in love with you. And being scared of that, I guess.' Someone walks right past in the gown and flipflops, so close that their hip catches the corner of the table, and she reduces the volume of her voice. 'And not knowing what to do about it.'

'You don't have to do anything right here and now.' It is strange to hear myself talking this way – like I am the one who is fifteen years older, has seen the world. 'I just have to know that you want it to change, that you want this.'

'I do want it.'

'OK. Because if you want it, you can get there.' I am almost impressed by my own words. Sure, I am making it up as I go along, but that goes for everything: that is how I came to be sitting here, in London, with a beautiful woman who loves me. If I can walk into the unknown, so can she.

'Damir Kovačević.'

She says it perfectly. I say her name back to her. Decca and Damir. The words sound like they go together. There is a music in the combination of the names which feels more real. Decca and Damir. I lean forward and kiss her, and nobody takes even a second's look. They do not see a married woman, Female Customer, and they do not see my rider name and rating; they just see us, two people.

20

'Mary Christ, what a beauty,' says Goran, crouching down by Axel's bike and, with a tender hand, inspecting the pressure of the slender front tyre. The paintwork is silver, like on mine, but they could almost be different species. The body of this bike is just a skeleton of sticks, so thin that they almost look two-dimensional, the maker's name – PINARELLO – written sharply across the down tube. The saddle is high, designed for someone powering through the Pyrenees, almost vertical on the bike, juicing the pedals for every last drop.

'You like it?' Decca looks proud. Her hair is in a wet curly mass down her back. 'I'll go ahead to the pub and, I mean, don't rush.'

'We will not rush,' says Goran. He is wearing his Lycra leggings, brought all the way from Croatia years ago and hardly ever used these days. At one time when we were struggling a little, he talked about selling them online, and I discouraged him – shut up, nobody wants to buy your disgusting pants – because it would have been a sad moment, a step back, like if I had got rid of my guitar. 'I will finish the race, then I relax for thirty minutes so he also finishes.'

Decca laughs eagerly at the joke. I can feel her nerves. We kiss in front of Goran, who makes a joke of covering his eyes and shaking his head. All this feels good, feels like what it could be. Goran has hopped up onto the saddle and his feet are playing gently on the pedals, teasing the crank, a dreamy smile on his face like a gourmet about to eat a fancy meal. 'Come on, *gubitnik*,' he says: loser. 'Decca, we see you in the pub.'

We get quickly off the main road and join the pedestrian and cycle lanes as they weave towards the marshes and the reservoir. Here, we have to go slow; there are people out for walks, holding hands, dogs trotting everywhere. I follow behind Goran, seeing in the poise of his body how much he wants to power the bike properly, get going. He breaks into 'The One and Only', his karaoke speciality from back home, the words sounding even more ridiculous in his terrible English-rock-star voice. It flashes into my head that the lyrics express what I feel: a cheesy pop classic can sometimes do more for you than a clever song. Moments from the day keep coming back to me: the strange freedom of the road as we drove out of London; changing into the swimming shorts with her eyes on me. The track widens and there are fewer people around. Soon we will be on the marshes themselves, and can do whatever we want. Although we are still only a couple of miles from the sweaty burger place, from the stressful shitshow of Superior Pizzas, the congested bike lines and angry drivers, the marshes feel very far away from our usual beat. There are birdcalls from the trees, and the sky looks as huge as it should, not contained within a bell jar like it is when you are out on the streets.

In front of me, Goran starts to warble the Seventies song 'Magic'. The sun is beginning to set and the sky is now pink with a layer of maroon cloud. I want to stop and take a picture, but he is cruising further ahead, starting to extend his stride a little, and I have to work hard to keep him in sight even for this pre-race warm-up. His voice is very loud in the thin summer air. In Split he used to sing like this even during races, to emphasize that he was not out of breath, that he could win while playing a trumpet if he had to. A couple of guys come towards us, walking four big dogs, the smaller of the two men being dragged along at an uncomfortable speed by the biggest of the dogs. *Imam previše pasa*, sings Goran, improvising a tune: 'I have too many dogs'. I join in, like it is a well-known hit. We are bombing along together, my best friend and I, and nobody can understand the joke because, although we can speak their language, they cannot speak ours: it is just for us.

The light is low as we get to the marshes, crouch on our traditional start line, next to a fallen tree. This part of the marsh opens out naturally like a velodrome; it could have been designed as a racetrack. Four circuits of the course is our normal distance. We are about to count down from three, *tri-dva-jedan*, followed by a klaxon sound: the same way we have started races since we were kids. Goran turns his head towards me.

'Look, this is kind of an unfair contest. This bike is like a spaceship and I am already a cycling legend, whereas you are more like the French woman.'

'What French woman?'

'You know, the one who was the oldest woman ever in the Guinness World Records.'

'Ah – Jeanne Calment.'

'See, I thought you'd know, that's your kind of age bracket for women.' Goran dings the bell twice to congratulate himself on the joke. 'So, why don't we swap. You can ride this monster and I will race you on the Fox.'

'Isn't the whole point that you want to ride it? You were all excited about it.'

'No, the *whole point* is that we are Dama and Gogo, and we do this every year, and we will be doing it every year until we are old men.' Goran has dismounted, and is rubbing the Silver Fox on its side in a friendly way. 'Come on, old friend. We're going to beat him even on that thing. You've got it in you.'

The klaxon noise: BLAAAAAAAAAAAA! We set off, Goran shadowing me, then jinking ahead, then falling behind again. The bike is so light beneath me, especially compared with the solidity of my trusty Fox, that I hardly dare to move through the gears; it feels like the top end of the range would take us off the ground and into the air. My limbs should be relaxed from the day in the pool, but if anything it seems to have encouraged them to shut down altogether; I feel slightly spaced out and absent, like I could just disappear into smoke. It is a pleasant kind of feeling, so different from the focus of the road, and I watch fondly as Goran starts to open up a lead. Tree roots and ruts in the path make the Fox buck and rear up; he yells in delight like someone on a rollercoaster; raises his front wheel in a wheelie.

When he has finished the four laps, he lies the Silver Fox down on the ground and curls up next to it, mocking me with snores. I lean Axel's bike against a tree trunk, thinking about the mud on the tyres, and the little spots of dirt on the paintwork: is Decca going to clean it, or does she not care? A third possibility enters my head, not for the first time: could it be that she wants it to come up, is looking for an opportunity to be caught, to get everything out in the open? It would fit with the way she has started to meet me in public, the fact we are right now about to meet in a bar on the high street like we are as publicly out as David and Victoria Beckham. The truth will set you free. Again, this is something I remember hearing in a song.

I fall on Goran, making him yell out. 'Wake up, man! We have an appointment!' We wrestle a little on the ground. This moment could be any time since we were kids. But what we are going onto is something new.

★

ONE MINUTE AWAY

The St George's flags from the Euros are still in the windows of the Grapes, the pub that Decca has chosen – or maybe this is the sort of place where they never come down. I tie the Silver Fox up outside, but Goran indicates that we will wheel Axel's superbike in with us. 'You can't just leave something like this out here; it would be gone by the time we ordered.' Inside, there is a blanket of pub noise which makes the situation feel more natural, and a surprise: Mario has turned up, and is standing in the corner with Decca, a nearly empty bottle of beer in his hand. The two of them salute and beckon us over. It is surreal and fun to see him and Decca together, two people with nothing in common but me, laughing in a familiar manner as if they had been on a weekend break together. Mario, sleeves rolled up, slaps me on the back hard enough to dislodge a rib. 'I'm going to get shots.'

'Bartosz not here?'

'No, nothing from him. Just me and your lover, so far. She's fun, man. She's got a tab at the bar.'

Decca and I stand shoulder to shoulder, her arm stealing around my back. I think about her body next to mine in the water, and then for the first time about the fact that I will not be able to go home with her, finish the day falling asleep next to her. Still: I made my speech at the spa. Another life is possible, a better, freer life.

Four little sambuca shots on the table, in a square. *Živjeli!* yells Mario. What? says Decca. Oh, it is too late, we have downed the shots, we will just have to get more. Mario is already on his way. How do I say it? Decca raising her voice.

Zeev-eh-lee, Goran and I repeat, over the hum: say it with us. That's not how he said it, Decca objects. Ignore Mario, we say, he is from a different part of Croatia, he talks like a peasant. Oh, I love it, inter-Croat bitching! All these little jokes, bits of chatter, start to blur. The syrupy taste of aniseed. Decca's breath when I lean in to kiss her. Are you having a good time, she asks. Yes, the best time. Four more shots, this time brought by Goran, and followed by more beers, pints instead of bottles. Goran and Mario do not care that she is paying for all this, do not find anything wrong with it. Or they are impressed, even. Or – there is just no need to think about it at all. I message Bartosz to see if he wants to join us; I have gone from being anxious about this gathering to wanting it to go on for ever.

'Now I sing a song,' Goran is saying. 'I say 'OI!', you must drink.'

He drums on the table with his hands and starts to sing the stupid song, 'Kad Čujem Tambure', in Croatian.

I think of my mother, how happy she would be with this life I have found, even if right now it is very different from anything she would have imagined. Of my dad when I am able to send him an audio track, say: I made this, it is out there on the internet. Goran is high-fiving Decca, very pleased with the way she threw herself in to the 'oi' chorus. This is what she is like, I want to say, but do not need to say. It is not 'us and them'. As if he is reading my thoughts, he grabs her arm.

'Hey, are you coming back to ours?'

ONE MINUTE AWAY

I start to cook up excuses on Decca's behalf: she cannot do that, she has work in the morning, she has family stuff. But her dark eyes are full of mischief, dancing in a tipsy way.

'I could. If I'm invited.'

'*Could* you?' I take her arm as if playfully claiming her away from Goran. 'What about . . . ?'

'I'll just say I've got pissed and I'm staying at Sap's. I've done things like this before.'

We totter back, under the streetlights, laughing. It is the opposite of my usual experience, the gradual smartening of the neighbourhoods towards Laurel Gardens; on this walk, I am conscious of how everything becomes narrower and darker. There seems to be more litter on the corner of the street than I normally notice: the Cecil Court door creaks more unnervingly than usual, the pile of leaflets on the stairs looks scruffy through a visitor's eyes. But Decca seems delighted by everything; this is an adventure. She laughs when I give her a brief guide to the kitchen to make sure she avoids doing an Alice in Wonderland, and when I forbid her from looking into Goran's shambles of a room. We sit on my bed, giggling like we have never been out in our lives before.

*

A rustling next to me. My head hurts. Decca is already up, in a T-shirt. She leans down to kiss me, the empty beer bottles clustered in one hand; I get an unwelcome breath of their smell, of last night.

'I'm going to get up and out and I'll see you – Friday? Before?'

'You don't have to take those out,' I croak.

'I think I can manage that, Dam. I love you.'

Quack! Quack! Quack! Quack! Quack!

An hour later. The alarm seems to be going louder than usual, is coming from two separate compartments of my brain. I am looking at the skirting board and something is different, wrong. There is still the dull pain in my head: my God, I remember, I got drunk, hard drunk. Goran is muttering and swearing across the hall.

'Make coffee, Dam. I'm going to die.'

Through the inadequate shower curtain, as the water trickles and splutters out, I hear a familiar old clattering noise and a flat laugh from Goran. 'Fuck me, seat's off again.'

'Completely off?'

'Literally in my hand. Your girlfriend just dodged a bullet.'

'Well, the usual then, I guess. We sit on what's left of it and wait for Caroline to save us.'

'Good old Caroline,' says Goran.

Bump-bump-bump, the bike down the stairs. The light a little too bright; both of us squinting into it, blowing out our cheeks. The first couple of delivery guys zipping by in the cycle lane, our competitors, our rivals. People who are not idiots and did not drink a dozen shots last night and have been already taking food off our plates for an hour or more. But the hangover pain has a satisfaction at the core of it, like the ache after ten hours in the saddle. We earned it, it means something. Goran reaches across to squeeze my shoulder in his spade of a hand.

'Last night was fun, brother. Decca is great.' He rubs his nose. 'I mean, for someone who remembers the Beatles getting together.'

'Fuck off.'

'She is hot, I admit. She doesn't even seem old. You're a lucky bastard, Dam.'

I can remember those words very sharply, can hear them spoken aloud in my head any time I stop and let thoughts flow in, because of what came straight afterwards. Getting to the corrugated-iron door of the lockup and seeing the padlock hanging, useless, undone. 'Mary and the disciples, which one of them keeps doing this, and are they actually thick as pigshit or . . .'

Then somehow a change in the air before we even saw it, like we somehow knew two seconds before we really knew.

'Oh no,' says Goran, his hands going to his head, 'oh no, no, Jesus Christ, no.'

PART THREE:

SOMEWHERE ELSE

21

Be your own boss. Work when you want to work, earn as much as you want to earn. Stop when you want. Quit giving your days up for some guy in a suit; be free. Everyone wins. The customer gets what they want, faster than ever before. You get paid, you have a flexible lifestyle, beers in the evening, you are part of an exciting city, providing an important service. On your bike all day, wind in your hair. This is the twenty-first century. This is the modern world.

Everyone wins, if you do not look at the picture too long. Everyone wins until they are one of the losers.

*

The police officer has small, sharp eyes and spiky blonde hair. Her accent is from somewhere in Western Europe. PC BERMAN. She quickly notes, on her keyboard, everything I say. It almost seems too quick, like not much of it is being recorded, like she could be writing: *pair of idiots lose motorbike, nothing to worry about here.* Despite the crisis, the idea of going to the police station was kind of fun, a distraction, for a moment. I had imagined someone screaming at the cops, writhing in the handcuffs as he was brought in. An interrogation down the corridor, a voice shouting that they will never get anything out of him: all the stuff we see on our pirated Netflix. In fact, the only sound in the room is her vigorous pressing of the keys, and – in the orange chair next to Goran – an old guy, with no mask, coughing every half a minute in such a nasty hacking way that it feels almost deliberate.

'So this – garage – was it broken into?'

'No, the – it was not locked properly, we think. We share it with two other guys.'

My stomach rumbles miserably. Behind me, Goran's face is pale, pinned to his phone, his fingers sliding over the screen: refresh, refresh. Someone must know something. The WhatsApp group. Even being in his head as I am, it is hard for me to know if he really means this, or is just saying it to fill the space. As a mantra until his brain recovers from the punch.

'So the last time you saw the motorbike . . .'

'Goran – my friend – put it in the lockup last night.'

'At what time exactly, would you say?'

'It was about seven.' Hard to believe this was only last night; that I had spent the day floating around like a hippo, come home smelling of oils and spices, was looking forward to a bike race, to going out to get drunk with my girlfriend and best buddy. Part of it almost felt too good to be true, and now this is our truth: the yellowish light, the posters about keeping your neighbourhood safe, the old man coughing again and again in the corner. Goran, hunched over in the corner, shaking a little, his feet jiggling unstoppably back and forth.

'Why is your friend not speaking himself, by the way?'

'His English is not so good,' I say in a lowered voice, 'it's better this way.'

PC Berman nods slowly. For a second it crosses my mind that she might be wondering if this is some sort of scam we are pulling. But if anything, that would be giving us too much credit. We are not confidence tricksters; we are two people who have lost one of the only things we possessed.

'And did your friend leave the . . . lockup open at that point?'

Give me some credit, I think, what am I going to say? *Yes, and then I put a sign up saying UNLOCKED, PLEASE STEAL MOTORBIKE.* But, when it comes down to it, the officer is just doing a job. She knows the bike is not coming back, and so do I. This is not the Fifties; a detective will not go knocking on doors to check if anyone has seen 'a suspicious character'. We are reporting this because without going to the cops we will not get a crime number, and without a crime number we are in even worse trouble.

'No, he definitely locked it up. But like I said, there are two other people who use it, and sometimes they leave it open.'

Berman nods slowly once more, again seeming to be on the verge of saying something less than flattering about our system. 'So he wasn't working yesterday evening? It's just, I would have thought the night was the best time for people doing your job.' I find myself wondering where she lives, whether she sometimes uses our app herself.

'Normally we would always work the evening, but it was my birthday.'

'Ah,' she says, typing again. 'Well, happy birthday.' This almost seems sarcastic in our situation, but her face seems genuinely to have relaxed; she is half-smiling. 'And did anyone else know about this? That your friend – Goran – wouldn't be on his motorbike, that it would be sitting there?'

The hacking cough again. It is stressing me out, Goran sitting next to him, in the cloud of those germs; I want to go and get the guy a cup of water from the machine and then ask him politely to fuck off. The cop is passing me a form to fill out. Another cough. I make myself think more kindly about the ill guy. Whatever he is here for, this cannot be where he was hoping to spend the morning, any more than it is for us.

Yes, we are among the losers here; this is where you end up when the game goes against you.

'Yes,' I say, 'yes, a few people did know.'

My hand is shaking on the little blue pen she hands over. The man's rasping cough echoes around the room again. I make a mistake writing 'CECIL' and have to scratch it out. I glance up towards the desk, embarrassed in case PC Berman noticed and has formed an even lower opinion of me. But she has no opinion of me at all; her phone is out, she has moved on to something else.

*

It is the longest we have ever walked in silence. No joke seems like it would be anything but an insult to him; no practical comment about the situation in front of us is quite bearable yet. It is just one foot in front of the other and, without bikes, those footsteps feel heavy. We get all the way back to Cecil Court without any conversation. Outside the door, a sort of duty takes hold of me. I have to be in charge here. I am forever following him, but now I have to lead.

'So, I guess what's best is – I guess I go out as normal, right, and then when there's a break, I could text Decca and try to borrow Axel's bike again, the Piranello. And then, when we stop tonight, I could ask her to lend us some money to get you something even just for now, a . . .'

'*Damir.*' Goran gestures helplessly with both hands, like a tennis player who cannot believe the umpire's decision. 'What are you talking about? You think I am going to just do what, lie on a sun-lounger? We are fucked. I need to get going now, I need to be out there till two in the fucking morning or something, I . . .'

Even on this app, nobody is ordering at two in the morning on a weeknight, but that is not the main problem, very clearly.

'Out on what, Gogo?'

He shakes his head; the reality of the situation is still too much to fit in there. 'OK, well, give me the Fox for the rest of today.'

'What?'

Goran's eyes are wide, and his face is still worryingly white. Our hangovers have given way to a much deeper sick feeling. 'Not – like, no jokes, obviously you are fast, but I'm faster, you know this. If I'm on your bike, at least I am making *some* money. And you could borrow the one from Decca. You could go to hers and do that, yeah? I need to get going. I have to, Damir.'

I look at my friend. It is probably true that if only one of us can be on a bike in the next couple of hours, Goran will make marginally more money than me, especially with the adrenalin pounding through him the way it obviously is. But he would be better waiting until I can get my hands on Axel's bike again: he can reach speeds on that which would make the Silver Fox break apart into tiny pieces. I could have that bike for him in almost no time, if Decca is in. There is no point in him racing off now on my faithful but creaky bike just so that he can put four pounds on the scoreboard, then another five pounds. We have to take stock.

But after ten seconds examining his face, I understand that it is useless saying this to him. Goran is doing what he has to do.

'OK. I love you, yeah?'

He half-nods in response. I have wheeled the bike all the

way back from the lockup, via the police station, since our awful discovery. Now I put it into his hands, for the second time in less than twenty-four hours. As he climbs onto the bike, making a cursory inspection of the gearstick, I want to say something. But no words volunteer themselves, and I watch as he pedals away, only one hand on the bars, phone upturned in the other. Pedals quickly, anyone would say, if they saw him; but slowly, too slowly, compared with what Goran has got used to.

Last night, the race, was all about fun; we created an obstacle for him where it did not exist before, because he was too good, too fast, had to be slowed down artificially. Now, he has been slowed down for real. And – knowing him like I do, like nobody else does – I am scared to think of how he will try to make up the time.

*

There are twelve messages from Decca, because I have not looked at the phone since we made our discovery. They started off with a picture of her half-covered in the bedsheet, her breasts bared to the camera, a mug in her hand. I recognize the mug – the design is some sort of famous watercolour painting, windmills in a field – and, in normal circumstances, it would have sparked a daydream about serving her coffee in bed, especially as we were together on my mattress only a few hours ago. The messages then go from playfully worried to actually worried.

Well, it's been an hour and a half so I'm worried you're either dead or have lost your phone. I hope it's the phone.

Hey, I'm sorry for being so pathetically fragile but it does all feel a bit too good to be true – I mean, YOU do – I was thinking that literally last night, about how you looked in the pub, handsome as all hell, and how I felt part of your circle, of your real life, your mates. All of it. So, anyway, will be a shame if it *is* too good to be true, but at least I'd rather know so I can find another guy on a bike, might even order tonight.

And, twenty minutes later: *Fuck, that was a joke. You know it was a joke, don't you?*

Dam – please reply? Are you okay? Xxxx

'I'm worried you're dead'. I have that thought again which struck me on the night of the football. That we have nobody in common, nobody to talk to if something happened to the other one, no reliable way of even finding out about it. Last night, with her world connected up with Goran's and mine, was the first taste of something different from that, and better. But the thought of Goran leads straight back to the nightmare we have woken up in.

Goran's motorbike was stolen last night. Or this morning. Anyway gone. Sorry for no messages but everything a bit fucked. Can I borrow yours again even though you only just brought it back home.

The 'typing' begins immediately. There is the usual frustration as it stops, starts again. Can we not just talk on the phone, I mutter to myself, feeling like an old man when the thought comes. But when the message pops up, it makes my heart a little lighter.

ONE MINUTE AWAY

Oh, how terrible. Of course you can have it. I can be back in an hour, is that OK?

I did not know you were not at home, I say: *are you sure it is all right to come back?* It feels like the right thing to say, even though, in fact, I need the bike and cannot think what I am going to do without it.

Don't be stupid. I'd do anything for you. See you in a bit.

I send a single heart in response to this, and lie on the mattress feeling like I can still smell her skin here, thinking about how I would even begin trying to explain the situation to Decca. 'Everything a bit fucked' is a start, for sure, but it is not just that Goran has lost the main thing he loves, or even just that our way of earning money is going to be massively compromised – bad as these things are. Whoever took the bike has taken away something bigger than any of this.

I think about the first time I saw the Empress, the day I flew to London. As soon as Goran had helped me carry my things up the stairs into the flat – the case, guitar, the Silver Fox taking its place in the kitchen – he marched me to the lockup and ordered me to sit behind him, clinging to his waist as he hurtled us around a circuit of streets I had never seen before. The roads were busier than I could have pictured them, and I had never ridden on a motorbike, let alone on half a motorbike with a madman in charge, weaving through gaps that hardly existed. Twice I cried out and shut my eyes, my body bracing for a crash. But as soon as I jumped down, I wanted to do it all again.

The Empress was shinier, faster, more like a magic carpet even than Goran had described it, and it seemed to confirm everything he had said about life here. The things I had read on the delivery apps' websites, in the study with Mum's electric piano folded up in the corner, as I tried to find the nerve to make the move. *Be your own boss! Be free!* Everything they said was big on freedom. To hell with living on office time, earning office wages. Say goodbye to doing what someone else tells you: set your own rules! Goran had been parroting all this for the months we were apart. You can just keep earning. People will always want deliveries, night and day. Look, I have already earned this motorbike. And now here we were, laughing and panting as he locked it up, and everything he had promised me was coming true.

We never intended to be here for ever. It is about building something for the life we want when we do go back home. For me, to be a musician; for Goran, maybe a family, a stable home. It is easy to imagine him swinging a couple of little kids around with his long arms, living something he did not get with his own dad. Over the months and years, we have always seemed to be moving in the right direction: doing a little bit better, a little bit better again, even if sometimes there were dips. A better ranking, slightly more money week-on-week, month-on-month. A motorbike for me was always going to be the next step, and even with what I send home, that was beginning to seem realistic. Sure, we were not going to return to Split with people lining the streets like in a movie: the boys have come back with their fortune. I would not be able to say, fuck you all, I will never work again, see you for the album launch. But we would have got somewhere. Even if in six months we were back in dead-end jobs, we would have dared to follow life somewhere exciting, lived abroad, have stories to tell.

For me, it would not be a disaster to go back to Josip's shop, or some equivalent; it would just be a little depressing. Goran, though, really has nothing to 'go back' to. The job prospects in Dalmatia have certainly not got better while we have been away, and he is older. Goran has to keep moving, not just because that is the only way he knows himself, but because every revving of the engine is an inch closer to a happy future, whatever shape that takes. Now there is no engine.

*

The kids' playground on Roundwood Street is busier than usual, the wild shouts of children, parents sloping along looking at phones. It crosses my mind that, like Goran, I would maybe like to have children one day, and with Decca that feels unlikely to be an option. But people adopt, of course. People have fertility treatments. People do all sorts of things I do not know about; if this summer has taught me one thing, it is that. People have many options in life, if they can afford to explore them.

It is weird sitting here, ignoring notifications as they come and go. When I am at Decca's, my shift is over, the phone is quiet; the world of deliveries does not exist. Here, it is difficult to pretend it does not exist. A rider goes by, on a motorbike, backpack just like mine, two minutes after I have sat down. The bike is not Goran's – of course it is not – but I think of someone riding it in another part of London, sitting where Goran has been for the last six years, on the machine he took care of like it was a living thing. It is a bitter thought, and the probable reality is even worse: by now, someone can have stripped it down to a bag of parts, can be selling it piece by piece. The Empress, as we knew her, does not exist anymore. And it is stupid to be so attached to a chunk of metal, sure, but Goran is, and he is going to feel this like the loss of a person.

And it is my fault. If I had not persuaded Goran to have a night out with me, he would have left the Empress safely locked up as usual. Or if the theft was this morning: still, if we were not hungover, if we were not clocking on an hour later than usual. We have a routine that works, and I disrupted it – for my birthday, to make things about me – and now the bike is gone. It is gone, it is my fault; I have to fix it.

22

The sun is on my back. I can feel my eyelids wanting to slide down. This is dangerous. We are so used to the feeling of not stopping, of pushing through the fatigue. The more we do it, the more it becomes who we are. We do not recognize tiredness, the same way the bike itself does not.

Yesterday, though, in the warm water of the spa, I caught a glimpse of the opposite feeling: if I stop, my body wants to stay stopped. Since I came to London, I have been living like the driver in *Speed*: forced to stay in top gear or everything will explode. But what if things did *not* explode. I am playing the guitar, Decca and Goran looking up proudly at the stage. The words are new, a song I do not know, even though I am the one singing it. *Love is something we say, love is something we do.* People already seem to know the chorus.

The guitar is coming out of my hands. No, my phone is coming out of my hands. Someone has got hold of it. I snap out of the half-dream, alert again. Decca is standing over me, in a white shirt and grey trousers; the first time I have seen her dressed as if for business. She leans in and kisses me on the mouth.

'Sorry, I thought it would be funny to pretend to mug you, but in the light of recent events, not the best joke.'

'I went kind of asleep, just for a minute.'

'You must be exhausted.' She reaches an arm down to help me up. 'Let's get you home, get you a cup of tea or something.'

'A cup of tea, and you take my arm – *you* are meant to be the old one.'

'And yet look at me, practically sprinted back from the tube.' We cut down Laurel Gardens, side by side, like any couple coming back from some trip. It is strange to be walking without the Fox; it is like a piece of me is missing.

There are a couple of different feelings running through me. Probably just because of the disconcerting rhythm of the day, her saying *get you home* has made me feel a little emotional. The word strikes a note which is different from if Goran and I discussed it being time to go home, *kući*. That word is functional, we use it every day: it just means a flat, a little box we sleep in. 'Home' in English means Decca, it means the bed, the bath, the feeling of being in love. At the same time, I am checking my pocket for my phone, checking compulsively again and again, even though it has only been two minutes. Although it was only a piece of fun, and it really meant nothing, the brief moment in which I thought my phone was being stolen *did* shake me, a little. Today has been a reminder of how easily we can lose the small amount we have, and how helpless it feels if that happens.

'Oh, darling!'

My eyes are moist, I cannot help it, and she slams the blue door behind us and folds me up. I shudder a little and try to compose myself.

'Sorry. Just a terrible day.'

'Don't apologize, never apologize.' Her hands are up and down my shoulders; her body feels so good, so full and warm. We are into the living room, onto the sofa, without having to discuss it, without having to look or think. On top of her, I have flipped quickly from vulnerability into control. She cries out and moans. As always, the world outside these walls vanishes to nothing; the phone could be blaring as loud as an ambulance and I would not move. We hit a perfect moment, in perfect sync, collapse, sweaty, breathing together.

'That was the best ever,' says Decca, 'again.'

I sit on the yellow sofa in a daze. She gets up and walks to the kitchen. The kettle is hissing, cups are clinking in her hands; the sounds reach me with the edges taken off, as if I were underwater all over again. The phone gradually becomes a real object to me once more, something demanding my attention in exchange for money. Decca, still naked, sits beside me, puts the mugs of tea in front of us. The sight makes me smile, even though I do not drink tea with milk, or really at all. The phone pulses. The WhatsApp groups are lighting up with talk about the stolen bike.

Was it locked up?

We don't know.
I will keep looking out.
Me too.

This is all meant well, but it will do no good, and Goran will hardly have the energy to read the messages at all. He knows as well as I do how likely it is we will ever see the Empress again. And he knows, as I know, that pretty soon the conversation will move on: someone will alert the rest of us to a road closure, or a restaurant with a special offer on today. There will be ten texts about that, and Goran's motorbike will slide up and off the screen, just like it vanished from the lockup – not because Goran is not popular, or people do not care, but just because work is work, and work goes on. Decca, not for the first time, seems to read what I am thinking, and we glance together towards the conservatory.

'So, look, about the bike.'

She clears her throat and swallows. I can guess what is coming, and the reality of the situation is building again in my stomach.

'I was thinking, would you – or Goran – would you be OK taking *my* bike. It's just, Axel . . . like, I got away with it yesterday, but it is going to be weird to explain if it's gone for more than a couple of . . .'

'I know. Of course.'

'I have to be a little bit careful with Axel, with . . . everything.'

A little pause. I squeeze Decca's hand, but I am really

thinking about Goran: imagining his disappointment when he sees, not the superbike, but Decca's ordinary one. It is still better than the Silver Fox – everything that lives in this house is better than our equivalents, obviously – but after how it felt to ride the Empress, it will be like an adult having to sit and do lessons in kindergarten again.

'I get that it's not the same, it's just . . .'

I squeeze her hand, staring at the paint on the nails, newly topped up. 'No, no. It's kind you even let me do this. Without you we would have no . . . choices, no options.'

'You don't think they'll find the bike?'

'They will not be calling in Hercule Poirot for it, I think. And, I mean, the place was not even locked up half the time. The thief probably felt like leaving us a thank-you card.'

'If they do catch them, they should chop their fucking bollocks off.' Decca's hand is hot and tight around mine.

'I don't think the police have the power to do that.' Because today feels like a day where rules do not exist – and anyway, we have not really established rules for this – I risk a joke. 'I don't know, maybe your husband can have someone killed? If you say it is for you?'

Decca's face changes a little, goes cloudy, and I regret saying this, and wonder what is in her head. 'What *are* your options, then?'

'What do we do next?'

'Yeah.'

'Well.' I spread my hands. I can feel the Fox's handlebars beneath them, the way they cut pleasurably into my skin, the marks left on them after gripping hard in heavy traffic or racing the clock. 'In a way, it is not about "options", it's just – we keep doing what we do.' As I am saying this out loud, I can hear the desperation of it, hear my voice becoming defensive. I feel like I am under questioning with my story starting to break down, even though *I* am not the one who has committed any crime. 'The algorithm – once you are an elite – you can do more and more. As you know. So, we need to make sure Goran stays in that group, keeps doing enough drops. So he has to do as many drops as he can, while we – while we work out what comes next.'

'Do you – does he have insurance?'

She asks it tentatively, but the question still claws at my guts, because it has been buzzing around in there from the moment we looked at the space where the bike should have been. 'Honestly, I don't know. Like, you cannot ride without some kind of insurance, not legally, same as a car, and he would not be *that* stupid. But his English is not great, was definitely not great when he got here. Seems pretty unlikely he has a policy which pays out if someone steals your bike, especially if it was not properly protected. More likely he has an email that says, hey, now you are insured, which might as well be from Krusty the Clown.'

She laughs, and it breaks the tension. We are quiet for a moment. She takes a long breath. Moments before she speaks, I sense what she is going to say.

'I mean: what does a motorbike like that cost? I honestly wouldn't have a clue.' She rubs her nose and her eyes focus on the problem with that particular, dazzling intensity they sometimes have. 'This is a difficult subject between us, obviously, but it would be weird if I didn't ask.'

'Lots, new. I think he paid about ten thousand for it, but that's 2016. Used, it would be cheaper, but it would be hard to even find one like that used, and then you would have the worry about what happens if it breaks, and . . .' Her eyes are looking right into mine, in that way which has been able to stop me talking, or start me talking, or do whatever they wanted, since the first time we caught sight of one another. 'Decca, you cannot just give us ten thousand pounds, or five thousand, or whatever you are trying to say. I cannot just – Goran would not want to feel like it is charity. You know?'

'I do know, but look. I know it's complicated. I just hate seeing you like this, Dam.

'I love you, don't I, and it seems like you love me, so then "charity" isn't what we're talking about. It becomes something else. This is *us*, a partnership. I want to look after you. And Goran. Because he comes as part of that. It's not charity, I'm just talking about pragmatism.'

'OK, well I can use Google Translate to tell Goran that, once I know what it even means in English.'

'You already know,' Decca replies, 'you live it, much more than I ever have.' She plays with a strand of my hair, lifting the teacup with her other hand. 'You don't have to decide anything this second, just – it's a conversation we can have. I mean, any conversation is.'

Her phone jumps around on the table, startling both of us a little. I can see the name: NIALL HUSBAND. His face fills the screen, a glass of something raised to camera. I am reminded unpleasantly of how good-looking he is, as I was when she made her Instagram post. Between the brief moments I have had to look at him, he has not really had a face in my mind. I can see her glancing at the phone. 'Go ahead. You can answer it.'

It comes out sounding like a challenge, and in Decca's eyes I can see it land that way, too. To my surprise, maybe a little to her own surprise, she stands up and presses to accept the call. 'Hi?' The tone is a little clipped, but almost normal: you would not imagine that she was naked, ten paces from the lover he does not know about. 'I've just popped back home to pick up a couple of things.' Niall's voice comes through to me as a series of half-sounds; he talks for at least thirty long seconds. Decca makes a face at me, her eyes dark, frowning as she concentrates. I want to get up and kiss her on the back of the neck, I want to hold her as she talks, but there are some limits to how many crazy things we can get away with. 'No, I didn't – let me finish, Niall. I didn't say I would be there *all* day. I'll be back in an hour.' Another pause for him to complain. She has one hand in her hair, curling a strand around her ear. 'Well, they're just going to have to wait for that, aren't they. All right, see you.'

She puts the phone back down on the table, a hard crunch against the glass. Her hand is shaking a little and she walks back and lets me take her in my arms. I want to have sex with her all over again: the way she spoke to him, refused to take orders from him, even though she takes orders from me. I remember her saying 'such a dick', rolling her eyes to the sky, the first time we ever discussed Niall.

'You are mine,' I whisper in her ear.

'I was just waiting for you, but I didn't know,' she whispers back.

We look together at the silenced phone, hear ourselves breathing. And stronger than ever comes the feeling that I could just stay here, like this, let the night fall around us, forget about everything that normally makes up my life. But one of those things is Goran, my friend, just the other end of Roundwood Street, wishing someone would help him. Whilst we have been in London, there has never been anyone to help him, or me. That is no longer true. We are a three now. We have to let her help us.

*

Goran is not back until late, more than an hour after me. He wheels the Silver Fox slowly into the kitchen, takes off his shirt, but does not even seem to have the will to dump it on the floor; it trails from his hand like a handkerchief. Although it could be my imagination, the Fox looks like he has worked it into the ground. The back tyre appears slightly deflated and there is a small scratch on the body paintwork which I do not remember being there even this morning.

But it has been a very long day. The spa, my birthday celebrations, could be a week ago. Goran puts out a hand to touch the saddle of Decca's bike.

'I couldn't get Axel's,' I say, 'I couldn't get the Pinarello, but . . .'

'No, this is cool,' says Goran. Just as expected, I can hear the disappointment in his voice. I want to tell him what Decca said. I want to say to him, here is why we have to take this chance. But he is not in a place to hear it, not right now.

'I've made you pasta.'

'I'm not hungry, bro,' he says.

'Yes, you are.'

'Yes I am.' He half-smiles, slumps down in the chair, which I have vacated for him.

'Are you OK?' I ask, hands on his shoulders.

'Yeah.'

'Tomorrow, when you're rested, let's – we can look at your insurance stuff, yeah? Get that going.'

'Thank God I've got you, man.'

'Obviously you've got me, loser.'

Petra has sent a funny meme: a guy back home who tries to do a dramatic dive into a pool, but misjudges the angle so badly that he hits a rock and hops away clutching his dick in agony. *Thought of you.* Goran laughs, makes me show it to him again. We watch it again and again. Each time it begins, we are convinced that somehow the diver will escape this time – the outcome looks so unlikely, even when you know it – and we end up laughing, a little bit more wildly each time, the joke getting better as it feeds on itself. *Laku noć*, goodnight. From across the hall, the babble of his wrestling videos. It could be any other night.

But an hour later, when I have texted kisses in response to Decca's, and put my phone in the wall, I wake from half-sleep to another sound, one I cannot immediately place. It sounds like he is laughing – as if he is watching the video all over again – but in a lower register, almost a gurgle, like someone putting on a dirty laugh. After a few moments I understand he is weeping.

I want to go to Goran and tell him things will be OK. But I cannot quite tell myself that and believe it. It comes into my head again, the way Axel looked at me, that air of amusement rather than shock as they processed my presence and what it meant. 'Now I've seen everything.' Perhaps after all they *have* seen much more than me, understand things about the game we are playing which I could not.

'I'm sure he'll find a way of doing a fucking Alan Muse on you', Axel said. I tap it into the phone, but you can tell it is a dead end even before clicking 'search', from the way that it does not auto-fill the phrase. Nobody has typed this into the engine before. I try just the name. Alan Muse. There are some results, but it comes down to the same three men over and over again: a CEO, lanyard round his neck; an actor; a botanist who writes books about cacti. I shuffle fruitlessly between pages about these people, not even really knowing what I am looking for.

MARK WATSON

When my dreams come, I am back in Croatia, but it is Yugoslavia, my childhood; a home I do not really remember any more.

23

Bloop-bloop-BLOOP. We-can-WIN, I tell myself. My brain prodding away at lyrics, picking up words and throwing them against other ones.

Everyone can win, that's the way I try to feel
Now I've met you and the

. . . and what? And the 'something' seems real. Maybe it will not stick because there is an English word which I do not know. Maybe it is just that my heart does not fully believe what it is trying to communicate: the missing thing is not a word, but a piece of the puzzle. It could also be that the problem is that I cannot work out if I am still using the same tune – the same beats, the same chords in my head – or trying out two or three at the same time: the words are always in the same rhythm, because that seems to be how they come naturally, but the tunes are sprayed over each other like graffiti. What I need is to record the original tune – *you wake up and you think you know the day*, that one – but when am I going to get into the studio? It is absurd to think of taking two hours out now, after what has happened, to mess around with my guitar. Really it would make sense to sell the voucher to someone else, someone who does have that time.

Also, the issue could just be that I am a shitty songwriter and do not really have any business composing these stupid little rhymes in my head. This is the kind of thought I try to drive away, but it is that sort of day. Rain is drizzling down, soaking my hair, running into my eyes. So much rain this summer, and the summer is not far from being over. My hair is too long, now; maybe I can get at it myself with scissors. Or Decca could cut it, but she seems to prefer it long. Decca has already told me she is not in London today, will be back home very late. With or without Niall, I do not know, cannot ask. Mud on the Silver Fox tyres. Pedestrians drifting across the cycle lane, oblivious to the ting! ting! ting! of my bell. The afternoon drizzles away and the phone starts to liven up with the rain. I cannot be bothered to go to the shops, people are saying. Maybe we skip the restaurant. Let's just stay home. You can get everything you want on the phone. Your order is half an hour away, twenty minutes away, ten minutes away, one minute away. Relax.

Another cyclist, one I have seen before in our company's jacket, risks being turned into dog food by weaving around a pair of slow walkers right into the middle of the road, and gets a blast from a lorry's horn so loud that it almost makes me fall out of the saddle. He is in a different colour jacket now, and backpack. I wonder whether the 'elite' categorization

ONE MINUTE AWAY

really has as much value as it used to; whether Goran and I would be better off just jumping between whichever app we can work for. But all these apps are so overstaffed, now. Every bike in the bike lane, half the motorbikes, scooters are delivering. Half of the cars are Ubers. You can almost imagine that nobody really lives in London anymore; that we are all in some sort of theme park, or a game show. That some sort of sadist is going to appear on our screens, like the super-villain enemy of Sherlock Holmes, cackling away: *there were never any customers! You are doing all this for no reason!* On my way to the dark kitchen, where three sweaty men stand over three sweaty pots and the dream of authentic Goan food comes straight to your door, I see a guy in an Amazon fleece sitting in a doorway, his trouser leg rolled up, shoe off. He winces as he dabs at his foot with something, then scowls in annoyance as I catch his eye. I think of the stupid searches last night, the brick wall of my ignorance.

The drops have dried up by early evening, but when I look in My Jobs, there are a few tips from the past couple of days. Two pounds, three pounds, two pounds fifty. No fairy tales, but not nothing. Keep going. A couple of messages from Decca. One extreme close-up of her eyes, as if she is looking at me as I go on my rounds of the city, which I set straight away as my wallpaper. And one which says: *Female Customer here. When you do eventually give the bike back (and it can be whenever you need to, however long it takes) – can I make a request? Will you sit on it before you bring it back to me? I just want to think of your bum being on there when I'm wheeling it back into the conservatory. I want to have that in my head.*

My Google session comes briefly back into my head again, but I push it away. Her business is her business. I imagine how impossible it would have seemed, even at the start of this year, for a woman like her to be having such thoughts about me. Yes, I will sit on the bike naked. I will *ride it back to you* naked, if you come with me. I press send, but she does not see the message right away, and the bloops are starting up. Someone wants dinner. Someone does not want to go out in the rain. We are a team, and we keep going until we cannot continue.

★

Almost midnight, and I am sitting at the table, alarmed. Goran is not here. It would not be that late to finish on a weekend night, but this is midweek, and things got pretty quiet after nine-thirty or so, at least around here. Much weirder than his absence, though, is what *is* in the kitchen with me. Decca's bike. It leans in the corner next to the Silver Fox. It was a jolt to see it and realize that Goran was not back; I knew without even checking his room or the bathroom, I can always tell. Maybe he came back here, dumped the bike, went back out for drinks with someone. But that makes no sense, not right now when he is desperate to claw back a little of the damage. And anyway, with whom?

Does he have a relationship he feels the need to keep secret from me, because I have made things strange by pursuing mine? Is there a new friend somewhere, something I do not know about? The thought is strange and uncomfortable, but all the other explanations seem worse. He is not looking at my messages. The ticks will not turn blue.

Decca has replied to say she wants me, and is missing me, but that was three hours ago, and there is no detail about what she is up to; I understand by now that this means she is out with Niall, and even if she might wish we were together instead, the reality – as I sit here in the tiny kitchen – is that we are not.

The WhatsApp group is talking about roadworks, as usual. The theft of the Empress is such old news already that you might as well try and start a conversation about the breakup of the USSR. I try to concentrate on a game on my phone, press the screen as fast as you can to kill aliens, but even this is about money: after I have saved half of the earth's population, the app asks me for five pounds so I can save the rest. I can hear Decca saying, *I want to look after you.*

Finally, the door downstairs: the two-part noise as it holds firm and then finally gives way. My heart gives a little flip of relief. I wait to see Goran's face in the doorway. I go to meet him like a housewife in an old movie, but instead there is the sound of further struggle: the thump-thump-thump of a bike on the stairs. What does this mean? Is it Goran with some other bike, or someone else entirely, a stranger with a key? For five seconds a shiver goes through my bones.

You could do anything to me here, if you wanted, and nobody would ever know.

Thank God. Goran. Under his hands, an e-bike, sleek grey frame, paintwork chipped here and there. A moment and I identify it.

'Is that Bartosz's?'

'It sure is, *Sherlock*.' Goran's voice is thick and strange. Drunk, but not like we were the other night. A harsh tone, like someone doing an unflattering impression of Goran. He wheels it in, through the hall, props it against the wall next to the Fox and Decca's bike. Three of them there looks wrong, and leaves very little space for us. He takes a beer from the fridge. Drinks a first mouthful with the disregard of someone already resigned to not enjoying it. The rest of the can.

'Why . . . why have you got his bike?'

But in the moment before the response, I know what Goran is going to say.

'Who do you think has mine, Dam?'

24

We are out of beers, and although it is probably not a good idea for Goran to have any more, I go to the little shop and buy six Moldovan ones, ignoring Goran's protest that we cannot afford it, cannot afford anything. The guy at the till has a bad cold and sneezes on the beers as he scans them through. I wrestle with the door, eventually putting my shoulder against it. When I get back, Goran is not in the kitchen where I left him, but walking up and down in the hall like a zoo animal. I have never felt so conscious of how small this place is. It never seemed to matter until I saw something else.

He takes a beer, sits in the chair. Bartosz's e-bike is slumped in the corner where the soft piece of floor is; it looks like Goran has shoved it over. We sit for two or three minutes in complete silence.

'So you think Bartosz . . .?'

Goran slides his phone across the table for me to look at: a message. It just says *sorry man*.

'Fucking hell.'

'Yeah.' Goran spreads his long hands, laughs with clenched teeth, shakes his head. 'I guess you have to say well played. All that time, I was worried about Mario leaving the thing unlocked so anyone could come in and take it. But we could have had the bike in a fucking bank safe behind bars and, as long as Bartosz had a key, one day it would have gone.'

He reaches for another beer. I already slightly regret buying them. 'You know, like . . .' He is on his feet again, pacing off into the hall, nowhere to go. He gestures towards our front door, his words still landing with a certain heaviness; like he is playing a guitar badly, which is what would happen if he ever *did* pick up a guitar. 'I mean, everyone out there, we cannot expect them to help us, sure. We live here, we ride our bikes, we stay out of the way. Fine. But, I mean, there were two people we trusted. *Two* people in this entire place, two out of a hundred million or however many of them there are in London.'

'I don't think it's a hundred million, Gor.'

Nine times out of ten the humour would work here, but this is the tenth. 'Well, I don't fucking know, do I. I don't know anything.' He looks like he is considering going into the bedroom, trying to get away from me. Goran is not himself, and I do not know what to do.

'Have you – like, I know it wouldn't work, but have you messaged back? Tried to call him?'

'Of course I called him, I called the son of a bitch as

soon as the text came in. I sent him ten messages, not even being a bastard, not even aggressive. Just, don't do this, man, bring it back, we can talk about it. I thought maybe that was a better way to do things, you know, try to understand. Be nice. *Be kind* – he says in English – like is written by the fucking tube station there, with the hearts. That's Goran Đurić for you. Kind, does his best not to be an asshole, helps people out a little bit where he can. Stupid idiot.'

I do not like the way he is spiralling into self-pity, I do not like all the big statements. There is no point making further enquiries about the conversation with Bartosz. Bartosz will not even be using that phone any more. You can get a new SIM card pretty easily, in a new place. Money tends to make things easier. An expensive motorbike, something you can sell, makes things easier. It is no use thinking about the three years we have been friends with Bartosz, the good conversation I had with him just the other week. He is gone, disappeared, the way anyone doing what we do can just disappear. I have to think of the next step.

'So, look, your insurance – have you . . .'

'I don't want to think about it, Dam.'

'I don't either, but we have to think about it. The only way we're going to get another bike is if we go through and check what the deal actually is with your insurance, get in touch with them and . . .'

'It's all in fucking English, isn't it.' He is moving away from me, towards the bathroom.

'I can read English for you, and Decca . . .'

'Sure, you can do everything for me, you two. Everything will be OK when you are in your fantasy relationship and we live in Hawaii.'

The sarcasm stings me, breaks my stride, and – just like before – he shuts the bathroom door.

The silence is piercing. There is no sound of the shower running, no sound at all. Just the door between us. I want to start the conversation again, say: just give me your email, let me search for it, let me call them up. At the same time I do not want to do this at all, because of what I am surely going to find, based on his reaction: that Goran never did the work properly, did not get a policy that covered theft.

Above all, I do not want to be standing here outside the bathroom door, waiting for him to open up and say sorry, feeling that I am not welcome here. Only two people in London we trusted, except each other.

And except Decca. This is when I need her, and when I go back to my phone she has sent a message. *I love you, I wish I could see you. That is all.*

I feel a little like crying, again. The message was sent half an hour ago, and there is no sign of her online. My trick of summoning her to the phone does not work, even when I stare as hard as Paddington Bear in the films when he is angry with someone, et cetera.

Goran goes into his room, shuts the door once more, and turns up YouTube. My phone is almost out of battery. I shove it into Decca's power pack, watch the numbers crawl away from the danger zone, and write:

Please can I come tomorrow. I know it is the wrong day. I just can't do things right now without you. No, delete this; it sounds like a sixteen-year-old wrote it. *I need you, I just need to see you.* Delete the second half. *I need you.* Send. Wait. All this messing with phones, living from one stab of dopamine to another. It was a good way to fall in love, but it is not a good way to be with her any longer. I need everything, and we do not have for ever to wait around. Maybe I will tell her that tomorrow. Maybe I cannot keep going unless I find the courage.

I am tired all the way through my body, and I resent these feelings, and Goran for making me have them, and Decca for not being next to me on the mattress. I cannot, for once, even find the effort it would take to plug the phone into the wall. The phone can feed off the power pack, next to the bed, which Decca gave me at the same time as the bike.

I have been tired many times since I came to London, but this is a different kind of fatigue. For the first time in these past three years, my body is telling me that it does not want to get up. Does not want to get on the bike. More: that there is no point in getting on the bike. That something else needs to happen, something big needs to change.

★

'Dama.'

Goran is standing over the mattress, already in his uniform. My brain smiles at the sight of him, and then cycles back quickly through the news feed of the last twelve hours, reminding me of the miserable conversation last night, and all the unanswered questions, the mountain of shit we have to hack through.

'What time . . .?'

'I'm going out early today. Sorry about – sorry I was drunk and being a dick. I've got a plan, OK.'

'A plan, what do you . . .?'

'Love you, man.'

I check the phone: half past seven. What is he doing? Shifts do not even start until eight, and it is not worth being logged on for at least the first hour of that. If his 'plan' is just to do five hours' more deliveries than usual, and keep doing fifteen-hour days until he drops dead, he must know this is not going to work. Even in this city, with its craze for deliveries, there are not enough people in their pyjamas calling for coffee. Maybe if you lived in Soho or in the City, there would be bulk breakfast orders from offices where the employees have stopped working from home. But if you could afford to live in those places, you would not *be* riding around with smoothies.

Or maybe he is talking about a side gig, like some riders have, but where is he going to find one of those, without a car, without that much English, and with no CV except this? Is he going to walk into the Bank of England and demand a managerial position? No, the only kind of side hustles I can imagine for someone in Goran's situation are things you do not want to get mixed up in.

But the way he was pacing around last night, the mixture of anger and despair, the helplessness of the situation as he sees it: my stomach slides at the thought of what escapes he might be thinking of. And, again, at the question of how we got to this, why there would be things he did not want to tell me. The answer to this mess is me and Decca, we know this, and this is also the thing that gives me hope, and as I flick through the phone there she is, her code name, her face.

Biker boy. Of course you can come. I'm sorry things are so tough, you two are still shell-shocked, but we can come up with a plan. Maybe this time I can actually do dinner. Or whatever, takeaway (but not from Goran). Sorry, is it super middle-aged of me that every time I invite you round, I immediately get onto dinner plans!? It's the company I want. Your company. And the sex. And to be with you and tell you everything is going to be OK. I love you, Damir K (little bit drunk, won't attempt the surname). Xxx

Sent at 2.20 a.m. Hardly five hours ago. She will not be awake for a while, and that thought drains the will from my body. All I want is to lie back on my side, facing away from the brightening window, and think about her hands on me. It is unusual to obey an impulse like this, and it feels so good to let it creep over me, to let all other thoughts out of my head. Soon she is in the room with me, or somewhere else, a public place, the unfocused crowd of a dream. When my eyes snap open, it is half past ten.

Ajme! I feel like a boy who has skipped off school. I take the phone into the bathroom to reply to Decca, to say how excited I am to see her. There, in the bright light, realities start to catch up with me. The shower gives a particular stinger of an electric shock, like it is telling me off for being lazy. And the phone battery is only at 54 per cent: the bar is so low that I wonder for a second if I am not fully awake, my eyes are too gummy to make it out properly. By the time I am getting dressed, I have grasped my mistake: I failed to put it in the wall overnight, the battery pack itself is out of power, and so now I have a dead charger and a half-dead phone. Somehow it feels like another sign. In the kitchen I see that Goran has taken both bikes – the cursed e-bike Bartosz left behind, and Decca's. This again is a puzzler: the man is fast, but he only has one backside. You can ride one bike while pushing another one along in parallel; we call it 'ghosting'. Is he going to try and perform double deliveries? Does he hope to meet a wizard who will clone him?

It is a slow day, which means the battery is less of a problem than it could be, but also increases my lack of motivation. What am I going to make today: forty pounds, fifty? Just about enough to be able to send the invisible landlady her money and continue to exist within her four walls? I am counting down to Decca, to being able to put everything in her lap, say: tell me what to do, tell me how we do it. By late afternoon, when my battery is into its final breaths, I am ready to stop, even though it only the start of dinner orders time. Goran has messaged to say that 'things are going good today', and that is enough for me right now. I complete a lengthy delivery from an Indian place to an address almost twenty minutes' cycle away, and the smell of it through the plastic bag as I hop off the bike is enough to finish me off.

'Have a nice evening,' says a woman with short spiky hair as I hand it over, and although I know she is just saying it, will forget the whole transaction within thirty seconds as she gets out the knife and fork, my brain somehow takes it as permission, even a request, to be happy.

'I *will* have a nice evening,' I say, surprising myself. The woman turns back, laughs.

'Good!' she says. 'I'm pleased to hear it!'

It is a fun exchange and, when I check my phone to find the screen black, the juice finally gone out of it, it feels like a release instead of an annoyance. Without it, of course, I cannot be certain what time it is, but it feels too early to be knocking on Decca's door. I am cycling at a speed which is almost unknown to me: not even Pogačar's elderly aunt going for the newspaper, more like his great-grandfather suspiciously testing a bicycle soon after they were invented. Idling my way past Superior Pizzas, its power over me temporarily removed – like when you see your school in the holidays, remember that there are no teachers, it is just a building. The Cork pub. Without consciously making the decision, I slide down from the saddle, tie the bike up on a post and go inside. A young man in an old-fashioned velvet jacket is behind the bar. He narrows his eyes in confusion for a moment: this is not a place that does deliveries.

'A red wine, please.'

The barman blinks. 'Which one?'

It feels like a test. I point at random at one of the bottles behind him, say the name as casually as I can. He nods with a little smile, fetches the little silver measure and starts to pour the wine. Tracy Chapman is playing over the speakers: not 'Fast Car', but 'Talkin' Bout a Revolution'. The way she sings 'run' over and over again. I touch my card against the machine to pay. Two deliveries, gone in a heartbeat, just like that. The rashness of this is part of what makes it feel good. I am breaking free of this whole way of calculating. I am not just a bike. Say it to myself again.

I take off my jacket, hang it on the wooden chair, sit in my shorts. There is a big clock, like one that would be hanging outside a station. Twenty minutes to seven. I think about the clock in Decca's kitchen, the smell of cooking, the bottles of wine – better, more expensive wines than this. I am not thinking about Goran or his motorbike, not about the argument, or his latest 'plan', whatever it is. I am thinking about the person who is going to make it all better, the smell of her skin, the feel of the duvet in the dark bedroom.

Half past seven. Almost an hour just sitting in a neutral space, enjoying the taste of the drink, raising my eyebrows in a friendly way as the barman goes back and forth to the

ONE MINUTE AWAY

bar. I could almost just get another drink, I think, show up to Decca's already with a couple inside me – not weary and sweaty as usual. Take her up to bed without even saying a word, because we understand each other. But no. What I want is not really this escape; this is just a miniature version of the real thing waiting at number 40.

Strange to be on the bike after even a little bit of wine: my reactions and judgement a little off, a little slowed. My foot slips off the left pedal for a moment as if I was just learning to ride in the park. It was Mum who taught me, holding onto the back of the seat, saying 'I won't let you go until I tell you', and then letting go one second before telling me. The adrenalin sparking my feet into actions they did not know they could do. Moving along for the first time, instantly in love with this new thing.

My eyes, freed from their usual jobs – no phone, no ticking clock – notice sights on the approach to Laurel Gardens which have not come up before. A large painting up one side of a brick building, a Black guy with a pen in hand, someone remembered around here, maybe. A poster on a tree for a kids' art competition. As I turn onto the street, I see the old man is in his deckchair again. I spring off the bike opposite number 28 and am wheeling it towards the place I think of as home. But it is not my home, not yet, not at all.

The blue door has opened. Someone is stepping onto the path. I slow to a walk, almost to no pace at all, but too late: I am looking through the doorway at the Bevans together, Decca and Niall.

In front of me on the path, Axel does one of their ironic facial expressions, a grimace, like someone watching a sitcom.

'Your friend is here, Mum.'

25

The mustard-coloured sofa. The huge TV, switched off at the moment; the remote controls neatly lined up. In the conservatory, two bikes, one missing. From the kitchen there are noises which should be familiar, sexy: the door of the huge fridge, clinking and pouring. But this is like a nightmare, in which a loved one's voice comes out of a different person's mouth, or going up the stairs in a well-known house leads to a totally different place. Decca and I sit side by side, waiting for her husband. Her eyes are huge, dancing with a strange light. Her hair is piled up on her head and she has the rainbow top on, just like the first time I saw her. I want to take her hand and squeeze it. At first she lets me, but at the sound of Niall approaching she slides it out of my grasp.

'I messaged you a million times he'd changed his plans,' she whispers.

'My phone is dead,' I say, thinking of the pub, how restful it was to look at the blank screen. All that time, Decca frantically typing, sweaty fingers, getting no reply. Why did she not make some excuse, come down the street, intercept me? She could not know which of the two ways I would approach, but there was a chance, at least. There is only one answer that makes sense, and it makes me push my chest out a little, steel myself for what is coming. Hiding me away is not the right thing for her anymore, not after all the conversations we have had, not after what was said at the spa, and after the bike was stolen. The big conversation has to happen, however frightening. I feel like I am standing on the rocks with Goran, watching him disappear into the water with a yell, then turn to look back up, his hair matted, beckoning to me. Come on, loser. The same tingling in the limbs. This is the moment, this is 'Fast Car'.

Niall is wearing a tight black T-shirt, his arms quietly full of muscle, his face humorous, bags under his eyes. He waves the bottle of wine in my direction, having already put a glass down in front of Decca. Her leg is shaking a little; I can feel the vibrations as if it was my own body, and again I am longing to touch her, just to calm her. She stares at the wine-glass without moving and I carry on in the role he has put me in, like a parody of the kind of dinner party they must have had here plenty of times.

'Can I tempt you? Or would you prefer a beer? We've got pretty much everything, as you're probably aware already.'

Again, it is like the cracked mirror of the beautiful things that have happened to me here this summer. I hold his eyes: blue eyes, almost Scandinavian-looking, I think again.

'That's OK, thank you.'

'Are you sure? You must be tired, doing that all day.' He gestures vaguely at my uniform. The Silver Fox did not even make it in here; it is propped just inside the front door, where Niall first greeted me – 'a new friend! Come in!' I remember the taste of the wine an hour ago, and think: hell, why not? Everything is coming to a climax. Everything is on the table. He thinks he is in charge, because it is his house and she is his wife. But those things are only true in name. Maybe he thinks it is funny, even, offering me a drink: I am just the delivery guy; he is a millionaire. Fine, we will call his bluff.

'I will have a wine, then, thanks.'

Niall nods, seeming almost impressed by the move. He pours a glass, sets it down in front of me, just the tiniest whisper of force in the way it lands on the glass table. He picks up his bottle of beer from the TV cabinet, takes a swig, and gestures like a TV chat-show host.

'So! To what do we owe the pleasure?'

This is not a phrase I have learned before, and it feels like it has been chosen to put me at a disadvantage: he has heard my accent, he knows I am not 'from here'. No, fuck that, protests the bolder part of my brain. Go where this is going. I look at Decca: are you going to speak, or am I? She is still rigid, breathing fast. I have heard that breath so much before; I know her.

'I mean, I did wonder if there was someone.' Niall laughs briefly; it almost seems like genuine amusement. 'You're not brilliant at hiding things, Dec. I've seen you glance down at your phone at the side of the bed, I've seen you texting someone at two a.m. You've been a little weird about your comings and goings. And, I mean, both of us have had our dalliances, haven't we . . .'

What does this mean, 'dalliances'? I do not get the impression, from the way Decca flinches, that I will be wanting to add it to my phone note.

'Not like this, never like this,' says Decca, so quietly it hardly comes across.

'Not like what?' asks Niall, still with his eyebrows raised, looking between us with an expression on his face which still does not seem serious enough for what is happening here. I understand: to him it is *not* that serious. His wife has had some sort of weird hook-up with a younger man she met somehow. This is embarrassing for her because here he is in his uniform. Niall has caught her. There is not that much to talk about here, he thinks. He is underestimating me, like he did the other time.

'We fell in love,' I say, 'we have fallen in love, I am sorry.' Another breath from her, sharp, like she caught it halfway out. 'Tell him, Decca.'

She is staring at the coffee table, staring at the floor, her face paler than I have ever seen it, all the usual flush gone from it. She nods, without meeting his eyes. Niall snorts, another sarcastic little laugh. He has had everything exactly the way he wanted for so long. It is going to be hard to make him imagine not having it.

'I'm sorry,' he says, 'I'm confused. Let's back it up a bit here. How did you two even – I mean we'll put aside the "love" thing for a moment, because, well, with the best will in the world.'

Another new phrase for me, but again it does not need a professor of linguistics to work out the intention. He still thinks everything he is hearing is delusional. It is time to give him the facts, give him the history: not the version of history in which he is king of everything, but the one that has actually happened.

'How did we meet? Is that what you were going to ask?'

'Yes.' Niall's eyes go between our faces. I can sense that his assurance is wavering a little. Things he did not know about have happened in his house. I can almost feel a little guilt, for a second, or at least sympathy. But there is no space for that. He had plenty of time.

Decca crosses one leg over the other and sighs. 'Niall, do you seriously not remember . . .'

He screws up his face, like I am some sort of insect he is being asked to identify; like I am one of the ants swarming around the chair legs at their garden table. The hard-working guys he just wants to get rid of. 'You're going to have to help me a bit more, I . . .'

'You threw away edamame beans in front of me,' I say, almost smiling at the memory, because it has such a different shape in my mind now. 'Does that help?'

He blinks a couple of times. 'Wait, that was *you*?'

'Damir Kovačević, yes.' I extend my hand as if for a handshake. Decca glances at me nervously and I suspect I am overdoing things. He is the one who made this into some kind of amusing play, with the wine, with his sarcasm, but I cannot rise to it too much. We are not here to play a game.

'We ordered Tokyo Kyoto from you and you were insanely late? So late it had gone cold and then it wasn't even the right—'

'Sorry,' I interrupt, feeling my pride flaring up even in this situation, just like it did when the incident happened. With his words in my ears, and the sound of the black bin slamming. 'You did not order *from me*. You ordered from them, from the restaurant, and they were late, and they gave me the wrong bag. All of it was their fault but you blamed me.'

Niall Bevan swigs from the bottle again. Everything he does is designed to look cool, and the annoying thing is that it works. 'Right. You came with the order, delivered late – we'll gloss over the culpability, I bow to your superior knowledge – and then, what? Love at first sight on the doorstep?'

'I came back another time,' I say. 'You were not here. Decca and I got to know each other.'

'*Got to know each other*,' he repeats.

The mockery of his tone is beginning to bite at me. 'Sorry, am I not speaking English well enough? It's my second language. Would you find it easier in Croatian?'

'Croatian.' Niall raises his eyebrows again. 'No, your English is very good, Dav – sorry, Damir, was it?'

'Damir, that's right.' I can feel adrenalin building again, feel my pulse in the side of my neck. 'If you look in My

ONE MINUTE AWAY

Orders, if you go back into the history, you will see my name there. Or it is also there quite a lot in your wife's phone.'

Decca makes a little noise at this, Niall laughs in a less relaxed way than before, and the atmosphere shifts. He goes into the kitchen and we hear the bottles jostling together, the huge stash of liquor in the bottom compartment, always full no matter how much you take. Decca gulps from her wine. I put my hand on her arm, touch her behind the ear where the little tattoo is. 'It's OK,' I whisper. 'We have got this, we can do it.'

She nods. 'I know. Yeah. I know.' My hand stays where it is and she flinches as Niall comes back into the living room. Finally he is rattled. Finally he feels this. He looks directly at Decca and I feel conscious for a moment of his physical presence. He is probably as tall as Goran. He has the body of someone with the time to work out every day. It was one of the first things I noticed about him. I feel my hand tighten on Decca's shoulder and Niall's eyes go towards it and back to her.

'So maybe, Dec, if you take up the story from here?'

He stands with his arms folded, very still, very poised, challenging us.

Her voice is quiet. She still cannot look at him. How much I want to take her somewhere safe, lie with her. However difficult, it can be done. I repeat my own words in my head: *we have got this*. Looking back, it is impossible to say how much I believed it.

'We, we started to see each other.'

'You started to have sex, you mean,' says Niall.

'Yes. And texting. And – we'd meet and say hello.'

'You had sex here? In our bed?'

He takes a step towards us, and I feel myself sit up a little straighter.

'Does it matter where?' asks Decca.

'What the fuck are you . . .?' His voice is still calm, his eyes are bright. 'Do you think you're still a teenager?'

'We went to a spa for my birthday,' I hear myself say. I want to be in this conversation, not an outsider as usual. This is my story, not just hers, and definitely not theirs. 'We talked about being together. She isn't happy with you. *You* probably are not happy either, because how can you be? You are both just going along like everything is fine, but you would both be better if . . .'

'I think that's probably enough life coaching from a fucking pizza delivery boy!'

Niall's voice has gone up another level. Decca tops up her glass; a little bit of wine misses the glass and trickles onto the coffee table, next to the big glossy book of places to visit before you die.

'Let's just . . . forgive me if I've got any of this wrong,' says Niall. 'You meet on the doorstep here, what, a couple of months ago. You start sexting or whatever. You fuck a few times, you – whatever else you do. You have a funny little fling. Decca, you're bored, you're at home too much. *You* – Damir, I believe – you presumably think this is all fun, and I guess it is. You go to . . .' Here, he gives one of his horrible laughs. 'A *spa*. Jesus Christ. What's planned next? London Zoo, Madame Tussaud's?'

'I am in love with her,' I say. 'Whether you want to hear it or not. This is a real thing. Tell him, Decca.'

She nods, looking at her feet. It is not enough. I can hear how this sounds, to him: like a fairy tale. And that is how it began, sure, but that is not where we are now.

'Decca,' I say her name again, but he talks over it.

'Dec. Listen. I don't doubt you've had a lovely time with this . . . this lad. And, obviously. Yeah. Things have been sub-ideal between us in some areas.'

Maybe there was a time – I think to myself – when he felt the things I now feel about Decca, and the other way round, too. When they were going to art galleries, restaurants. When he was first making money, they were running all over London, everything new, everything an adventure. Foreign holidays, business-class travel, beautiful pictures on Facebook. These images race through my mind without causing any pain. They are from fifteen, twenty years ago. It does not matter what they did then; they are not the same people now. Decca certainly is not, or why would she have come this far down the road with me, why tell me that this is happiness for her, that this is different and better than what she has?

My brain is issuing all these thoughts – logical and rational reactions to everything that has happened between us – and trying to drown out the feeling lower down, in my guts, a swirling, twisting feeling. Their house. Photos of them and their kid. Their belongings around me. Their money in the walls. I have to push all this back down into me as he keeps talking, that horrible little smile on his face.

'So, look, this is for us to sort out, me and you.' Without it being obvious, he has slowly moved closer to Decca, is almost standing right over us now, and I feel vulnerable sitting on the sofa. 'I imagine there are various ways I could take revenge, I imagine I could get your employer to drop you like a stone with one email. But I can't really be arsed with all that. I reckon if you just fuck off out of my house now and the two of you stop this stupid shit, we can draw a line under it.'

My heart is loud in my chest. I look at Decca: she is resting her head in her hands; her eyes are hidden from me. This is the moment, looking down from the rocks into the water. The moment to leap. I touch Decca's shoulder, as gently as if she was someone I hardly knew.

'Get the fuck off her,' spits Niall.

'He does not get to talk to you like this,' I say, even though Niall is now even closer and it feels for a second like he could hit me. 'He doesn't understand you, or the situation. Just come with me, leave with me now.'

'And go where?' Niall thrusts an arm out at the Silver Fox, perched in the hall like it is a person eavesdropping on the argument. 'Just going to hop on the back of that, are you, Decca? Ride off into the sunset with your lover, back to his beautiful home? Dinner in KFC, is it?'

'You don't know shit about me,' I say, getting to my feet

now, looking at him. It is stupid to be toe-to-toe like this, fighting over a woman, like we think we are in a cowboy movie. Again I address her, not him. 'Decca, we could go anywhere, do anything you want. You know this. You don't need to live in a house like this, you don't need any of this.'

'But I do need to work, Dam.' Decca's hands are clasped together. Her phone throbs, a text; all of us flinch for a half-second, then forget it. 'My job is . . . we have a company together. We earn money together. There's Axel, there's a whole load of things.'

'These are just . . .' I am grasping desperately in my brain for the words, for the English. 'All the things you're saying are just the condition your life is in now. The current things. They aren't how it *has* to be, they . . .'

'Of course they're how it has to be if you are living on planet Earth instead of in some fantasy,' says Niall, his voice impatient now; he wants this done, wants to be having the conversation he needs with his wife. Not with this stranger in a green jacket whom he can still, it seems, not really take seriously as a person, certainly not as a rival. 'She is not going to run away to Poland with you, pal. You've had some fun, sure.'

'I am not from fucking Poland. Decca.' I reach for her hand, but she will not give it to me; Niall is very still, as if he is daring me to try again. 'You want to be with me, I want to be with you. You have said you want it. It might seem like it is crazy difficult . . .'

'*Crazy difficult,*' Niall echoes, in something like my voice, what he believes is my voice, and now I am the one who wants to hit *him*, but I continue. I am playing for the biggest prize there could be. I have to let my words go wherever they go, even if they come out stupid, even if I cannot speak English the way he does, the sarcasm, the sense of superiority.

'But you can do it, we can do it. I said to you before, another life is possible. Or you can just live and die this way, like in the song. Come with me now, walk out of the door with me. And you will feel then that it is possible. Whatever you need to do to make the new life happen, we can plan, we can talk about and make it happen.' I am repeating myself, I am tripping over words, but I press on, like I am on the bike going through heavy rain. I look at her wonderful dark eyes, think about seeing them every morning. Somewhere, anywhere. 'Come with me, because I love you, more than he can love you. It isn't anybody's fault, but that's how it is. You know that's how it is.'

I am expecting Niall to laugh again, or mock, or to tell me again to leave his house – maybe even to take hold of my sleeve, make his point physically – but there is genuine silence for a moment. A motorbike goes by outside, a delivery, and I think about the time we summoned Goran, and everything that has gone wrong since, and everything that could go right now, if we are brave. It is all rushing through me. But Decca looks me in the eyes and I can see her backing away and I feel a little sick.

'I can't just do that, Damir.' She turns her eyes away. 'I want to, but I can't, not just like that, not straight away.'

ONE MINUTE AWAY

'You can.'

I make as if I am going to take her hand again, pull her up towards me, run out of the door with her like in a movie. But this time Niall mutters 'yeah, no, I don't think so,' and manoeuvres my arm away, twisting it gently behind my back and then releasing it, with an elegance, like someone demonstrating a martial art. It is not painful, but it knocks the breath out of me, and he is piloting me towards the doorway, out into the hall. 'I think we've probably done enough of this for the time being, pal.'

'I know things about you,' I say. I see him stumble on this for a second, and arrange his face back into its mocking composure to cover it. 'You know fuck all about me, but I know about you. About what you have done. I—'

'Off you go, I think!' Niall says again, in a louder voice. 'Fuck off now! Five stars, excellent service!'

Decca is on her feet now, coming towards the door, saying my name. But it is too late; she does not get to say anything else. There were so many chances, in there. If she had wanted to enough, or dared enough. Niall is standing between us. My hand is on the bike, the only thing I still have in this situation. I am bumping it onto the path, the blue door is slamming behind me, just like the first time.

It will not open again, and I do not look back. The screen of my phone is black, there is nothing to see, nowhere for me to go. I cannot even review what has just happened, or not happened.

I do not want to get on the bike. I wander into the little

alley that runs alongside their house. This is right where we met. There was a moment I stood here having never spoken to her in my life, and now it is as if I am back there, like it never happened.

VINTNER MEWS. I stare at the sign. The words are written in an old-fashioned-looking typeface, different from the standard ones on the main streets in this area. 'Mews'. I did not think, when I first saw the word those couple of months ago, how it would sound. Have never heard anyone say it. Do not even know the exact definition. But what if it sounds the same as the word 'muse'? If Axel said Alan *Mews?*

'I know about you' was an empty threat: it was me clinging onto the scrap of power I still had after that conversation. And maybe it is too late. But it is something to think about, and God knows, I need something to think about now.

*

I push the Fox, I walk with my head down, not looking where I am going. When I reach the Turkish shop, I buy the cheapest vodka, get it back to the kitchen, and drink straight from the bottle. It tastes like something a chemical plant would dispose of. Another slug from the bottle. If Goran was behaving like this, I would probably intervene; if Petra was acting like this back home, as she occasionally did after Mum died, I would tell her to stop being a maniac. But I have always been the person to do that, not to receive it.

ONE MINUTE AWAY

I finally load up my phone with enough charge that I can turn on, see all the doomed messages from Decca. Into the search bar: Alan Mews. Showing searches for 'Allen' Mews, says Google.

Allen Mews brings up a lot of pages. The words are not familiar, still. But it turns out they are familiar to a lot of other people.

26

Quack! Quack! Quack! Quack! Quack!

I do not move.

It starts again. I lie there like a slab of concrete and my brain catches up with the past eight hours. The Google tunnel: Baxters, scandal, Niall Bevan, Allen Mews. 'While our thoughts go out to everyone affected, we must make it clear that we take no responsibility for . . .' Slept in three or four bursts of an hour, with periods in between of moving side to side on the mattress, onto my back, front again, never quite asleep or awake, a kind of fever state. At some point must have put the phone into the wall, or we would not be getting the quacks, which now begin for a third performance. Goran is looking in, quizzically. He does not come all the way into the room, like he would have done even a few weeks ago. He does not loom over me grinning, or grab my foot, or clown around. He just stares.

'Are you going to stop that, or is it your favourite song now?'

ONE MINUTE AWAY

'Can you do it for me?'

He comes into the room, scoops the phone out of the wall, stops the terrible ducks. 'What's up with you, man? You want a coffee?'

'I'm not going out for a while. Maybe later.'

Goran blinks. I hear how strange the statement sounds: how unthinkable it would have been, so recently. We sync our alarms, we get up together, we go out together. But he does not even react as if it is strange, just nods. 'Uh-huh.'

The water sloshing down the drain is all money, everything is money, but I cannot get out of the shower quickly as usual. I think back to what I read about Niall. The jet of water dies away for thirty seconds, and even this is not enough to make me leave. I stand, my arms wrapped around my body, shivering.

Finally into my uniform, but still no energy; no will to get out and on the bike. There are three messages from F CUSTOMER, the first so long that it cannot all be displayed at once and I have to select 'read more'. All energy seems to have left me since I walked out of her house, and even this reading task feels too much. The spy name is another thing which has gone hollow, now. All the fun, the sexy drama, code names, hidden folders, but when it came down to it last night she was not F Customer any more. She was Decca Bevan, Jessica Chloe Bevan. The wife in a wealthy couple, a mother, the owner of multiple properties, a landlady, and the business partner of a crook. This is the official biography and none of it has anything to do with me; I am not in the story. It feels idiotic to have believed that the story could change.

Out of the door, holding a cereal bar I cannot be bothered to eat or even unwrap.

Damir.

I'm sorry. It was so much, I wasn't ready for the conversation. I wasn't brave enough. It's going to take so much courage to talk to him, tell him. And so much courage to take the leap. I thought I had that in me, in fact I know I HAVE got it in me. But I just froze, with everything that was happening, with the way he was talking, his energy. I'm sleeping in the spare room and I've been crying for hours. I want to call you but I know I can't. I no longer have a right to ask anything. Either of you or of him, really. I've somehow fucked this up as fully as it's possible to, and I've got nowhere to go. I'm not asking for pity, either. Just don't give up on me. Please. Xxxxxx

The next two messages just say, please reply, please just say something. The idea of her lying in bed alone, thinking of me; then the idea of her staring at the phone, waiting in vain for me, doing the 'typing' trick I do – all this makes my heart clench. But I cannot let myself believe in her. It is bad enough I sat in their house and waited for something which was not going to happen. That she allowed him to humiliate me, let me feel that he'd won. Sent me away as if I truly was the hopeless guy on the bike he thought I was on that first night, and still thinks I am, and always will think I am, no matter what has happened between me and Decca.

Her bike is still in our kitchen. Her hands have been all

over me, so recently. My phone is full of pictures of her; my insides ache at the thought I will not see her today, will not see her tomorrow, or anytime soon, unless she finds something new in her. But I delete her messages, and delete her from my thoughts, at least enough that I can bump the Silver Fox down the stairs.

Bloop-bloop-BLOOP. Fuck-my-LIFE. The first notification of the day. The drop is at Escape Studios. Four coffees, a bag with the stupid pastries. I buzz twice on the intercom before footsteps come to the door. A hand comes out, the usual man in his sweater thanks me without looking at me. The memory of my birthday morning, the voucher, is like a bad taste in the mouth now, and when my brain tries to force the tune into my head – whipping up the whirr of the pedal into a bass line, the cries of the market guys into an echo pedal, like when I first met her – I close it down, block it out, hear only my own flat breathing. On to the next job, and the next. Your order is in the oven. Your order is one minute away. Your order has been delivered by Damir. How did we do today?

Bloop-bloop-*BLOOP*. Superior Pizzas. Order number 234. They have told the customer the order is 'being prepared' as soon as the credit card details went through and the money went into their account. Even if there are twenty pizzas to cook before this order gets anywhere near the oven. Everyone is lying a little bit. There are already two riders waiting in front of me, but the situation turns out to be worse than it initially looks: two more, who showed up *after* me, are given their bags before I am. The familiar sticky feeling of the customer's impatience, the app's assurance that everything should be there any moment – unless the delivery boy, Damir, has fucked it up. I show the guy my phone and he nods like he has been waiting to deliver bad news.

'This is a mad big order, man, will take more time. Five twenty-inch.'

Five twenty-inch. One hundred inches of pizza. What is happening at this address, a meeting of the United Nations? Quite apart from how long it is going to take to finish off this giant order on the wood-burner, I do not have capacity for an Empire State Building of pizzas in my backpack. The app should have broken it up into two separate orders for two different riders – when I started, this used to happen all the time – but of course it takes that little bit longer to find two separate riders, an extra thirty seconds or a minute, and now there is so much competition, you could just close the app and open a new one. So it is all on me. The clock is ticking. Every delivery is reviewed, rated, to improve the service for you – our valued customer.

When I finally get the five boxes, I have to lay three of them flat in the backpack and the other two in my lap, holding them steady with one hand, the other on the right-hand handlebar. This, ironically, is the sort of cycle challenge Goran would probably love, I think to myself as I battle towards the address. Ampadu Court. I am not sure precisely where this is, so I have to keep glancing at the GPS dot on my phone in its little perch, even though it would be more relaxing not to see the exclamation-mark notifications which are now popping up to tell me I am late. Rain trickling into my eyes again. Yes, maybe that is the key to making Goran feel OK on a regular bike, I am half-thinking to myself. Appeal to his ego: anyone can ride fast on a motorbike, but doing it with the pedals is where you can outperform them. I entertain a sort of daydream in which we are able to hack the system so that he gets these sorts of orders, hero jobs. Too many pizzas to carry? Roads too dangerous? Send for Goran! A one-man SWAT team of the food delivery business; a *true* member of the elite.

These frivolous thoughts are skipping across my mind and maybe take 5 per cent off my concentration, enough to be slow to notice that the traffic has come to a stop. A van has turned sideways into the road ahead, and two men have got out and are unloading a mattress into a flat, unbelievably slowly, chatting and laughing like two buddies on a pub crawl, one of them with a lit cigarette poking out of his mouth. Cars around me honk furiously, but the guys are on their way into the building, could not care less, and the road is blocked.

If I had spotted this three seconds earlier, I could have done a 180-degree and escaped, but now the cars are all turning around at the same time, the street is a mess, no space for anyone. By the time I get back around the corner and re-plot the route, a bad situation has got worse. 'Six minutes added to journey,' says the GPS, not sympathetically but – in my head – like I am a moron.

Finally out of the queue and towards traffic lights, but

they are about to turn red. Red also on my phone screen; by now the app will be going crazy, more or less flashing up a picture of the customer shaking their fists at me. Every second counts. Go go go. I step on the pedals, try to slip through the lights like the ghost I am, but my timing is just off: a woman with a long bobbing ponytail is jogging across the zebra crossing. It is my fault, not hers; I slam on the brakes and the rucksack slides halfway off, hanging off my shoulders. Honks behind me. I have to slide out of the seat with the pizza boxes in my hand, hold my hand up to stop anyone from running me down, haul the bike across the lanes – more honking, the race is going on, it never stops – and rearrange myself by the side of the road.

My breath is uneven and I do not even dare to look into the backpack. The boxes in there will have been thrown around; it will be like a crime scene when they get them open. As for the time, we are lost, this is now the disaster zone.

As I pedal down Coldharbour, I am bracing myself for another scene like Edamame-gate, another lecture from a bastard like the one which began everything. Maybe I am almost hoping for that, in fact. I am ready to say: hey, fuck *you*. Has it killed you to wait half an hour longer than you thought for dinner? Have the pizzas disappeared from the box, like in a magic trick? No, they have just got a bit shaken up, and you may have to spoon some of the stuff back onto the pizza bases. Really sorry for your suffering! All that has happened to *me* tonight is that nobody on the road, or in your city, gives a shit if I live or die!

ONE MINUTE AWAY

Of course I am not going to say these words out loud. They mean nothing. I know the rules. Anyway, there is nobody to deliver the imaginary speech to. Nobody is waiting on the doorstep. Nobody even comes out straight away when I bang on the door; there is enough time for me to ride away, into the night, before they emerge. The punishment will be delivered in a different way: a hit to my rating, maybe even a complaint, all done via the app, nothing personal. Slither a little way down the snake, back down the board.

Decca's house is less than half a kilometre away. She could walk out of there right now, call me, find out where I am, tell me what she wants to say, come with me to the other life I told her about. But instead she is sitting, pressing buttons, hoping to bring what she wants to her door, just like everyone else here. There is another message from her; I take a deep breath and delete it without looking. I text Goran, just nonsense, how are you, look at this video of a man sliding down the handrail of an escalator. I find I am staring at the screen, willing him to answer, the way I do with Decca in the night. Or did. The hollow feeling in the core of me tells me he is not going to reply, even if he sees the message. We are not those people now; something is broken, and it feels like my fault.

Bloop-bloop-BLOOP. I stare at the screen, an order not far from here, and cannot make my finger do the two seconds' work of swiping to claim the job. I let the screen go blank as someone else takes it, then return to staring at the caption: 'waiting for orders . . .' The picture of the frying pan, a burger flipping up and down in it. Like this is just as mouth-watering for us, the deliverers, as for the people who actually get to eat the food. For a second I feel real hatred for the phone, the way I am tied to it like a sheepdog to a whistle. I imagine just throwing it into a hedge, or giving it to the next person I see. *Here, you want this? You can have the job too, that comes with it. Just pick up the phone and do what you're told.*

Where do they leave me, these thoughts? Sitting here, on this wall, as the sun passes behind the cloud to leave me in shade, I think I know where they leave me, but the words will not quite form, not in English, not even in Croatian.

Two women are sitting on the wall next to me now, with big paper cups of coffee, facing the other way as they watch their children in the playground. 'People say it goes fast, but *those* people don't have kids this age,' says one.

'Seriously,' the other one agrees. 'The moment when you walk past your first "Back to School" display in Asda.'

'It's like a water stop in a marathon,' says the first one, and they laugh and move onto talking about running, and I shuffle away a little bit to pretend that I have not being listening in, even though it probably has the opposite effect. I have probably missed some of the nuance, but I understand that they are talking about the school holidays – they will be over soon. Summer will be over soon.

I slide off the wall and take the handlebars. I am going home, whatever that means now.

★

ONE MINUTE AWAY

Nine p.m., and I am already done for the day; I just cannot find anything else inside me. I hear the door downstairs. My heart jumps a little, maybe even more than usual. I have missed him. I am missing him.

I wait, a beer in my hand for him, but our door does not open. What is he doing out there? Has he brought back something even stranger, this time? I cross the hall, open the door myself, and catch my breath.

Goran is standing there, the e-bike trailing from his right hand across three steps, like it is a sack he is dragging. His face is completely white and his right leg is a horrible sight. There is a huge angry cut down the side of it, dull red, like meat hanging in a butcher's window, and around it the skin is white where it has been scraped away. He takes another half-step forward, gasps and winces, lets go of the bike, which slithers down the stairs behind him.

'Jesus, Goran.'

I go to collect the bike, feeling shaky on my legs, and follow him into the flat. He has gone into the bathroom and is hunched over the toilet, throwing up. I put my hand on his shoulder. When he is done, his face at least looks a little better, but I cannot take my eyes off the blood, the raw wound, and I feel sick myself. He shuts the lid of the toilet, sits down, gives me a sort of desperate smile.

'Well, apart from that it was a pretty good day.'

'What the fuck happened?'

He shrugs, like it is normal for him to have an accident so bad that his leg looks like it has been through a mincer

– and the other one, I can see now, is not much better. 'Just hit a pothole and came off.'

'Came off?'

'Yeah, I was lucky, could have gone under a car, the guy stopped. He looked like he would have *liked* to finish me off but still, thanks dude. *Ajme!*' He gasps again in pain, and I am scared by the look of the leg, and by the way he touches it very softly and then flinches like he is stifling a scream.

'Christ. What if you've broken something, or . . .?'

'I don't think so. At first I couldn't move it at all. Now, I can kind of drag it. It just feels a bit – it feels a bit weird.'

He rises from the seat, gives a strangled sort of yell and sinks back down with a clatter. I feel like I want to hide. The room is spinning. I sit down on the floor so I am now looking up at him. Goran's expression is concerned like *I* am the injured one. He reaches out an arm and ruffles my hair.

'Don't worry.' Even the voice is pain; it sounds like every sentence is costing him an effort. 'I don't even need two legs. The whole point of the e-bike, you can do thirty-five an hour without even moving your feet.'

I glance for as long as I can bear at the leg – which is only a few seconds – and think again about what he said. A pothole. Everyone riding a bike in this city has hit a pothole, a crack in the pavement, a bump. You do not come off your bike badly enough to do this sort of damage, especially if you are Goran, a gymnast of the saddle.

'You cannot do thirty-five k an hour on an e-bike.'

Goran looks into my face for a minute, and then down at his feet.

'Fuck, you haven't hacked the bike?'

He pulls himself up, like an old man, one hand on the sink, and edges a little at the time out of the door.

'Gor. Was that – when you talked about "I've got a plan"? Was the plan you hacked the bike?'

I am talking to his back. He shuffles along the hall. 'A guy did it for me.'

'A guy, what guy? How much did you pay him? Because . . .'

'Why does it matter who it was, and what it cost? I had to pay for it because if I carry on riding around on a baby's bike, I won't have enough money until I am a fucking hundred. You think I can just sit around on a pushbike while guys who can't even ride properly zoom past me getting all the jobs? Maybe that's good enough for you now you have your rich girlfriend, but . . .'

We stand in the hall, in the little space we have always shared, where we have depended on each other. I do not feel in control of what I am saying.

'Well now you aren't going to be riding around on anything, are you? You've fucked your leg coming off a bike which some total stranger messed around with so it can go faster than you're fucking *legally allowed* to go. You're going to make it worse and worse if you go back out. Seriously, what are we going to . . .'

'*We* aren't going to do anything,' says Goran.

'What are you talking about?'

He shoulders open the front door and starts to haul himself down the stairs, holding onto the wall for support, dragging his damaged leg. I follow him, again. 'Where are you going? Gor, where are you going?' My voice rises to a shout. The neighbours' door opens on the ground floor and the guy looks out, up at me, with some pity in his face.

'Everything all right out here?'

I manage some sort of noise in response and turn away before he can see I am crying. The street door slams and Goran, even though he can barely walk, is gone. My hands are shaking. I go into the kitchen, open a beer, drink it in one go.

The windows rattle as a lorry goes by. I pick up my phone and bring up F Customer and begin to type.

OK. See me tomorrow. I don't care where. Find a way. One chance. Find a way.

27

From that bar at the top of London's tallest tower, which I am not likely to visit again, someone with a telescope could see me weaving Decca's bike through the streets, around the big cars as they lumber forward and come to a stop again, around the red buses. I wipe rain out of my eyes and look up at the tower, half a kilometre away. Things felt very different when I was sitting up there with Goran, after our supermarket bonanza. It felt like the beginning of something. Tonight, one way or another, is the end of something.

The hotel has a red awning; the flags of the United Kingdom, United States, European Union. There is some sort of conference going on this evening: people are getting checked in, being given little plastic lanyards. In a meeting room just off the main reception, there is a drinks reception for them: staff members in jackets buzz in and out with silver trays. A lot is happening, and I am in ghost mode, nobody looking at me as I follow Decca's instructions: all the way through the lobby to the far end, turn left, across the shiny floor to the lift.

She is standing with her back to the lift, hair down, in a dark green jumpsuit I have not seen before. The old thrill runs through me like mercury, whether I want it to or not. We brush hands very lightly, hers against mine, like we did in the kitchen that first time. We say hi, step into the lift. Mirrors either side of us, thousands of Decca and Damir pairs going off into eternity, or into nothingness.

Out into the hall. Carpet under our feet, a long corridor of identical doors. Numbers in the seven hundreds. Decca presses her card against 721. Inside, a huge bed, a long window looking out over rooftops. Her overnight bag is on the desk, the laptop and phone charger plugged into the wall. It is not clear from the scene whether she is staying the night, whether she thinks we are both going to. I do not want to ask what she said to Niall, where he believes she is, how much time she has. Enough of this has been on her terms. But when she sits on the bed I have to sit next to her, and when she turns her face to mine – eyeshadow, the smoky smell of the perfume – I can hardly bear the thought of what I am going to do.

'I didn't know if you would reply. If we were done.'

She looks down at her fingernails. The paint is chipped and faded.

'I had to give you your bike back.'

Decca nods, sniffs with a sort of grudging laughter.

'Thank you.'

ONE MINUTE AWAY

'It's locked up outside,' I say. 'I couldn't really bring it through the hotel.'

'No, of course. Thanks.'

It is a strange sort of silence in here, high up away from London. Different from our flat, obviously, but different even from the peace of Laurel Gardens, where at least there were occasional bikes delivering outside, the wind blowing in the trees. Up here we could be in the International Space Station. Everything is neutral. Although it does not come as a surprise now, all the money, it is still strange if I stop to think: this is another level again. This is where you can go if you own a big house but you want to sleep somewhere else, or have to sleep somewhere else, or talk to someone you should not, because with all that money you have still managed to make a mess of your life. I feel sorry for her as much as frustrated with her. In fact, maybe more sorry. But feelings alone are not going to help me, now.

'And is that it?' she asks. 'Is that all you . . .'

'No, you know it isn't all.'

My hand goes gently to the straps of her outfit, easing them down off her shoulders. She takes a shaky breath and is kicking off the jumpsuit, wriggling clear of it. Her hand goes to loosen my jeans, but I push it back gently. I lie her down and turn off the lamp by the bed, so that the only light is what comes in from the long window, blueish and far-off, belonging to a city I am not really part of.

'Do you want this?' I ask quietly.

'Of course I do. It's all I want. I haven't been sleeping. Look, it was my fault, and . . .'

'Yes, it was your fault, and we don't have to talk about it.' The smell of her skin is as charged for me as always. I am kissing her breasts; I am on top of her. 'But maybe we should.' I can feel her writhing in pleasure, can hear her breathing as it accelerates. Whatever I might have been wrong about, I was not wrong about this, about how it feels; I was not imagining this. 'Maybe you quite like it when we talk about things you have done wrong?'

'I do, you know I do.'

'OK.' The conversation in short sharp breaths. 'So tell me why you did not speak up for me. For us. Why you let him think he won.'

'Because I'm weak, I'm scared.' Our bodies are moving together like they always did. I can see us on her bed with the summer light slanting in; I can feel us in the swimming pool together. There could be so many more of these, still. 'I'm scared of him.'

'Scared of what you really want, too. Scared of making changes. Cowardly.'

'Say it in your language,' she asks.

'*Nemaš hrabosti,*' I say. You have no courage. '*Kukavica si.*' You are a coward. She is breathing hard. I mutter some more choice phrases in Croatian: this is disgusting, you people are disgusting. She groans, she is mine. Of course she does not understand the words; I could be reciting the lyrics to 'When I Hear the Tambourines'. But just enough of my heart wants to say the words, too. I think of all the bad, dangerous, expensive little buildings people like Goran and me pay money to stay in. I know I have to go further.

We lie on our backs, naked, London beneath us, a ceiling fan purring gently. I had not even noticed it before; its breath is cool on our skin. I reach for her hand and hold it close to my body. I feel like I have known the touch of this hand for years: the little freckles on the back of it; the long, lovely fingers. And everything else, too. The tattoo on the back of her neck, the one on her bottom. Her breath, her voice, the dark, dark eyes, the way we laugh together. Of course it is not right. Of course it has only been two months, and what kind of idiot believes in true love after two months? But my heart will not be told this. It wants what it wants. Even as I write this now, it is twisting itself into the same shape, feeling the same things, crying out in the same way.

'Are you hungry?' she asks, just like she did when I was first in her house. The answer is the same as it was then: yes, I am pretty much always hungry. That first time, of course, I said no, thank you, I am fine. But the game has changed a lot since then. At this point, it is finally true that there is not much to lose. Not for me.

*

A man knocks on the huge door and wheels in a table with two covered plates on it. Ever since Decca made the phone call, I have been imagining the guy – basically a more highly paid version of myself. It was an old-fashioned telephone ringing on the desk, instead of *bloop-bloop* on his phone; he picked up the meals from a fancy kitchen, and he has only had to bring them upstairs for two minutes. No sore thighs, no rain in the face. He is higher up the ladder than me. In time, I could climb as high as he has; I could also be in a smart shirt, setting up a tablecloth and cutlery in an expensive hotel room. But you do not really want to be on the ladder at all; you want to be looking down from a window, watching people climb it. There are people who order food, and people who deliver it, for ever.

'I have your sirloin and chips, I have your sea bass, and your wine,' he says; 'if you can just sign for me here, please.' The accent is a little like mine, I guess: the voice of people who deliver. Decca swishes her signature for him. It is sexy even watching her do that; watching her turn back to me, in the clothes she only put back on half an hour ago, sit opposite me, look at the piece of fish, her tongue touching her lips in hunger. Her hands on the knife and fork, her eyes up to meet me.

'Did you ever go fishing? Back home?'

I am grateful for the unimportant question, even though it is not where we need to be. 'No, too much waiting around. Me and Goran went on his buddy's fishing boat once, and after an hour we were so bored we just jumped off and swam home in our clothes.' I can remember him whispering 'I have a plan'; smell the salt, which never really came out of those jeans after that day. The sun is shining in all my memories of Split, whether it really was or not. 'I think Dalmatia is meant to be pretty amazing if you do like to fish, though.' I am thinking back to talking about it in her bathtub, trying to push it to her like a travel agent. 'Millions of little caves and . . . little pools, I don't know what the word would be, little bits of the river, you see people getting all kinds of fish out of there.'

'Inlets?'

'Maybe inlets, I will ask Google Translate.'

For a weird moment I am about to be polite and say: what about you? Do you fish? But the question would really be, does your husband fish and do you sometimes go with him? Even if she did not mention him in the answer, really every conversation comes down to that. I look again at the menu. With the wine we are now drinking, all this was about seventy pounds. Seventy pounds, about seven hundred kuna. Lots of people all over the hotel spending that sort of money with a stroke of the pen. And it is still true, what I thought before: anger is not the point. Judgement is not the point. It is just about playing the game the way they play it. Not everyone can win at once. But anyone *can* win.

'If you're thinking about the prices, obviously, don't be . . .'

'I am thinking about them,' I say, 'but not in that way, not in a guilty way.'

She laughs, cautiously. 'I guess that's progress? Is it progress?' A deep breath. A speech is coming, which she had been working herself up to – I can see it – but I already know it will not be quite enough. 'Look, about the other night. I know I've said it, tried to say it, by text. I let you down, I was weak. I just wasn't ready for it. I've hardly spoken to him since, he doesn't want to; he's not really interested in making things better, even if they could be better. I just have to have the guts, find the guts to . . .'

'I know. Always courage, always "I am not quite there". Listen, Decca.' I hold up my hand to stop her from saying something else. 'Can I ask you a question?'

'Of course you can.'

'I said, when I left, when you let me leave: I know about you. I said it to your husband.' Her eyes dart up nervously to meet mine. Those eyes, I could happily look at every morning, if she was truly mine, if I could know for sure. 'I just wonder what happened, what your version of it is, with Allen Mews.'

My tone of voice is gentle, I think, not like an interrogator. My hand is very lightly resting on the back of her neck, among all the curls and folds of her hair. She swallows hard, loudly.

'What *do* you already know?'

'Well, I know your husband owns four flats in somewhere called Allen Mews, in Hertfordshire.' She seems about to correct my pronunciation and then change her mind. 'I know in one of these flats, a man called Hari lived and worked in an Amazon place, a warehouse. Got behind with his rent. Had threatening emails from – well. From "Baxters", but everyone online says, your husband. And then one day they found Hari had hanged himself in the lounge room. So that is what I know.'

She pours herself a second glass of wine; offers me the bottle, but I shake my head.

'He – Niall – he didn't think that was going to happen. They weren't *threatening emails*, I don't think. He didn't know that the guy was in a mental state where the pressure . . .' Her voice trails off.

'You know,' I say, as gently as I can, 'that was a man like me, just someone doing his job.'

'I know.' She is looking at the carpet. 'It shook him up. He's not a bad person, like, not . . .'

'I guess it depends how you see it.' I take her hand in mine, squeeze it. 'I am going to go back to Croatia. Going home. Like, very soon, immediately.'

Her mouth opens a little way. 'Please don't do that, Dam. I know it's . . .'

'Listen to me, let me say this. I'm going back. Me and Goran. This is what I think we should do. You keep saying you will be with me one day, all you need is time, give you time. But time is my money, time is all I have, you know? I do not have time just to play with. For a little bit, when we were first meeting, I maybe forgot that. It all felt good, right? We had found each other. Now, since he lost the bike, Goran is not doing good, both of us are not doing good.' Decca is trying to say something again, and I have to raise my hand. She is holding one hand in another, her knife and fork on the plate, food half-eaten, like mine is. Thirty-five pounds' worth.

'You are always saying you would be with me if you could. That you *will* be. Here's what I think. What about if you let me have a really big amount of money, just like that. You have always suggested it. I could help you with this, with that. Buy you lunch. Buy a new bike. And it was kind, but most of the time, almost all the time, I said no. Because I believed something was happening, I believed, OK, this is love, or whatever stupid thing—'

'It was love. Is.'

'Well, OK, but the name we have for it, that is not important anymore. The important thing is what we do, what actually happens next.'

'How much money?'

I name an amount of money. It is an amount which I have made up on the way here, which sounds insane spoken out loud – as I knew it would. But Decca's face hardly changes. She nods, thoughtfully. I can see her working out whether she can do it, how she would do it in secret. So many secrets.

'And sure, maybe Niall will notice, there will be an argument, but if you want me, you will do it, have the argument. You can see it like a deposit. And then, if you ever come to Croatia, if you ever actually go for the better life, if you find me and we start again – then you have it back, because we share everything. Right?'

ONE MINUTE AWAY

'Is this . . . why did you bring up Hari Shah? I mean, are you – is this some sort of blackmail thing?'

Her eyes flash at me. I have to look down at my feet for a moment, but I do not let go of her hand.

'Of course not. Even if I wanted to, I could not blackmail you and him. All I have is what is on the internet. And, sure, there are lots of people on Reddit saying Niall is at fault, and if I wanted, I could get in touch with them and make it not so nice for Niall. But, first, of course you guys would still win, because money is what wins. And also, much more important, I love you. I want you, that is what I want. Wanted, want. But if I can't have what I really want, then I would like the next thing – the next best thing.'

'Don't just walk away. Don't go back to Croatia.'

'I might not *stay* there; it depends how we go. I could go to Belgrade, there is a big music scene there, take Goran with me. I mean, I could go to America, like I always imagined doing. Japan. That is the point. Without money you are trapped in one place, you are like – kind of like those ants who can only really go up and down one space. But I would not be any more. I could be anywhere. And you won't know where, you will have to find me.'

'You have to stay in touch, at least.' Decca's hand goes to grab my arm, fiercely, just above the elbow. 'I wouldn't be able to cope if I couldn't text you. If I didn't know what was happening with you. Couldn't talk to you. You wouldn't do that to me.'

'I will not stay in touch.' It is important that I do not let my voice shake like it wants to, that I do not cry until I am out of here. I feel sick, but I have to stay strong. Decca is gnawing at the sleeve of her jumpsuit. I stand up and put my arms around her back, press her face into me, feel her heaving into my chest, shaking. I know that this version of her will haunt me; that every time I have a happy memory of Decca, this one will be waiting right on its heels, wiping it out. 'If you want me, you will find a way. If I do not do this, we will never know. You know "Fast Car". It's that.'

'When are you going to go.' Her voice does not even lift at the end of the sentence. She chokes the words out. My hand is in her hair. We will not be together again like this; it seems impossible to believe that I am making it that way. But it has to be.

'If you transfer me the money, straight away. Days. We send a couple of weeks' money to the landlady, or a month, whatever she wants. Book a flight. We are gone. On the day, I will send you a heart emoji, just that. Then the SIM card goes for good. You have no number for me. You look up in the sky and you think maybe I am on that plane, or that one. And then after that, you just wonder what I am doing, in the day, at night. Where I am. But you cannot know.

'We could have, literally, anything. You and me. We could start something totally new. But it is up to you, not me.'

She looks limp and cold, as if she needs me to scoop her up like a child and put her in bed.

ONE MINUTE AWAY

'Can I have a kiss?'

She says it in a tiny voice. I wrap her up and we stand there, kissing, slowly and tentatively, then more urgently. When it stops for a moment, she pulls me back towards her and we begin again.

'It feels so right,' she whispers.

'It is right. Just, the way it is *now*: that is not right. You know that.'

I glance towards the door and it seems to pierce her. 'Don't go right now, Damir. Stay. Stay the night? I've got the room. He's fucked off somewhere. I'll turn off my phone, I . . .'

Very gently, I shake my head, touch her arm. Even though there is nothing I want more in the world than to do what she is asking, even though walking through that door is going to mean breaking my own heart.

'Every minute I stay here is a minute you are not making things better. For me, for you. It can start tomorrow, you could start changing tomorrow. But not while I am still giving you what you want. You know that.'

She shakes her head. 'I love you. Please don't go. Please.'

'I love you too, Decca. Take care of yourself and be happy. Work out how to be happy.'

'And come to me', I want to say, but I will not finish by asking for something. I do not want to be a person doing that. I have asked for enough.

I close the heavy door behind me.

The best thing to do would be to walk down the corridor

right away, not glance back, keep going. But I find I cannot do that, not immediately. I stand quietly outside her door and I can hear her frantic, panicky breathing and then crying, crying, almost wailing. I stand there as if I am frozen. The crying means more, now that I am not there with her. There is nobody to see it. Maybe, as always, I had to know that it was real.

I force myself to walk slowly, then more quickly, down the corridor away from her. I think to myself: it is a strange thing about goodbyes that however huge and crushing they feel, most of the time you can take them back straight away. When I was in tears because Goran had flown to London, part of what seemed unbearable was that he was only the other side of the PASSENGERS ONLY doors, the security checks; for another two hours he would still be right near me, and in theory I could easily get through there and see his stupid face. Even in the moments after Mum died, after the most final goodbye of all, she was still lying there on the bed – like she had been for a few weeks. At any time I wanted, I could walk back in and see her one more time. Goran understood this, and that it would not be a good idea; that was why he dragged me out to the sea.

This is the same. Even after everything I said in there, I could reverse it all by just turning around. *Please don't go.* I can hear her saying it. *Please.* I can see her face, streaked with tears, and feel her in my arms. My heart is pleading with me to go back, but I cannot.

ONE MINUTE AWAY

Since I started the job, it has always been about driving the distances down. Ten minutes away, five minutes away, one minute away. Push those pedals, watch the numbers go down until zero, start again. Now, it is the opposite. I have to put minutes between myself and her. I have to keep moving.

As soon as I am outside the hotel, looking back up at the awning, the flags, and the many layers of luxury, it feels as if it was never real: like it was just painted against the sky. Sure, Decca is still in there – is still only about fifty metres above me right now – but there is no way back. I put my head down low over my phone, glancing up to get out of the way of a bike, one of me, zipping across two lanes on a life-and-death mission to deliver a couple of Indian meals.

The silence on my phone gnaws straight away at my stomach. I have not been logged in to the app, of course, so no notifications. But nothing else either. No message from Goran. He stormed out last night, nearly twenty hours ago. I was not too concerned that he was not back this morning; fine, he crashed at someone's house, he was pissed off with me. But not to have messaged this morning, or at any point in the day. I send him three texts at five-minute intervals. He is not receiving them; no ticks.

I ride the underground: the first time since our trip to the highest bar in London, and one of only a few times ever. The adventure of that night, the way we laughed: every memory leads back to Goran. Everything leads to him. It is not just that the breathlessness, the reckless fun of that night has vanished; our whole friendship feels like it might have. Maybe I imagined that if Decca did not work out, we would just go back to normal, and 'normal' was pretty fun. Now that too is gone. I have reached out for something beyond me, toppled over, and sent everything crashing to the ground.

These thoughts are no use. Come on, Damir. Out onto the platform, the whirl of people back from work. Some of these people have probably been my customers. On the escalator I stare at my phone, willing the signal to come back. TIRED OF BEING TIRED? asks an advertising board. Energy drinks, expensive branded ones. Put money in, get energy, use the energy to make more money. My signal is back; I go to WhatsApp, I go to my other messaging services, everything. No Goran. Nothing. Even a message from Decca would be some sort of comfort – *please think again, I need you* – although there is no way of going back. But there is nothing from her, either. I had two people and right now I have none.

I stand around outside the burger place. No point in putting the app on; the Silver Fox is still at home, and there would be no sense in starting a shift now, anyway. The usual frying smell hangs in the air; I can feel the rich hotel food in my guts. The riders come, wait for their packages, go: the whole thing carries on. It will be exactly the same in a couple of weeks, a couple of months from now, a new Damir in my place. It is a relief to see the looming, sweaty figure of Mario approaching. He removes his helmet and chugs on a Coke. 'Hey, bro. You not out?'

'No, I . . . done for today. Hey, have you seen Goran?'

There is a hesitation in his eyes; the guy has never been a master of emotional disguise. 'Please, Mario. You don't have to tell me where he is, if he doesn't . . .' It is degrading to have to say it. 'If he doesn't want me to know, if he is pissed with me. But just tell me he's OK? He's been acting pretty weird since the bike; he's fucked his leg up . . .'

'I know, man. It looks fucking gross.' Mario glances at his phone. I am scared he is going to get a drop, leave without giving me anything at all. I am desperate.

'Mario, please.'

'Listen, I don't know where he is. Nobody has seen him all day. Nobody has heard. I do know, there's a van leaving some time, tonight, tomorrow, whatever. Going to Europe.'

'A van?'

'A few guys who want to leave, find somewhere better, where there are not so many riders, more money. Where this is still more new, maybe.' He fingers the logo on his jacket. 'Me, I think fuck that: it is the same everywhere now. Anyway, plenty here still. You just got to be fast. Earlier today, man, I swear to God, ten pounds tip because I got talking to the girl on the doorstep and said it is hard working on my birthday'. He smirks. 'I have had, like, ten birthdays this year.'

I reach up and grip him by the shoulder; it is as firm as marble. 'You think Goran is in this van, you think he's gone?'

Mario shrugs. 'I just know they were talking about it in

a group; I think he is in the group, so.' *Bloop-bloop-BLOOP.* I reach for the phone, instinctively, but of course it is his notification, not mine. His fingers on the screen, swiping, muscle memory. Job Accepted. He gives me a wink; his huge bald head disappears under the helmet. He is on his way.

The guy from downstairs has just finished his Uber shift, I assume; with sheer bad timing he is approaching the door of Cecil Court at the same time as me. He looks at me with a kindness I do not want at the current moment.

'How are things, you guys OK up there?'

I almost want to laugh. 'We're good, thank you.'

'Well, have a good night.'

'You too.'

Maybe he will have a good night, he and his wife. Maybe some people just have life worked out properly; I thought I did, for a little while. Up the stairs, feeling each one. Another little struggle with the door. Our flat feels so empty. The e-bike is gone from the kitchen; I expected this. But Goran's room sends a chill through me; it hardly looks like his room. I can see more of the floor than ever before. He has been back at some point, picked up at least some of his things. Can he really have left, left me to deal with this place? Or has he done something else, something I do not want to think about? How has it got to this?

Anger, fear, heartbreak that is partly of my own making: hard to say where one begins and another ends. There is no beer in the fridge: nothing at all in there. Almost nothing under this roof belongs to me. When I have dragged the mattresses down the stairs – hopefully, sold them on some website – and bumped the Fox out of the door with my stupid guitar slung on my back, the flat will go back to being an empty box. The property of Caroline, whoever she is. A roof to sleep under for the next idiots like us that come along.

I plug the phone into the power pack. I never gave *that* back to her, but she could get someone to bring another one by lunchtime tomorrow, if she wanted. I rest it in the corner, far away from me, so I will not be tempted to look for Goran. He will make contact, I tell myself. He has not done anything stupid. But I cannot stare at the phone all night. Instead, I stare at the ceiling, the shadows, the glare of the lights outside. I try to summon Bačvice beach, the sun and the seabirds, the water like a bath, but he creeps into every image, splashing around in the sea, dunking my head under, messing around throwing a tennis ball, balancing it on his nose like a seal. Waiting for me to leap from a rocky shelf a little too high for me, his arms outstretched like a father. I fall into some sort of dream in which I have been told he is in a market square, a little like the one in front of the burger place, but there is a time limit to find him. Nobody can help me, Mum has her hand on my arm trying to tell me something bad, and I am awake, knowing – although I did not hear anything – that it is the phone.

★

No messages; just a new notification. It is my banking app. The phone screen light is harsh in front of my tired eyes. 'You received a payment'. The updated balance has the same unreal quality as when that tip came in, that night in June. Decca has given me what I asked for, what I forced myself to ask for.

It is hard to know what it feels like. Not the surreal joy of that night, for sure. Maybe not happiness at all. But something: a release, a full stop. I bring up Decca's number, count to ten, select 'block', and then delete it. In a matter of seconds, it is the same as before we met.

28

I am my own boss, that was what they always said, so for my final day, I will throw myself a little party.

Bloop-bloop-BLOOP. One-more-time. Now that there is nothing at stake, now that for the first time ever I technically do not need the drops, they come continually from the moment I swipe Begin Shift. Sod's Law. When End Shift comes, it will be the last time I see that screen. Maybe it is because I know this is it, that I have so much energy for the work – almost an appetite for it, again. More likely the energy is kind of manic, is a by-product of trying to force all other thoughts out of my head. Avoid thinking of the person who can no longer contact me, and the one who seemingly will not. Be the bike, one more time.

Coffees and breakfast items, the local council building. Your order will be delivered by Damir. Thank you very much, have a good day. Fast food breakfast, someone hungover down Fishbourne Road. Your order is in the kitchen (although it is probably not yet). Your order has been collected by Damir (although it has not been, yet, because the number has not come up). Your order will be delivered by Damir, whose stomach growls as the smell drifts out of the package he is zipping into his backpack. You have requested a contactless delivery, so you will not see him. Have a good day. Sandwiches for lunch, your order will be delivered by Damir. I stop for lunch myself: why not? I cannot face the burger place, because it reminds me of her. I sit in a little Japanese place and order edamame beans. In a way, of course, this is stupid because that is only going to remind me of her ten times as much. But somehow, as I eat them – slowly, one at a time, savouring the saltiness of each one – that is not how it is. Instead I think about the trap she is in with this man, the trap she has dug herself into. I wonder how she felt this morning, waking up without me.

When I come to pay the bill – two little bowls of edamame, a Diet Coke – I hardly even glance at the price, and I do not think about the money leaving my account. For the first time, really in my life, there is enough in there that the purchase is almost irrelevant. The way it must feel to be them. It is not a totally positive feeling, because part of that means being in some way dirty like them. But it is something new, something I can build on. I have already checked at a cash machine that the money is definitely there; I even took ten pounds out, just because I could. Soon of course this account, like my rider account, my phone account, will not exist. The money will vanish across the sea and turn into kuna, but it will still exist. It is real, just like her tears were real, even if not everything else was, in the end.

Bloop-bloop-BLOOP. Yes-of-COURSE: of course there is an order for the Escape Studios, where I never did end up taping my doomed song. It is almost in a spirit of masochism that I pounce on it: do I need to pedal sandwiches over to them, or the stupid pastries they love so much, for about three pounds fifty, at this stage? Something makes me do it, though. It is not the usual guy in a sweater who collects when I buzz: it is a different, almost identical guy in a similar sweater. Maybe they only interview people who look like this. Something in his manner is a little friendlier than I am used to from the other man, though, and he looks pleased to get the bag, and not in a hurry to get away.

'Everything good,' I ask, 'everything is here?'

'Yes, I think so, thank you,' he says.

'I was pretty quick to get here, I think.' Why not, my brain is saying: we can have some fun, now.

The recipient blinks. 'Yes – it *was* quick, thanks.'

'If you ever want to give a tip, you can,' I tell him. The guy looks very surprised by this – it is hard to blame him – but his hand goes, politely, to his pocket. 'No, I just mean on the app,' I clarify, enjoying myself. 'Not many people have cash with everything that has happened; none of us expect cash. You can do it but it isn't usual. The app, though, you just go to My Orders and, where it says "your order was delivered by . . ." under that, there is a little pound sign.'

'Oh. OK, thanks.' You would expect him to want the

conversation over with, to be backing away from me, but he seems interested, just like Decca was interested that night. 'Yeah, it wouldn't – I guess, it wouldn't occur to me most of the time.'

'No, of course, that is just how it goes. Everyone just got used to having everything.' I am warming to the theme. I can almost picture myself writing these words, in the future. 'It is nothing personal, but it makes a real difference if you are doing this, and you find someone has given you some pounds. Once it kind of changed my life, a little bit.' My helmet is going back on. 'Don't worry about tipping *me*: this is actually my last day. But for people in the future. If you feel like doing it, do it, you know?'

'I . . . yeah, I will,' says the guy, nodding slowly.

'Tell people, too!' I shout over my shoulder. 'Everyone can help each other a bit!'

The man stands in the doorway watching me go, and it is a little bit like he is in some movie and has been visited by an angel or a person from the future, et cetera. Just an hour and two drops later, I see in the app that – despite what I said – he has tipped me five pounds. For a while, I stay in the strange, slightly heady mood I have had for most of the day. I imagine giving my lecture on tipping to more customers, letting that be my final sign-off, my little legacy.

But the sky clouds over and the dinner orders begin, and my mood darkens too as reality starts to push its way back in. Leaning against a wall, my hand goes to the phone to message Decca, and I cannot; I have literally no record of her number left, of our conversations: just the photos I saved, which I have not been able to delete yet. Of course, I would not really have texted her. It is just, that is what I have got used to doing. It was the thing I looked forward to, those messages, the build-up of suspense, the knock on her door, Narnia. And, above everything else, still no Goran. Like the sorrow over Decca, a fear of what might have happened to Goran moves in, a missile, and smashes me in the middle. If he could contact me, he would, surely; it was just an argument, just a stupid argument. If he cannot, then why not? Where is he? Is he still in the country, is he still here at all? I let myself stare at the phone, at his name; send another couple of messages. Nothing.

I go around the back of the burger place, where the drains are, where steam pours out of a window and pipes creak and there are huge industrial dustbins containing God knows what, and I cry for a couple of minutes. All that stops me is a *bloop-bloop-BLOOP.* Superior Pizzas, my old friends. Swipe to take it. Jolt myself out the blackness, at least for the twenty minutes it will take.

It works, because sure enough they are not ready, even though there are no other riders waiting, even though this looks like the only order they have had all day. *Ajme!* I will almost miss these guys, this pizza place whose main angle is being really bad and slow at making pizzas. Of course the app has lied and said I am on my bike already, but what does it matter any more? 'Just need a few minutes here, pal,' says the sweaty guy in his apron. Fine, whatever. I try not to look at my phone, at the nothingness, but it is impossible. Brief hope, a couple of notifications; but no, just the group talking about a new Chinese place which has a welcome offer on: lots of orders tonight. Another new Chinese place. Another lot of leaflets through everyone's doors. There is something about roadworks, as always. There is nothing about what matters to me, no response to my occasional pleas about Goran, no news from the other group, the one which supposedly planned this escape to some other city. Maybe I was never that important even to the small community I thought I had around me; maybe even Goran had other people who were bigger in his life, even though it squashes me to think of it.

'OK mate, thirty-four.' I smile at the fact he still gives the number, despite the fact I am the only one in here. He is doing his best. 'Keep doing what you are doing, man,' I say. 'Good luck.'

'What?'

But the Silver Fox and I are gone: onto the main street, down to the bottom where it meets Station Road – and straight into a dead end. The very roadworks they were chatting about, I will find out later when I bother to read the message properly. Road closed. I am no longer afraid of the consequences of lateness, but I still have my pride. I do my work well; I make sure people are satisfied. Elite rider, 4.72 rating. Fuck this for a game of soldiers: I am not going all the way round. I will be the judge of whether the road is closed, thank you. I bypass the sign, pedal up the deserted street, come out on Coldharbour Road into a lorry horn so loud the vibrations feel as if they are going to throw me off the bike. The lorry has braked ten centimetres from me. The adrenalin crashes through me. The driver is yelling, swearing; fair, there is no way he could have expected me. I raise a hand in apology, wait for him to roar away, shaking his head, talking to himself. Let two, three more cars out in front of me, even though I could sneak past them. My legs feel shaky. I do not want to ride any further. The notifications are flashing up, red exclamation marks, by the time I tie up the Fox outside the address.

The doorbell sounds that three-part tone that is like a fragment of a pop song. A girl is standing there who does not look much older than a uni student. Barefoot, wearing pyjamas. Her hair is streaks of pink and blue over blonde. I can smell drink on her breath as she takes a step towards me.

'What kept you?'

'I'm sorry, what?'

'Why did you take so long? You took ages.'

'They were not ready for a while,' I say. 'The app always claims that they are, as soon as . . .'

I am building up to another one of my lectures, Damir's Final Thought, but she has taken the box from my hands and is looking inside it like a bomb disposal expert. 'This is cold, man. I can't eat it.'

Do you not have an oven, I want to ask. Or a microwave? Do you not have any means of heating food, are you taking part in some sort of social experiment?

'You can't eat it?'

'I need another one,' the woman says. 'I didn't order it to be like this. I wouldn't have bothered if it was going to be like this.'

Wouldn't have bothered, I repeat to myself mentally. I take the pizza box back out of her hands. She looks at me in surprise. There is a moment in which the Devil is on my shoulder, like in a cartoon, saying: do what you want. I grab the pizza, let the box fall to the ground. I take a big bite into the stuffed crust, chew it while she watches me, bewildered.

'It seems OK to me,' I say, through a mouthful of cheese and dough, and as she starts to protest I hold the rest of the pizza in my right hand, draw back my hand, throw it like a frisbee. For an unforgettable moment we both watch as it soars towards the row of parked cars, hitting a silver Volvo and sliding slowly down in a smeary trail. The silence between us is so pure, for a moment, that I can hear birds chatting to each other in the treetops; I feel like I can hear the humming of the phone wires. My customer makes a noise like two half-words soldered together.

'Are you out of your fucking mind?'

I am already moving away from the scene of violence, back to my bike, the one thing I can trust. 'I think all of you are,' I say over my shoulder.

She is shouting she will report me, I will be in so much shit, I will lose my job, I can only make out fragments of sentences as I put my feet on the pedals. They do not get it, these people, people like her and Niall. Because things did not go exactly as they expected, they want to put me 'in the shit', like the kid at school who puts his hand up and tells the teacher about you. What they do not understand is that there is no teacher. Sure, if I were not leaving anyway, the company could remove me from the app. If someone complained to say, hey, your rider is a madman who threw a pizza. Or, hey, your rider is a bad guy who gave my wife better sex than she had had in her life.

But very likely they would not do that. Because I am just a name on a screen. I am a collection of statistics and so are you. If they shut down my account, they know, we both know, I could just sign with a rival company and be delivering to the exact same people in twenty-four hours. In fact, I could re-register with *them* by just using a different login, different phone number. They would not know, because they do not know me, because the company is not a real company, which buys and sells things and says thank you to its customers and knows them by name. It pretends to be all these things, but it is not. The company is just a few people checking bank balances now and again, selling shares of an imaginary product to people who are, themselves, using imaginary money. Nothing personal.

'Be your own boss' was not true, I think to myself as I head back down the main street, with nothing left in my legs now. And the video game comparison – that was not really true, either. Or if it was true, I was never the player. I was the character, and the whole city was the one playing the game. The person holding the controller, at any time, is just whoever is the next person to pay ten pounds for me to bring them a bag. The boss was not me; it was literally anyone else, anyone who wanted to be.

I sit on the wall across from the burger place, the Silver Fox tied to a post. A plane rumbles far overhead and I think about what I have to do, what comes next. The sight of my beautiful, weary old bike makes me feel stupid emotions, as if it is a pet, a person even. The Fox is all I have left. *Just you and me now, buddy.* Tears come into my eyes again; fuck, this is pathetic. Come on, Dam.

Bloop-bloop-BLOOP. Time-to-GO. I do not glance at the phone, at its invitation. Someone else can have the job. Your order will be delivered. And your neighbour's order, and her brother's order, everyone's order. Your Uber is on the way to take you to the train station. That album you want to listen to on the journey: that can be delivered straight to your phone, via a streaming service; you do not have to pay the musician, those days are gone. Your weekly shop will be delivered, and separately, a four-item grocery shop will be delivered to save you from going out for the things you forgot. Your Amazon order of a celebrity autobiography, a set of guitar strings, a lampshade, all things purchasable within ten minutes of your house – that will be delivered at the latest one p.m., or first thing in the morning if you pay a little more, or even the same day if you have a special membership, whatever it does to the people who have to carry this out.

But it will not be delivered by Damir. End Shift. I swipe carefully. I press the button to turn my phone off. The screen is black.

I look across the square, see a familiar figure sloping around near the sleeping market stalls, the big iron frames where in a few hours the shouting men will set up their tables again. It is the crazy dancing guy. A bottle of something is in his hand, but he is not drinking from it. He is not doing anything at all, in fact, just standing there, like he is a toy from which someone has removed the batteries. But when we have made eye-contact, he starts to wander in my direction. I avert my gaze, staring down at the wet pavement.

There is an ant. I watch him scuttle mysteriously along the base of the wall I am sitting on. I train my eyes hard on him, doing my trick to make other ants come to life, but there are none: this guy is a lone operator. *Like me, pal*, I think. I expect the ant to double back at the end of the wall, make his slow trip back the way he came, but he continues: down off the wall, across the cracks of paving stones, on a journey somewhere. Ants can find their way with landmarks like humans can, I imagine myself saying to Decca. He knows what he is doing, where he is going.

Something shifts in my brain and I have an idea which does not seem like it can be right, and yet somehow has to be.

I am leaping off the wall. I say good luck to my small friend and I am walking fast, feet landing hard on the pavement. Back towards Cecil Court, but not quite. A right turn by the coffee shop, down the little alley. The padlock is hanging off the lockup. My hands are trembling as I slide the door up. Inside, pitch black, the smell of engine oil, the bulk of Mario's big bike in outline. But something else too. I can feel it before I see him; I can feel it as soon as I am inside.

*

My damp hand on the phone, finding the torch. A sharp small light. I aim it at the back wall. He is there, a heap of clothes, face-down. My heart feels like it will smash through my ribs. I go over to him, put my hand on him. He is very cold, not moving. I shake him. He is breathing. I move him around like a doll, with more and more force, until finally he moans and protests and they are the best sounds I have ever heard.

'Wake up, you idiot.'

Goran sits up slowly, groans, lies back down. For a few seconds it is as if he does not know who this is, who I am. But he does. We have always known each other.

'Dama,' he says, in a low voice.

'Mary and Joseph Christ and the . . . the fucking wise men,' I say, trying to keep my voice from cracking. 'Couldn't you have just told me, hi, my brain has exploded so I am going to live in a shed now? Or whatever the idea of this is?'

He sits up a little again, gives a horrible cough like all the dust from this place has been stacking in his lungs – what, all last night, today, and it was going to be tonight as well? I am either too relieved to be angry, or the other way around; hard to know.

'I have no phone now,' he says, 'sold that. I am no use. I've got nothing; it is all gone. I'm done.'

'You are not. Listen . . .'

'How did you think I got the Empress?' he rasps.

'What?'

My eyes are getting used to the dark in here. I have him by the wrist. His skin is cold.

'You think I could ever afford that, just from doing drops? It was pretty good when I was first here, but I would have needed to fucking *fly* to get that much money, bro.'

'I don't know, I just thought you got it not too expensive and you had saved up for six months . . . I didn't know how it worked. Why are we talking about this now?'

'Because,' says Goran, putting his hand on my arm, 'my best friend, you need to understand the level of shithead I am, and the amount I am now finished. I had to borrow money to get that bike in the first place, borrow it from some bastard who made me sign something, and I am still paying the fucker off now. Was. When I was still earning money.' He gives me a horrible, frightened grin, his eyes tinged red in the torchlight. 'So it wasn't just, I lost the Empress, now I cannot earn shit. It's more, I lost a thing I hardly even really owned. My whole plan was shitty from the start; it would have taken another five years before I was actually putting money away. I was just desperate to do something, be someone, whatever. But I am not someone, am I?'

We sit with this for a few moments. Yes, I want to say, you are more than someone, to me. We played the game, that is all, and now I have found a hack, and we will play a different, better game. Me and you, together. But all that can wait.

'You know *why* I bought such an expensive bike?' he continues.

'Because – we've covered this – you are an idiot?'

'Well, sure. But more specific. It's because I had to get you to come over. It needed to look so good on the pictures that you would be like, wow, OK, London will work for me. I needed you to be here.'

He winces as I help him up to his feet, his long, long legs uncoiling like rope. I take him by the shoulders. 'London did work for a while. But now we can do better.'

'Better how? What do you mean?'

'We are going back to Split.'

He snorts. 'And, what, I will get a job in government? We find buried treasure in the sea? There's nothing back there for us, Dam. Without money, you . . .'

'Who said we will be without money?' I say. 'Come with me. I have a plan.'

EPILOGUE

I played a show tonight. It was in Ritam, the club in Split. About fifty people came; it could have been more. Of course, Goran, Dad and Petra – at the back, because I would not let them sit where I could see them – but also real, paying customers too. Some of them were probably people who go there every night. Some of them maybe did not even enjoy it. But it was my show and they cheered me at the end, and the booker invited me back next month.

Outside, Goran had never looked so proud, Petra hugged me harder than I can ever remember, kissed me on the cheek. Dad introduced me to his date, Ludmila, his online chess opponent, and they both denied that it was a date. Someone tapped me on the shoulder and I swung around and started in surprise. It was Josip, from the record shop.

'That was very impressive,' he said, 'really, very good indeed.' I was almost too surprised to thank him. I recovered myself and offered to buy him a beer, but he shook my hand and said, no, he would have to get going, and walked slowly away to wherever he lives. I could not keep the grin off my face for half an hour. That night, even though it was almost midnight, Goran and I rode up Marjan and just stood there looking out over the city lights, the black water. I tried to work out if it had always been quite this beautiful. Sometimes you cannot see the place you are actually in.

★

Not contacting you, keeping it going for almost three years now, has continued to be very difficult. And not thinking of you at all is more difficult – in fact, impossible. There will always be someone in the street who seems to be you for ten seconds, they turn around, my heart falls again. We had the neighbours round for *Titanic* in our home cinema and she said the line about French girls, and I had to leave the room for a couple of minutes. I saw a mother entertaining a kid with the trick where you stab the fork between your fingers, and again, there you were. No sex I have had since quite compares to what we had, and nothing has been exciting in quite the same way as the feeling of going through your front door, shutting it behind me, smelling the dinner cooking, knowing the bed is upstairs. At night, here when I cannot sleep, I imagine what would happen if, just once, I sent a message. *Hi. Biker boy here.* I said I will not do that, and it was true. But, of course, the thoughts do not go away.

Sometimes I ask myself what would happen if somehow you did get my number, and I woke up to see you had sent

ONE MINUTE AWAY

something. But if you did, I would have to ignore it, unless it was a message saying, 'I will be in Split tomorrow, I have done it'. It would be very, very hard to ignore it, but sometimes you just have to do the hard thing, Decca.

You must sometimes – again, late at night – find your fingers going towards the internet. It is not all that difficult to find me, even without my phone number. Once you have started putting songs out on Instagram, you have to build a whole profile: pictures of you backstage, or with your guitar thinking about a song.

If you were to look at the pictures, you would see me and Goran on holiday in Naples and wonder: is he happy? (Yes, most of the time I am.) You would see a photo of me with a girl on the beach and think: is she his new girlfriend? (No: Goran's, actually.) You might see us in what looks like an upmarket bar, or – recently – at dinner on a terrace, and think: so the money has helped. And yes, it certainly has. We can do this because I met you, I guess. The fairy tale of me and you might not have been true, but a different kind of story came out of it.

Maybe you have even given in to temptation and listened to some of the songs. One or two of them have done quite well online, as you might have seen. Well enough that it seems worth writing more, allowing myself to talk and act like the person I want to be. Doing more shows, spending time in a studio, treating myself like a musician, just like Goran now treats himself as a cycling coach.

The best songs I have are not online yet; nobody will hear

them until I am ready. The old rule. The one I am proudest of, the one I think people will love, came from the half-dream I had sitting exhausted on the wall, just after the bike got stolen, when you came to save me. The line ended up being: *Love is a verb before it's a noun. You say it by doing it, not the other way round.* I do not know if it makes complete sense, but it sounds good; it sounds really good.

But it is like any other lyric: you have to hear it with the tune, hear the whole thing together, see the whole picture. And, Decca, maybe some people never do.

Damir
Summer 2024

ACKNOWLEDGEMENTS

A lot of people helped with this book. I'd like to thank early readers DJ, Vix Leyton, Owen Powell, Sam Craig and Lisa Austin; Dinky Donk and Ben Addy for cycling advice; Coop, for all those takeaways; Harry Wallop and my two anonymous riders for inside information; Kimberley Young, Charlotte Brabbin and the whole team at HarperCollins; Francesca Main for long-term mentorship; Cathryn Summerhayes, as always, for making it happen. Also, thank you to everyone who supported my work in Covid, including the period covered by this book. Stay in touch.

One man's last journey.
One hundred and fifty-eight chances to save his life.

MARK WATSON

James thought he had lost everyone.

CONTACTS

Now everyone is trying to find him.

'Funny and daring'
RICHARD CURTIS

'Beautifully written'
JILL MANSELL

'Heartbreaking and hopeful'
CHRIS ADDISON

Contacts is also available to buy now.

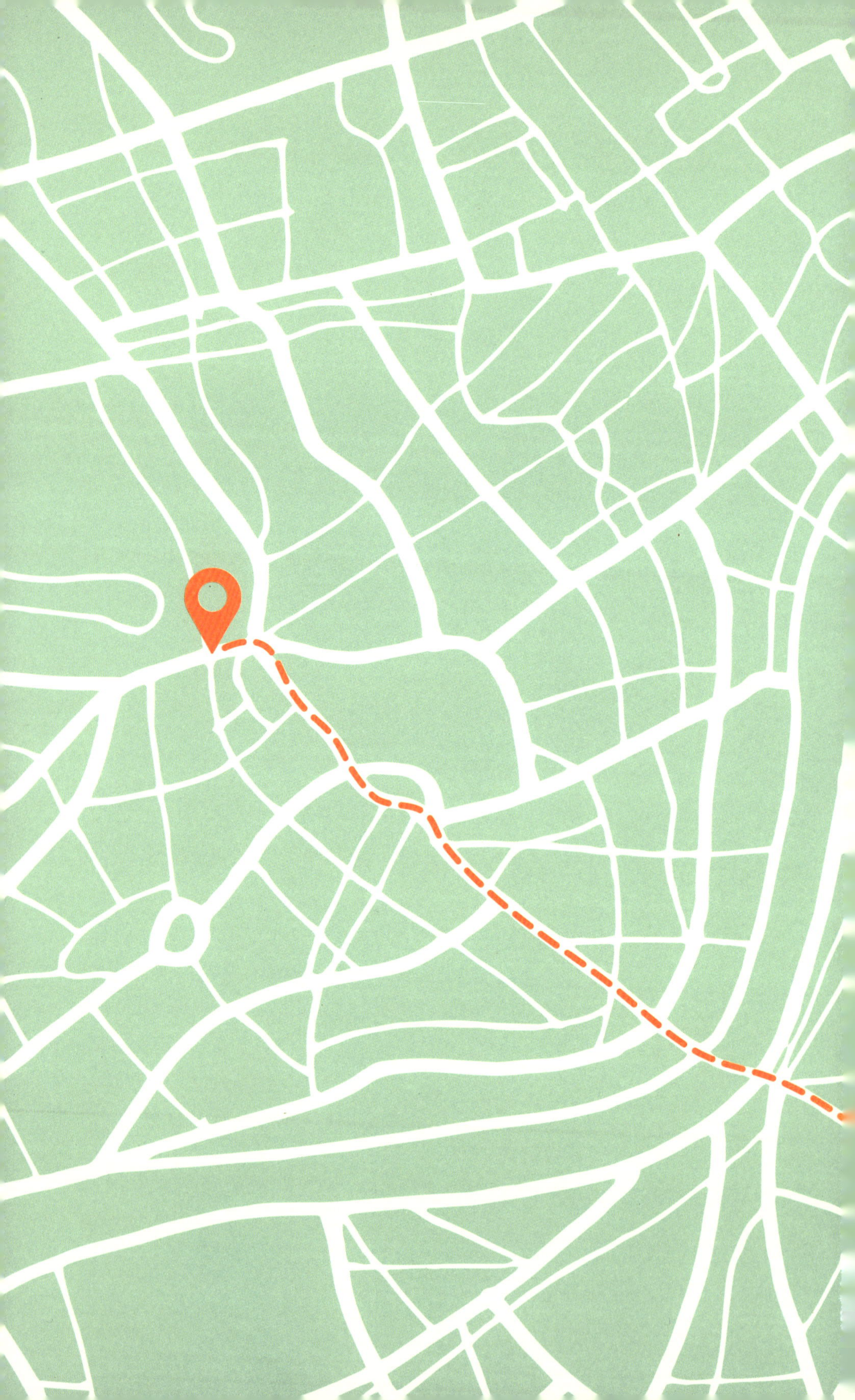